EMERGENCE

A GIDEON WOLF STORY

ERNEST DEMPSEY

138 PUBLISHING

1

GUADALAJARA, MEXICO

I stared out at the mob, terrified at the sight of so many eyeballs —all demanding the same thing from me. Every person in that huge room gazed at me with the same salivating expectation they might have watching a steak sizzle on a griddle.

A few of them even looked as if they might consume me like they would that steak.

In that moment, I wished I could turn and run. Or maybe put on some kind of invisibility cloak so I could just disappear. I wasn't made for giving speeches in a room like this, filled with my peers. Who was I kidding? Most of these folks were way above my pay grade.

So what if I'd been the one to locate several lost treasure hordes in the last year or two? I'd been lucky. None of these people knew that. Which reminded me of something a friend had said when we were getting ready to do our first ever rock show back in college.

I was the singer and had been nervous about standing in front of so many people with them all looking at me.

My buddy Mark had simply said, "Just fake it. Pretend like you're a rock star, and you will be to them."

The advice worked, though it took practice to get proficient at looking like I was a "rock star."

"Good evening, and thank you for joining me," I began. *Simple enough.* I stole a quick look at my wife, Amy, sitting in the front row next to some of the Mexican dignitaries who'd set up the event. She smiled up at me, immediately disarming my nerves like only her smile could do.

"My wife and I have spent years working on this project, and we are so proud to bring it to you tonight in partnership with the lovely folks at the Guadalajara Historical Expo." I swept my eyes across the audience—hundreds of well-dressed high-society types. Many had contributed significant donations to make this project possible, and I easily recognized the satisfaction on those faces. "This exhibit represents the work of so many people, and so many generous donations that helped make it possible. What you are about to see is the result of all our efforts, and a spectacular example of what can be accomplished when people from different cultures come together to try to accomplish something great."

The crowd erupted in applause, and I waited, doing my best not to let the swelling noise inflame my nerves again.

I nodded and waved, waiting for them to settle down again. Once the room quieted to a murmur, I grinned wickedly and motioned to the enormous red curtain behind me. "Ladies and gentlemen, I give you the lost treasures of the Purépecha civilization."

I turned and extended my left hand toward the curtain. Right on cue, the dark red veil swept to both sides, revealing a glimmering exhibit of incredible artifacts on the other side.

The display room covered an area of a hundred feet from right to left, and the forty-foot-high ceiling made the space feel even larger. It stretched another two hundred feet from end to end, with tables, display cases, and rows of gold, jewels, pottery, tools, weapons, utensils, and art—all from a lost civilization.

I smiled as the people proceeded around the stage to the exhibit entrance. My gaze fell back to my wife, who beamed proudly from the front row. Her golden-blonde hair dangled just to her shoulders, brushing the tight black evening gown's straps against her milky skin.

We'd been married for ten years now, and she'd been there with me through all the frustrations, and all the triumphs.

Hunting down lost treasures was one thing, but resurrecting an entire civilization turned out to be a monumental task of a scope I could never have estimated. The project took over seven years to complete, and now the historical community could enjoy the fruits of their labors.

Amy raised a glass of champagne toward me a split second before her attention zeroed in on one of the Mexican diplomats in attendance. Amy knew how to play the room, and she'd played no small part in getting the funding necessary to make this operation happen.

I nodded to her, and she tore her eyes from me to engage with the black-haired dignitary in a tuxedo.

I recognized the man. Alfonso Garcia had been influential in getting the project the necessary permits, and he'd helped me navigate the red tape provided so generously by the Mexican government. In truth, I was glad the project had been in Mexico. Most of the nations in the world had far worse bureaucracies to deal with.

With a sign, I took my eyes from my wife and the conversation she'd started with Garcia and made my way off the stage to the right. As I descended the stairs, I noticed three men standing beyond the line of people making their way into the exhibition room.

There were hundreds of people in the place, half of them men, but these three stood out. While they wore expensive suits, I immediately realized that something about these guys didn't fit. The tattoos sneaking out from underneath their collars, and climbing up their necks, was the first thing that caught my attention. Or maybe that was second to the cold, lifeless stares in their eyes, as if they were predators locked onto their next meal.

That last thought sent a shiver through my spine, especially considering my initial assessment of the men.

They were from a cartel. The only question was, which one?

The men watched me reach the floor and smile to the patrons as they passed, welcoming each to the exhibit with polite nods and bows. I shook a few hands for good measure, hoping that my read on the three men was wrong and that they were simply there to take a look at the treasures our project had recovered.

When the line started to thin, I decided to approach the men. I glanced over my shoulder and saw my wife giggling with the esteemed Garcia. These guys clearly wanted to have a chat with me.

I stepped through the stragglers in the procession and crossed the twenty feet to where the three men stood, each in black suits. The one in the middle wore a traditional white button-up shirt with a black tie. The other two wore black on black on more black, all the way down to their shiny shoes.

"Hello," I said, stopping a few feet short of the three. "Welcome to the exhibit. I hope you'll find it interesting."

The man in the middle didn't say anything at first. Instead, he wore the same chilling expression on his face he'd kept since I noticed him. It was a threatening, angry look and one that I'd seen several times on the faces of Las Vegas Raiders fans when they came to play in my hometown of Nashville.

"Do you know who I am?" The man in the middle asked. The bright lights overhead gleamed off the shaved heads of the men on either side of him. His black hair was cut short, spiked off to one side.

"No," I admitted, starting to think maybe I should know who he was. "But I am terrible with names, which is why my wife handles most of the fundraising duties."

The man's brown eyes shifted, and I didn't necessarily like the way he up-and-downed my wife's athletic figure. Still, I was secure enough to know who she was going home with later that evening, and so I let the gesture slide.

He brought his attention back to me and reached into his jacket pocket. For a split second, I thought the man was going to produce a gun, but I quickly recalled the security measures the museum used, including metal detectors at all the entrances. No one was getting a firearm into this place, short of barging through the gates in a full-on desperate sprint.

The man produced an unsealed envelope and extended it toward me.

I furrowed my brow in confusion, eyeing the paper skeptically. "This isn't a subpoena, is it? Because I would honestly prefer to let my lawyer take that."

"It isn't a subpoena," the man said in a thick Mexican accent. "It's a job."

My brow tightened. *Job? What job? I already have a job. And I'm not looking to work for someone else, other than the board that oversees my current projects, anyway.*

"What do you mean, job?" I asked, keeping most of my thoughts where they belonged, in my head.

"Open it."

I didn't like the forceful way the man issued his "command," but I wasn't about to argue. I knew from the tattoo on his wrist that my initial assessment had been correct—these guys were with a cartel. And based on the ink marking his skin, they were from the Los Zetas organization—a dangerous crew known for their brutality. I couldn't believe they were standing here in my exhibit, and I hoped they weren't there to cause trouble.

I plucked the envelope cautiously from the man's fingertips and pried open the flap. I looked inside, wary that it could be some kind of trick, but only a folded letter rested within.

Satisfied it wasn't a bomb, or whatever I was irrationally afraid of, I took the paper from the envelope and opened it. I immediately realized it wasn't just a letter. The pages were printouts, and one of them featured a fierce-looking wolf's head with sinister eyes that seemed to stare into my soul.

I shoved the picture to the back of the short stack and looked over the documents. The next one featured notes written in someone's handwriting, but in English. I frowned as I read through it and then shifted to the next page in the stack—a map with circles and notes drawn on it.

"I'm sorry, is this something you're wanting me to look for?" I said, finally starting to put together the pieces to the puzzle of why these three had approached me.

"Yes, Dr. Wolf. We have been searching for this talisman for some time now, without success. We need an expert, someone who is capable of finding the unfindable." The leader turned his head to the left, looking into the exhibit room, where most of the audience milled about looking at artifacts or talking over champagne.

I looked back down at the map then at the wolf image again. "This thing? That's the talisman you're looking for?"

"Yes," the leader replied. "Have you ever heard of it?"

"No," I shook my head, staring at the strange piece. "Never. And I've never seen this before, either." I shuffled the pages back to the map. "This map, it's here in Mexico, yes?"

The man nodded, as if the answer should have been obvious.

He wasn't wrong. I spoke fluent Spanish, and I knew some of the points of reference noted on the map.

"So, based on the circle here, you think that whatever this talisman is... that it's located in the Sierra Gorda Mountains?"

"Yes," the leader said. "But we haven't been able to locate it."

I handed the envelope and pages back to the man. "Well, you're looking for a needle in a haystack, my friend. I've never heard of that necklace, or whatever it is. But if it's out there in that jungle, or in the mountains, I doubt it will ever be found. Anything short of dumb luck won't be able to track down a single amulet. That's just my opinion, and I certainly don't want to cause you to rethink your project."

"I see," the man said, accepting the papers without emotion, though I thought I detected a hint of disappointment. He stuffed the papers back into his inner jacket pocket and then straightened his shoulders. "We are willing to pay you for your assistance, Dr. Wolf."

Here we go. These treasure hunters are all the same. Well, not *entirely* the same. This was the first time I'd been approached to do a job for a cartel, and I hoped it would be the last.

"I'm sure you would," I affirmed. "But we're still winding down a lot of things on this project, and frankly, I could use a little time off before I start a new one. These things take a lot out of a person."

"We will pay you five million, American," the leader continued, as if I hadn't turned down his offer. "And that's just to take the job. We'll pay another five when the medallion is found."

I hesitated. *Had this guy just offered me ten million bucks to find some lost necklace?* I could think of some priceless artifacts and jewels from antiquity, but even they often found a way to be priced, and the amount usually sat somewhere between stratospheric and beyond the stars. Still, I hadn't found any single item in my explorations that would command that sum. Based on the outrageous amount he was offering alone, I figured this guy was either insane or a con artist looking for my grant money through some scheme of his own.

"Sorry," I added, this time adding a touch of firmness to my rejection. "But I don't really do for-hire gigs. And besides, I would need a lot more information than a map, a picture of the amulet, and some notes from a random treasure hunter's journal to get started."

The leader drew in a long breath through his nose and turned his head toward where my wife and the diplomat stood. "Does it bother you?" he asked.

I followed his gaze and saw my wife laughing as she placed a hand on Garcia's shoulder. I brought my focus back to the leader. "Does what bother me?"

He didn't take his gaze off my wife. "That she is sleeping with that man."

The statement caught me off guard at first, but he never changed his expression, even when he locked eyes with me again. What had started off as something I took as a joke immediately turned sour.

At first, I was going to chuckle at the ludicrous insinuation. That quickly evolved into being offended as my father's Irish temper kicked in.

"I'm sorry? What did you just say?"

"That man," the leader said, pointing at Garcia without fear of being noticed. "I don't know what she sees in him. Power, perhaps. Women love that. And they're willing to look beyond rough exteriors to simply have a taste of it."

I felt my blood boiling deep down inside but fought away the emotion. This guy wasn't going to get to me. I wouldn't allow it.

"Well, I'm sorry I can't work with you, but I have a lot on my plate right now, and I need to get back to greeting my guests. Thank you for your generous offer, Mister..." I extended my hand and waited.

"Carrillo. Vicente Carrillo."

The name fluttered in the air for a second and then hit my chest like a cannonball. I tried to suppress my surprise, but I knew it splashed across my face as the color drained from my skin.

Vicente Carrillo was one of the most feared men in Mexico. I knew the name. Most people with a pulse did.

Carrillo's reputation for brutality carried beyond borders, and his name struck fear into the hearts of even the most callous. His methods for punishing disloyalty, or simply for making a statement, had been well documented over the last decade during his rise to power.

They had to come in with guns blazing, instilling fear, or at the very least, second thoughts through in any rivals' minds.

I recalled seeing something about a series of quarterings that had occurred about an hour from here but had always felt safe enough traveling in Mexico to various excavation sites or, in this case, to speak at a symposium to open an exhibit.

"Pleasure to make your acquaintance, Señor Carrillo," I said diplomatically. "Thank you for the offer. Now, if you'll excuse me, I need to get back to hosting this gala. Perhaps we will meet again and will have the chance to work together."

He inclined his head, and for half a second, I thought he was going to have one of his goons kill me right there on the spot. In front of everyone.

He reached into his suit jacket, and I felt the blood drain from my face. *The man smuggled in a gun. How had he brought a gun in here with all the security at the entrance? He could have bribed one of the guards. That sort of thing took place here more often than in the States.*

I felt a surge of relief course through me when he produced a business card and extended it to me. "Call me sometime. We'll have coffee and talk."

I accepted, knowing better than to turn Vicente Carrillo down twice in two minutes. The white card had no name on it, just a number in black text. "Thank you, Señor. I appreciate it."

I turned, nodding to his guards on either side, and returned into the mob of Guadalajara's elites to hobnob and schmooze—hoping the sheer numbers could protect me. As something of an introvert, I preferred not to do the social thing, but it was way better than facing off with Carrillo. I felt the sudden urge to hide, but I couldn't. Being alone was the last thing I needed. Instead, I plunged into the fray, glad-handing and backslapping people I'd never met, or only met a few times without cause for recollection.

As I shook hands with people, smiling and toasting to our success, a single thought kept ringing in my mind, twisting my gut like a screw.

I hope I never see Vicente Carrillo again.

2

The driver let us out at the front of our hotel and drove off. I imagined he was still palming the American hundred-dollar bill I'd given him. I wondered, for a second, if anyone had ever given him that much money as a tip, but I blew the thought off as vanity to even think such a thing. The way I saw it, anyone who was willing to work hard when so many weren't, deserved a little bonus every now and then.

The doorman smiled at us, pulling one of the glass doors open wide for us to pass. Amy hiccupped as she passed and patted the man on the shoulder in an idiotic display of drunkenness.

I looped my arm around her waist and eased her into the hotel. We passed the front desk, despite the knowing stare from the concierge on duty. She wasn't judging, but she wasn't impressed either. Honestly, my wife definitely overdid it on the booze. It wasn't often she had the chance to get out and enjoy a good time like that. We'd been so busy over the last few years—her with her fundraising campaigns to support the research projects and me with arranging for permits at dig sites, organizing the teams, setting schedules, the whole nine. Most of the time, we were both in separate places, often for days, and sometimes out of the country.

It had been way too long since we'd had a little romantic getaway for ourselves.

I helped her onto the elevator, and she leaned against my right arm as I pressed the button to take us up to the top floor, where our penthouse suite awaited.

Unfortunately, I knew too well that there would be no romance tonight. I'd seen her in this condition before, like the night of our wedding. She had too much to drink and ended up passing out within minutes of the last guest departing for the evening.

We both liked to party. I was slightly inebriated, too, and if I hadn't had to talk to so many people I probably would have been just as trashed as her.

The elevator doors opened, and I ushered my wife down the hall to the door leading into our room. I had to stop and let her lean on me again as I removed the key card from my pocket and used it to unlock the door.

One swipe and the little green light blinked. A click accompanied the light, and I pushed open the door, eager to get Amy into the bed and off my shoulder.

The door closed behind us as I guided her the last few steps to the king-size bed, where I slumped her off my shoulder and let her fall onto the soft mattress.

"Thanks, honey," she slurred. The slits between her eyelids barely let in any light, and I wasn't certain if she even saw me or not. She'd be asleep soon, so it didn't matter.

"Did you have a good time?" I asked, pulling the knot out of my tie. I set the tie on the dresser underneath the television and began unbuttoning my shirt.

"Wonderful," she said, putting her hands out wide on the bed as if about to make mattress angels.

I finished unbuttoning my shirt and let it slip to the floor. Then I stepped over to her, spread her feet apart, and slipped her shoes off one at a time, setting them against the wall in the nearest corner.

"You take such good care of me, honey," she said in a drunken voice.

She wasn't wrong. I did everything I could to make her life easier, more enjoyable. But I almost never got even a sniff of appreciation. Much less a kind word on regular occasions.

This one was nice to receive, but I also put it in context of her being obliterated, so it was more the champagne talking than her.

"How is Alfonso doing?" I asked. Carrillo's comments lingered in the back of my head, tempting me to press the issue further, but I decided to put out a feeler first and see how she reacted.

Her face twitched slightly. It was a subtle movement, barely noticeable by all accounts. Except that I'd been looking for it, and the psychology courses I'd taken as electives finally paid their dividends more than two decades after finishing them.

She frowned at the question, a gesture that should not have accompanied her answer.

"Oh, I guess he's fine. You know him, always talking about the next thing he's sponsoring with all his money."

Her response didn't give me any consolation. In fact, it made me far more suspicious than I'd been during the entirety of the evening.

"Looked like you two had quite a bit to talk about," I hedged.

"Oh, Gideon," she said, confirming her guilt with the beginning of what I was certain would be a gaslighting session of how I'm never around, how if anyone should be suspicious it would be her. I braced myself to face the onslaught, but it never came. Her eyelids closed and her head rolled to the side. Her chest rose and fell in a steady rhythm, and I knew she'd fallen asleep.

I sighed, knowing any chance at an explanation was about as possible as my chance for romance. At that moment, I wasn't sure I wanted it anyway.

I'd always thought she was lying to me, or at the most innocent, simply telling half-truths, possibly for my own protection. Not that I was okay with that reasoning. I'd always lived with the mantra that a person was innocent until proven guilty. *But how many times did they need to prove themselves guilty?*

Carrillo wasn't the first person to suggest Amy hadn't been faithful, but I insisted, both in my mind and to friends, that she wasn't the type to do that. Now, I was less certain of that than I'd ever been.

"Guess we'll talk about it in the morning," I said, knowing she didn't hear a word.

I slipped out of my clothes and stepped into the bathroom, turning on the shower so the water would warm up while I brushed my teeth. Aside from the disappointing ending with the wife, the night had been an unquestionable success. The historical foundation raised a ton of money for future projects, and word of the discovery and the exhibit traveled far and wide. I'm not a vain person, necessarily, but everyone likes to appreciate a job well done.

After finishing brushing my teeth, I stepped into the steaming-hot shower and let the water soak my skin. For nearly ten minutes, I just stood there, not washing, not doing anything except relaxing as the soothing water spilled over me. Finally, I snapped out of my trance and washed off. I stayed another five minutes in the shower before getting out. There was no hurry, and Amy wouldn't be needing the shower until the next morning, or perhaps late at night when she awoke half-drunk and feeling nauseated.

I dried off, slipped into some clean clothes, and planted my hands on the sink as I stared at the man in the mirror. I found myself loathing the image before me, not for the outward appearance but for the total absence of anything remotely close to courage. My entire life I'd never made a stand for anything, not even for myself.

Who was I kidding? I would walk out that bathroom door, lie down next to my hammered wife, and fall asleep. Then, in the morning she would tell me how much fun she had at the party, congratulate me on the success, and probably offer up a little of the abandoned romance from this evening. As if all that would simply make everything better.

In the end, it always worked. No matter how much I convinced myself that I was going to make a stand, demand the truth, put her on the spot, I couldn't do it. What if I was wrong? What if she really was being honest the entire time?

Nothing short of her confessing, or someone showing me a video, would convince me.

I shook my head in disgust, then turned off the lights and opened the door. Nothing could have prepared me for what waited on the other side.

3

The second I set foot out of the bathroom, someone grabbed me around the back of my neck, and before I could offer up even the most modest resistance, jerked me into the hallway between the door and the bedroom.

He slammed my face against the wall, mashing my right cheek into the smooth surface. I heard a squeak but nothing I could understand. It was a muted, desperate sound but also familiar. I couldn't move against the force pressing me to the wall, but I managed to shift my eyes enough to see my wife being held on the living room sofa.

"Let her go," I demanded through a swelling pain in my jaw. My words came out as smushed as my face.

Another figure stepped into my view, and my heart fell straight into my gut.

"What do you want, Vicente?" I demanded, struggling against the much stronger man behind me.

Carrillo smiled the way a tiger would before consuming its prey. Then he reached into his jacket. I winced, anticipating the cartel head pulling a pistol and pointing it to my head. A tepid relief washed over me when I saw him instead remove an envelope from his jacket. He held it aloft and met my gaze as he spoke.

"Do you know what this is, Gideon?" He wagged the paper around like a flag.

"No. Why would I?"

He bobbed his head. "No, I suppose you wouldn't." He turned dramatically and faced my wife.

She sat there with one of Carrillo's henchmen holding her down with his hands on her shoulders. For her part, she didn't struggle much. Her head rolled back and forth as she fought her internal captor—a high blood alcohol level.

"Let her go," I repeated. "It's me you want."

Carrillo stood still for several seconds, then he nodded. "Yes, it is you I want. Your wife, while she may have use to many others, has none in my plan."

"What's that supposed to mean?"

Carrillo's head bobbed one time, and the man holding down Amy stepped to the side. He drew a pistol with a black tube attached to the end and fired without even thinking. The right side of my wife's head burst open. Her body slumped in the chair, her cratered head falling to the right shoulder.

A surge of fury, pain, and a million other emotions pulsed through me. I started to scream, but the man holding me pressed my face harder into the wall. The words never passed my lips.

"Now, Dr. Wolf, I need you to calm down and take a moment to think about what just happened here. My man just killed your whore wife, who—whether you choose to believe it or not—has been cheating on you for a long time. And not just with the man in these photos."

He faced me with apathy in his eyes. It was a look I felt certain most sociopaths possessed, a glazed and disturbing combination of glorious purpose and total insanity.

I breathed hard, taking in huge gulps of air. Tears punched at the dams behind my eyes, but only insincere trickles fell down my cheeks.

"You don't believe me," he said. "I can see it in your eyes. Here, Dr. Wolf. Behold, the truth that sets you free."

He opened the envelope and removed several photos. Some of them were innocent enough at first, simply Amy talking with Alfonso. More graphic images followed, until I couldn't take looking at them anymore.

Then the tears came. Truthful, sincere sobbing that racked my body like a child in full tantrum. As I dropped to the floor, I felt the man holding me loosen his grip. Not that I had any intention of trying to escape. *Escape? Where would I go?*

Amy was dead, shot in the head just a few yards away from me. One minute, she'd been lying there in the bed, passed out drunk. The next, she was gone. Murdered in cold blood.

Carrillo peered down at me with disdain dripping from his eyes. "What kind of man are you, crying over a woman who you now see was disloyal?"

I didn't have a defense. All I could think of was how Amy and I met, the years we'd spent together, all the good times. Now they were gone. Blown away in a fraction of a second by this monster.

"Those aren't real," I spat as I knelt on the floor. "I know those aren't real. You Photoshopped those pictures. Amy would never."

"Except that she did. I'm not going to go around in circles with you over this, Dr. Wolf. We are running out of time, and discussing the virtues or immoralities of your wife at this point won't change anything."

I couldn't run. That much I knew. Carrillo had three men with him—the one who'd pinned me to the wall, the one who killed Amy, and a third over by the door. One look at the three, and I knew they would shoot me the same way they had my wife a few moments earlier, and they wouldn't think twice about it.

Maybe that's what I should do, I thought foolishly. *I don't have anything to live for now, anyway.* My wife was dead. In one second, I'd lost everything that mattered to me. Although those feelings swam in a confusing pool of information now. *Was Carrillo telling the truth?*

The pictures looked real enough, I had to admit it. But even if she'd done what he said, did that mean Amy deserved to die? To be murdered in a hotel room by a drug dealer?

I stood up, glowering at Carrillo. "I don't know what it is you want from me, but there isn't a chance in hell that I'll give it to you. You may as well kill me, too."

Carrillo blinked slowly, unimpressed by the show of bravado. "The amulet I showed you earlier this evening, Gideon. I want you to help me find it. Of course, my offer still stands. If you help me locate the amulet, I will pay you five million dollars. American, of course. All you have to do is help me find the necklace. After that, you will be free to go and live your life. You can tell the police I killed your wife if you like, although they will never find her. And the accusation will fall squarely on your shoulders. With my help, her murder goes away. All of it goes away. And you become a very wealthy man."

I barely heard anything he said. The man's hollow words bounced off me and reverberated around the room.

My wife still sat there, slouched on the sofa, blood spilling onto the thin carpet. Shock took over. For the initial minute, I was merely in disbelief. Then I lost all feeling in my legs and started to waver.

"I can imagine," Carrillo said, his voice distant, "you must be experiencing a great many things right now, Gideon. It didn't have to be this way, of course, but you left me little choice." The man turned his head and glanced at my dead wife. He huffed a laugh. "You should be thanking me. I'm surprised she hasn't brought home some kind of disease yet. Alfonso wasn't the only one; you can be certain of that."

For a second, I felt a surge of energy rush through me. It was fueled by rage, vengeance, anger, and righteous indignation.

I sprang forward, fists balled and ready to strike Carrillo as many times as it took before he stopped breathing.

But a stronger power than my own held me back from the man, and I realized immediately I was struggling against the same guy who'd pinned me to the wall. Now he gripped a wad of my T-shirt, using it like reins on a horse to keep me in check. Within two seconds, I felt the man's thick fingers slap against my shoulder, gripping me even tighter.

"You murderer!" I screamed. It was all I could think of. And I was certain it didn't have any impact on the man.

"Shh," Carrillo ordered, pressing a finger to his lips. "We don't want to cause a disturbance."

The guard at the door hurried over, producing a handkerchief from his jacket as he strode across the room. He quickly started to wrap the rag around my mouth, but Carrillo held up a hand, stopping him in the process.

"Don't make this difficult, Dr. Wolf. You are going to work for me. Sooner or later, everyone does. Find me the amulet, and you will be set free. And you will be a wealthy man. You'll have any woman you want. Live wherever you desire."

His face soured. "Or you can rot in a hole, sleeping on a cold, hard floor with the rats, eating whatever scraps our kitchen throws out every day." He cocked his head to the side. "The choice is yours."

"Doesn't sound like much of a choice to me," I fired back.

"No, I suppose it doesn't. But those are your options, nonetheless."

I continued resisting the guard holding me back from tearing into Carrillo, jerking and pulling forward with every bit of strength I could muster, testing the stitching of my shirt to its maximum capability.

"I will kill you," I sneered through clenched teeth. "Do you hear me, Vicente? I will kill all of you for this."

Carrillo took a deep breath in through his nose, then bobbed his head once toward the guard behind me. I'd seen him approaching with the kerchief as I'd whipped my head around in a wild, desperate attempt to free myself. The man holding me pulled harder, yanking me back in a show of strength that also told me exactly how feeble I truly was against such a person.

I felt two more hands wrap the cloth around my mouth and pull it hard against my lips. I tried to resist, keeping my mouth tightly pressed to keep the rag from slipping by, but it was no use. The fabric stopped at the corners of my mouth, and I found it much harder to produce any volume from my voice.

"Now," Carrillo said, stepping to the side so my wife's body was in full view again. But I saw immediately why he'd moved aside. The third guard, the man who'd killed my wife, stepped forward with a syringe and a needle that looked way too long for someone of my physique. "Since you declined to come peacefully, we're going to have to do things a little differently. Perhaps, Dr. Wolf, you will feel differently about my offer after you spend a night in the hole."

I struggled as the guard with the syringe approached. The tattoos peeking out from under his shirt climbed his neck all the way to his ears. More ink adorned his hands and fingers, covering them with skulls or symbols used by the cartels.

"No," I protested, my voice muted by the rag. "Stop!"

I resisted with one last, desperate struggle, but it was for naught. The two guards behind me teamed up and held me so tight I could barely move anything. I watched as the man with the syringe held the needle close to my arm. He jerked the sleeve up, finding his target.

Something deep down inside me grabbed my fear, my sadness, my utter devastation at everything that had happened in the last five minutes, and swallowed it whole. For a few seconds, all the emotions rocking me like a ship in a storm disappeared, and I was left with nothing but a numbness that I can only describe as serene. With it, my wit returned, and the shock paralyzing me vanished.

I relaxed and met Carrillo's gaze with my own, icy stare. "Aren't you going to sterilize the arm with some alcohol first?"

Carrillo's guard with the syringe looked at him, actually expecting an answer as if I were serious.

The cartel don laughed, snorting at first, then allowing the laughter to take hold of him for several seconds. His men didn't join in, instead staring at him as if seeing this sort of reaction out of their boss for the first time.

"Sterilize it," he said out loud, clearly with no intention of having the guard go through with that. "This guy is funny." He pointed a long finger at me again. "Sees his cheating wife shot in the head and makes a joke about rubbing alcohol on his arm before we knock him out. That's good, man."

My nostrils flared as I breathed harder, both from anger and to calm myself down. I felt something insane creeping through my body, seeping into my mind like a sort of venomous drug, intoxicating me to the point I could only focus on one thing—revenge.

"I'm going to kill you, Vicente. Do whatever you want, but you'd better kill me first. Or you'll regret it."

He smiled back at me, a sickly, wicked expression that could have scalded the skin off a lemon. "I like your spirit. You should use that to help me get what I want."

I struggled once more, trying to charge forward and break free from the men holding me back. It was no use. Just like my impotent threat to Carrillo, I was too weak to do anything. Now Amy was dead because of me and my inability to be a protector, a guardian, or at the very least a good husband.

"Try to relax, Dr. Wolf," Carrillo warned. "It will only hurt a second."

4

My eyes creaked open like a one-ton door on rusty hinges. Thankfully, whatever room I was in was dark, with only a faint flickering light reaching me from one side. My head hurt but nothing I couldn't manage.

Answers began flooding my senses. The first came in the form of smell. The scent of campfire smoke filled the room. I heard the crackling sound of the fire, and a man speaking in Spanish.

I sat up but immediately realized that was a mistake. My head spun, and the lights on the walls around me blurred again. To make things worse, my wrists were zip-tied together. The plastic cut into my skin. My fingers felt like a five-hundred-pound person had been sitting on them for hours. I wriggled my hands around and worked my fingers back and forth to get the circulation going, but the effort didn't do much.

As I worked to regain the blood flow to my hands, my head cleared a little more, and I could see around the room... namely, that it wasn't a room at all but the interior of a tent. It was one of those old safari-style tents made from a heavy light-brown fabric.

I heard voices somewhere outside and realized they were standing around a campfire. Their shadows danced on the fabric walls. They spoke Spanish, Mexican Spanish. And in that moment, all of the confusion cleared.

I remembered the hotel room, and my memory ran backward from there. They'd injected me with something. No, not just they; Vicente Carrillo and his men. I recalled with disturbing clarity how they'd shot my wife. Rational thought left me, and I felt a bomb of nausea go off in my gut. The queasy feeling squeezed my abdomen, and I felt it crawling upward. I leaned over to retch, but nothing happened. *How long had it been since I'd eaten?*

Even more concerning was my thirst. My throat felt cracked and dry, like dirt that hadn't tasted rain in weeks, baking in the summer sun. Focusing my attention on my parched throat took away the nausea, at least for the moment, and I searched the room for something to drink. At this point, I would have taken pretty much anything. A half-empty bottle of water sat on a rickety wooden table in the opposite corner. I wondered if the other half had been dumped down my throat while I was unconscious. Or if they'd even bothered to worry about keeping me hydrated.

I doubted they cared.

I struggled to stand, thinking I could make it over to the water bottle, but my legs felt weak, like I hadn't used the muscles in days. That caused me to wonder just how long I'd been out. The grumble in my stomach told me I hadn't eaten in a while, but it wasn't so bad that I felt like I was starving. With that being the case, I surmised I'd been asleep for less than a day. And since it was dark outside, there was a good chance it was still the same night the men had....

I felt the nausea tension my gut again, and I leaned forward, dry heaving once more, immediately regretting the sounds escaping my mouth.

Get ahold of yourself, Gideon, I warned. *These men could kill you.*

Not that it mattered. Amy was dead, and apparently nothing in my little world had ever been real. The pictures Carrillo showed me appeared in my mind—haunting, vivid images that squeezed every negative emotion from my being like a juicer squeezing a lemon.

Gravity tugged at me as I tried to stand, but I managed to overpower it. My knees felt sore, like I'd been praying on rocks for hours. I breathed heavily at the effort required to simply stand, but I fought off the aftereffects of the drugs and managed a single step forward.

The second my foot touched the ground, I nearly fell flat on my face, but I threw the other leg forward and steadied myself, avoiding what felt like a potential disaster.

Pausing for a few seconds, I straightened my spine and took several deep breaths to further purge the grogginess from my eyes and equilibrium. I stared straight ahead at the bottle of water. It stood there on the table like a mirage, calling to me in the scorched desert, begging to quench my thirst.

I swallowed, which only reinforced how thirsty I was, and then risked another step forward. This one was easier than the first, and I followed quickly with another, and again until I reached the table.

A matching wooden chair sat under it. I eased onto the seat and immediately felt like I was in the most comfortable chair in the world. I recalled watching the movie *Count of Monte Cristo* and how the main character had felt the first time he sat in a piece of actual furniture again for the first time in years. The actor had portrayed the scene perfectly, and now I completely identified with that sentiment.

I felt as if a fuel tanker had been taken off my back, and I breathed easier for a few seconds before grabbing the bottle and twisting off the lid. At this point, I didn't care who'd been drinking it before me. It could have been the lowliest vagrant, and I would have still downed the liquid in seconds, which I did.

The room-temperature water splashed through my dry throat, easing the ache that scratched at my nerves. I exhaled when the bottle was empty and set it back down on the table.

The room abruptly brightened, and I snapped my head to the right to see the flap to the tent wide open, being held by a man I immediately recognized through the thinning fog in my mind.

Dark eyes stared back at me, so black and full of evil they could have frightened a demon. But he was no demon, at least not in the literal sense. He was just a man, a horrible, wicked person who had killed my wife and who knew how many others.

"You're awake," Carrillo said in a matter-of-fact tone.

"And you're observant," I sneered.

He allowed a cynical smile for a split second and craned his head back in a single nod. "And your sense of humor has returned. The drugs must be wearing off."

"What did you do to me?" I asked. I started to stand up, apparently under the notion that I could charge and somehow take him down with my hands tied. It could have been worse. At least they weren't tied behind my back. As I stood, however, I felt a hint of dizziness smother my intentions, and I returned to the seat without fanfare.

"Not completely worn off, though, I see."

I breathed heavily, desperately. I needed to get out of this place, wherever we were. But where would I go? I was in a tent somewhere, which meant we were no longer in the city. If we were still in Mexico, there was no telling how far away from civilization we were, and without any sense of direction in a foreign place, any escape attempt would be quickly foiled. Then there was the matter of his men who waited outside. I could hear two of them still talking, and no telling how many more there were in reserve that I couldn't see or hear.

"You must be thinking about ways to escape," Carrillo demurred. "I know." He nodded. "I would be, too, if I were in your situation. By now you must have realized there is no escape. There is no way out of this, except through service to me."

I blinked, trying to comprehend what he was saying. Nothing registered. Then I noticed him clutching something in his left hand —a piece of paper, rolled up like a single scroll. Upon looking closer, I realized it wasn't just a piece of paper. It was old, and maybe not paper at all. Perhaps vellum, or maybe papyrus. The dimly lit tent made it difficult to tell which, but I knew definitively that it wasn't a piece of printer paper from Staples.

"What's that?" I asked, my eyes tracing to the scroll.

"Perhaps the drug we administered has thrown your memory off." Carrillo took a step closer but didn't fully commit to joining me at the table.

"Maybe you could refresh me." There it was, the snark, the irritation I'd been wanting to conjure since the man appeared in the doorway of the tent.

Carrillo took another step forward and placed the rolled-up document on the table before me. He spread it out with his fingers and pressed it down flat.

I stared down at the vellum, now realizing exactly what it was. I pored over the drawing, immediately recognizing it as a map of Mexico, but not one that was remotely current. Based on the material used, and the faded ink, I knew it had to be a few hundred years old, at minimum.

"What is this?" I asked. "And what do you want me to do with it?"

Carrillo cocked his head at an angle, glowering at me as if I'd asked the dumbest question of all time.

"It's a map, Dr. Wolf."

"Yes, thank you for that," I chirped. "And before you tell me, I can see that it's a map of Mexico. What I need you to tell me is, why am I looking at it?"

"You really don't remember our conversation at the gala, do you?" He peered at me with genuine curiosity, as if I were some science experiment he'd just completed and wasn't sure would work.

"It's a little hazy. Something about you wanting me to find an artifact for you. That's all I remember. Honestly, I stopped paying attention the second I realized you wanted me to do a job for you. I don't work for anyone. Especially murderous cartel kingpins."

I stood up, ready to punch him with my bound fists, but he pressed down on my shoulder with a quick hand, and I slammed back into the seat. The jarring shook the cobwebs from my eyes and mind, but I was still too weak to do anything about it.

"Do you remember the pictures I showed you?"

"The ones of my wife and Alfonso?" The words caused a knot to tighten in my stomach.

"No, but you should know that Alfonso will no longer be a problem. We took care of him for you. Call it paying things forward on your behalf."

"How charitable."

He ignored the sarcasm and kept going. "I am looking for this amulet," he said, pushing a familiar picture onto the table. Even in the dim light of the lantern in the corner, I easily recalled the image. He'd shown it to me at the gala earlier, and now the conversation started ringing the proverbial bell.

"Oh right," I said. I stared down at the picture of the garish thing. *Why would anyone want that thing? I guess it looks cool in a Halloween party accessory sort of way. Or maybe this guy has a goth thing going on.*

"I know what you are thinking, Professor," Carrillo grumbled.

"Yeah? How I'm thinking about how I could kill you and get out of this," I looked around the room, "whatever this is going on here. Why are we in a tent? And why do I hear the sounds of the jungle?"

"Because you're in the jungle, Gideon." He tapped on the drawing. "You really don't know what this is, do you?"

I stared hard at the image for several seconds, contemplating the answer. I didn't like the way he asked the question. There was a subtleness to his tone that others might have missed, but I didn't. Carrillo's unspoken threat was simple—if I couldn't help him, he wouldn't need me.

What did I care? In a single night, that monster had wrecked my world. Amy was dead. While my feelings on the matter of her infidelity muddled my vision on the subject, I still didn't want her dead.

I did my best to come up with a response, one that I hoped Carrillo would accept, but nothing came to mind. With every passing nanosecond, I felt the looming threat of death swelling over me like a brewing storm.

I was about to tell him I still didn't recognize the amulet, or anything about the man's request, until I caught sight of an image I hadn't noticed before.

"Wait a second," I said. I took the map and stared hard at a faded symbol in the bottom-right corner. "That's the symbol of Xolotl. The dog god of the Aztecs."

Carrillo inclined his head, peering down at me with what

appeared to be approval or satisfaction, although heavily tempered. "Go on," he ordered in hushed voice.

I exhaled, and for the first time since waking, I relaxed a little, falling into the zone where things made sense and where my mind could focus on what I knew—history and civilizations.

"In Aztec mythology, Xolotl is the sunset deity. He escorts the sun into the land of death every evening. It was believed that the world was destroyed four times before this present age. After the last cataclysm destroyed everything and everyone, Xolotl and his twin, the fifth son Quetzalcoatl, descended into the underworld to reclaim the bones of humanity. They used the bones to restore mankind to the Earth."

I took a deep breath before I went on. "The dogs we see today were supposedly created from those bones and given to humans as a gift from the gods. Men were instructed to watch over and protect their dogs, and in return, their dogs would guide their souls into the afterlife. The deceased and its dog companion would walk side by side beneath the earth for four years before finally reaching Mictlan, the final destination."

Carrillo listened intently until I finished. "Very good," he approved. "What else?"

I'd honestly given him everything I knew, and I wasn't sure what he wanted to hear. So, I looked over the map again and the words written in weathered ink.

"The one who bears the symbol of Xolotl will possess the power of a god among men."

I frowned at the text and looked up at Carrillo. "Who wrote this? Where did you find it?"

"That was written long ago, Dr. Wolf. And as to the author, he was a conquistador. Perhaps you've heard of him. Those words were written by the hand of none other than Francisco Pizarro."

Both of my eyebrows shot up. "Pizarro was too busy looking for the cities of gold, Vicente. And murdering an entire civilization."

"No," he said with a subtle twist of the head. "He found something. This map. He found an Aztec shaman and forced him to translate the symbols. The legend says that after the shaman gave Pizarro what he wanted, he cut off the man's head and threw it into the river. Some of the local myths suggest that his actions put a curse on the river, and that's when the fish became flesh eaters."

"Piranha?" I guessed.

"It's only a myth, Dr. Wolf. But the amulet is real. And I need you to find it for me." He pointed at the map. "You can see there is a temple in the jungle. This jungle. Based on this drawing, we should be right on top of it, or at least close."

I resisted the urge to tell him where to go, and instead stayed in my comfort zone as an archaeologist. "Have you used any aerial images? Lidar? Metal detectors?" I said the last with malice, but the joke slipped by the drug lord.

"We've done all those things. And I had my men scour this area. One was killed by a venomous snake. Another mauled by a jaguar."

"Sounds like maybe the curse wasn't just on the water, huh?"

Carrillo didn't laugh. He didn't even crack his lips until he spoke. "The curse is real, whether you believe it or not. It is said that three must die before the amulet will be revealed." He drew a long hunting knife from his side and held it out toward my neck. "If you can't help me, perhaps I should put the legend to the test and see if killing you will reveal the temple."

"Would be a shame if it didn't," I said, cooler than I expected possible. I didn't know where the bravado came from, but I went with it. "It's a big risk, Vicente. You kill me, and your theory doesn't work, then you just offed your best chance at finding whatever this is."

He stiffened his spine, twisting the blade around close to my neck, as if seriously contemplating shoving it through to the base of my skull. Then he abruptly withdrew the knife and sheathed it.

"Go on," he said.

I sucked in another breath of air, scanning the documents, the map, scouring it for something I could use, anything that might buy me some time. I needed to find a way to escape, but with Carrillo breathing down my neck and losing patience, I knew time was running out.

Then an idea emerged from the fog in the back of my brain. Carrillo had looked over all this stuff. He'd had experts analyze it, or so he suggested. If he didn't know what any of this meant, and he was keeping me alive to figure it out, that meant I had the upper hand.

Carrillo would have no way of knowing if whatever I told him was true or not. If I could somehow get him and his goons off me for a moment, I might be able to disappear into the jungle. While I didn't want to gamble with the local wildlife, my chances of getting mauled by a big cat looked a lot better than the fate I knew Carrillo had in store for me, no matter what he tried to promise in terms of rewards.

As I tried to assemble the lie, I found something interesting on the map. At the edge of where the Gulf of Mexico ended, I noticed a drawing that seemed out of place. Most maps had edges, and this one was no different, but typically nothing existed outside the map's boundaries. This featured a half circle with squiggly lines running from it in multiple directions. It looked like a sunrise.

I analyzed the notes on the map and the other documents. Within seconds, I'd concocted the story. If this guy wanted to believe in Aztec fairy tales, I would give him one.

5

"This," I said, pointing at the half sun on the vellum, "is the sunrise. Based on what these notes suggest, the temple can only be found at sunrise, just before the first rays of light touch the world."

His eyes widened, and his head began nodding unconsciously. "Yes. Of course. Why did I not see this before?"

"Because you didn't have me." I let him brood over the cocky statement. My heart raced. He was buying it, but that only meant I had a few hours to come up with a way to escape.

"That is why we haven't been able to find it. Do you think we are in the right place?"

I quickly conjured another lie. "I'll need to confirm with GPS and compare it to the map."

"We've already done that. This is the place. It must be near." Carrillo looked like a man possessed, eyes wide and ravenous. I half wondered if he was about to start foaming at the mouth. "Sunrise, then." He checked his watch. "We have three more hours."

"Okay," I said, nodding. "This suggests that you must look to the east. So the moment before the sun emerges over the horizon, the temple will appear. But it won't remain visible for long." I was rolling now, and the man was eating the lie right out of my palm. "I suggest you set up your men—however many you have—in a row, staggering them to space them out. That way, they can get a full view of the east. Surely, someone will see it in time."

"Yes. That's a good plan."

I could see him running through it in his mind, and he'd already fully committed to it.

"What happens when you're inside the temple?" I cautioned, "I can't say. I have no idea what will happen if you're inside and the thing vanishes."

The intensity in his eyes never faded, though a sinister darkness shadowed his face.

"Once inside the temple, the one who holds the amulet will be granted great power over men—strength, speed, heightened senses. He will be unstoppable."

At that moment, it all made sense, and yet it didn't. This man was hunting for a medallion that would give him supernatural powers. Just thinking it sounded crazy. Then again, look who I was talking to. I'd thought Carrillo was a madman before. And I just got my confirmation.

"Thank you for your honesty," Carrillo said. He spoke in a way that made me think he was about to end the conversation. "I wondered if the sunrise had something to do with it, and you have confirmed that suspicion. At dawn, my men will look for the temple. If it does not appear, then you die. If it does, I will let you live. How long is up to you, Dr. Wolf."

He turned abruptly and stalked back to the tent entrance without so much as looking back over his shoulder at me. He disappeared through the flaps and left me alone again. I'd thought I was being clever in the construction of my lie, but from what the man said, Carrillo had already built it himself.

Did that mean I was lying? Or was that really the mystery of the map?

I looked down at the documents again, realizing that Carrillo had left them there—either by mistake or simply because he didn't think he needed the map anymore.

I glanced over at a lantern in the corner and briefly considered trying to burn the things, but I couldn't bring myself to do it. If legitimate, these documents were important historical artifacts. I would need to analyze the penmanship against other samples from Pizarro, but...

I cut off my thoughts. *No, Gideon. Stop worrying about that right now. You need to find a way out of here.*

"Right," I muttered.

I stood up and walked over to the backside of the tent and knelt down on the ground. I started to lift the bottom edge but heard footsteps just outside. The sound was accompanied by a flashlight dancing on the ground and off the tent walls. I immediately withdrew, taking a step back.

A patrol guard.

Carrillo must have ordered some of his men to circle the tent to make sure I didn't try exactly what I was about to.

I stood there waiting for the next lap. I didn't have to wait long. Another guard, or the same one—it was impossible to tell from within the tent's confines—roamed by again going the same direction.

If I tried to sneak out under the tent's wall, I would risk being seen. Then there was no telling what Carrillo might do to me. I was already pretty sure he was going to kill me anyway, but I didn't want to provoke him.

I looked back to the entrance and noted the shadows dancing on the wall in the firelight. A Rage Against the Machine song echoed in my head about the ghost of Tom Joad. I could have used the help of a ghost right then. Maybe it could have scared away Carrillo's men. The most wishful of thoughts were always the least productive.

I knew that. Ghosts weren't real. Still, desperation often bred fantasy.

Resigned to whatever fate Carrillo had in store for me, I returned to the table and sat down in the chair. I twisted my hands around to keep the circulation going.

The least Carrillo could have done was cut these stupid things off me. It's not like I could do much with the bonds off. I was surrounded by gunmen and had no idea how many. Another scan of the room produced no potential weapon, and why would there have been one anyway? He wouldn't be that foolish.

The only item that could have passed for something swingable was the lantern hanging in the corner, and a small box of matches sitting on a nearby stool.

That's when I realized I had a weapon after all.

I stood up and walked over to the other side of the tent and picked up the miniature matchbox. I pushed open the side and discovered dozens of matchsticks inside. I looked back toward the entrance, then turned my attention to the lantern. I jiggled it gently and heard the sound of kerosene sloshing around inside.

A plan simmered in my mind. I rounded to face the back of the tent, and the idea started to boil. I could use the lantern and kerosene to set the tent on fire. Carrillo's men would rush to douse the flames, and I could slip out underneath on the other side.

It was risky. And it was predicated on the assumption that Carrillo's guards would go for water first and not rush into the tent's interior. Even if they did, if I was quick enough, I could maybe roll out under the flap and still make a break for it.

I'd rather die trying than die sitting here making it easy on them.

My mind made up, I took the lantern off the hook and walked over to the back-left corner of the tent. When I made my run, I would go east, hoping we were closer to the gulf than not. If I could get to the coastline, or perhaps one of the villages along the way, there was a chance I could get safe passage back to the States.

Now, all I had to do was wait. And not fall asleep in the next three hours. Carrillo's men had, apparently, taken my watch, so telling the time was going to prove difficult. I'd have to listen for my cue and go from there. That would make the timing of all this even trickier, but it was my only chance.

I went back over to the table and chair at the front of the room and sat down, focusing all my attention on the voices and sounds from outside. When the time came, I would be ready.

6

"Gideon."

I heard my name spoken like a hiss from the wind, as if the jungle wanted to tell me a secret.

I'd dozed off in the chair with my hand supporting my cheek. I looked around the tent and spotted the lantern in the corner and the same shadows on the wall cast by the fire outside. Carrillo's men stood around the flames, talking in Spanish about everything from women to beer to their favorite fútbol team. And the entire time, the same guard continued to circle my fabric prison.

I secretly hated the guy and wished he'd take just a one-minute break. That would give me enough time to simply squirm under the flaps and disappear into the night.

I calmed my breathing and looked down at the map again.

I didn't know how long I'd been out, but based on the darkness outside and the lack of activity, I figured I must have only snoozed for a few minutes. Although I'd heard that voice, that strange ethereal sound that seemed as if it came from a dream.

I rolled my shoulders and shook it off, and returned to indulging my curiosity with the map.

"Gideon."

I jumped to my feet, startled and terrified of the voice. My eyes darted around the room, but no one else was there. The voice hadn't been Carrillo's. And I doubted it was one of the other men.

The accent was strange, and it had the sound of an old man, but not Mexican.

"Who's there?" I asked, frantically spinning around in circles. *What was in those drugs they gave me?*

"Xolotl will rise with you." The words sounded as if spoken by a serpent.

"What?" I asked, hoping the men outside hadn't heard me. But I was speaking so loud, I felt certain they would come check the tent any second. Then they would see the lantern in the corner and become suspicious.

"They cannot hear you, Gideon Wolf." The voice grew clearer. A red mist seeped into the tent and surrounded my feet. It circled me as if guided by a mind of its own, swirling and wrapping around my ankles until my feet disappeared within. "It is foretold that Xolotl will rise when the wolf unites with him."

"What was in that shot they gave me?" I mumbled.

"This is no hallucination, Gideon. Find the talisman. Awaken the beast within. And rise to embrace your destiny."

I choked down my fear and continued looking around. "Who are you? What do you want with me?"

"Defend the innocent. Avenge those who cannot fight for themselves."

"What are you talking about? Defend who? I'm not a fighter." I stumbled backward, but the red mist grew brighter, and somehow I maintained my balance, as if held up by the strange fog.

"When the time comes, Gideon, you will know." The voice sounded more distant now, fading as it spoke. "Enter the temple. Find the chamber of Xolotl, and take what is rightfully yours."

"Rightfully mine?"

The mist retreated, slipping back out of the tent underneath the fabric walls.

"Hello?"

No response.

I tried again. "Is someone there?"

I snapped out of it and found myself sitting on the chair again with my elbow resting on the table and my chin in my hand. I heard the voices outside again, the laughter of Carrillo's men, the crackle of the fire, the sounds of the nocturnal jungle.

I immediately panned the room but found no sign of the strange fog or the source of the voice that had spoken to me. I blinked rapidly and rubbed my eyes. *Had I fallen asleep again? Or better yet, had I ever really woken up?*

"It was just a dream," I said to myself.

I shook off the grogginess in my head and stood up. Something stirred outside, and I listened closer to see if I could glean what was going on.

Someone was barking orders. Carrillo, I realized. He told the men to get ready, that sunrise would be in a few minutes and to organize themselves in a line across the camp, each facing east.

None of the men questioned the orders.

"You two," Carrillo ordered in Spanish, "get the prisoner. I don't want him trying to escape while we're looking for this."

"What are we looking for, sir?" one man asked.

"You'll know it when you see it."

Two figures near the flickering light turned and started toward the tent.

I had to act fast. My time was up. I couldn't believe I let myself fall asleep like that.

I rushed across the floor to the lantern and picked up the matchbox. I hurriedly slid open the matchbox, but I fumbled and the matches spilled them onto the ground. A few remained intact, and I took one out and struck it against the box. The match broke under the pressure, and the air left my chest. I looked back over my shoulder and saw the silhouettes drawing near.

I picked up another match and tried to be gentler with this one. I ran the red tip across the band, and the compound blazed to life. I reached over to insert it into the lantern, but the flaps to the tent flew open, bathing the room in firelight.

A draft of air shot through the tent, and the match blew out, leaving nothing but a thin trail of smoke wafting up from the blackened tip.

"Hey!" the guard in the doorway shouted.

A second later, a man's scream ripped through the tent. The guard turned and let go of the flap. That's when I heard the roar. It was a loud, haunting sound, and it sent chills over my entire body.

There was only one animal in these parts that made that sound— a jaguar.

The guard at the entrance slung his submachine gun around and fired. It was my chance—probably my last one—to light the lantern and blow this popsicle stand.

I picked up another match, slid it across the box, and watched as the flame bloomed to life. I shielded it with my hand, which was no easy trick amid the screams and gunfire outside. I held my breath as I stuck the match into the glass bulb and touched it to the wick.

The lantern flickered to life, and I felt a twitch of relief.

Outside, the men were shouting orders and yelling in panic. One screamed in what sounded like agonizing pain.

With the men outside distracted, I stepped back from the corner with the lantern in my hand and raised it up. One last check at the entrance, and I threw the lantern onto the ground in the corner. The glass shattered easily, spilling the fuel and flame onto the dirt. Some of the kerosene splashed onto the tent wall. The flames spread deliberately, crawling up the fabric as they hungrily consumed energy from everything they touched.

Satisfied that would do the trick, I retreated to the corner as the fire spread rapidly across the tent walls. I got down on my hands and knees and rolled under the flap into the chaos outside.

I stayed down for a second, assessing my surroundings. The fighting and shouting had shifted away from the front of the tent. Carrillo and his men were all facing west, firing into the jungle darkness.

I spotted a body on the ground by the fire—one of Carrillo's men. He didn't move, and I could see a huge bloody gash on his neck from where the jaguar must have mauled him. This was my chance. Probably my only chance.

I quickly crept around the backside of the flaming tent and around to the front corner, where I stopped and waited. I peeked around and saw Carrillo and his men still firing into the darkness to the west. There was no sign of the big cat, which was both reassuring and unnerving. If I couldn't see it, maybe it was gone. But it could also could have been right behind me.

I looked over my shoulder out of paranoia but found nothing but jungle.

Then I took a breath and darted out from behind the burning fabric.

I'd gone no farther than ten, maybe twelve steps, when I heard one of Carrillo's men shouting about the fire.

I didn't dare look back this time. I kept my eyes focused on the forest in front of me, and the dim light over the horizon.

Another shout came from behind and then more gunfire. This time, they weren't shooting at the jaguar. Carrillo's men were firing at me.

7

I jumped onto the narrow path and sprinted, pumping my legs as fast as my muscles would allow.

Huge leaves smacked against my arms and face. Branches from small trees and shrubs scraped against my skin, but I didn't slow down.

Bullets cracked the air around me, smashing into tree trunks and cutting limbs.

I just knew at any second I would feel one hit me in the back. Maybe if I was lucky, a round would hit me in the head and kill me instantly. That would have been better than being wounded and then subsequently tortured by Carrillo's goons.

Through the canopy, I saw the sky slowly brightening as the sun inched its way upon the horizon to the east. A bullet zipped right by my head on the right and clipped a tree. I ducked instinctively and kept moving.

A thought occurred to me as I ran: Staying on the path would make it too easy for Carrillo to catch me. While I didn't want to risk the dangers of the jungle, I also knew if I stayed on the trail I would eventually run out of time.

The decision made, I cut to the left and immediately met a broad, thick leaf with my face. I grimaced and swatted the thing out of the way, moving deeper into the untrodden jungle.

The undergrowth was thicker and more difficult to wade through. I hoped I had enough of a head start that the men behind couldn't see where I'd gone. If they had, there was no chance I was going to escape.

I listened as I navigated the trees and bushes, still moving east toward the rising sun. The bullets didn't fly around me anymore. The loud pops grew distant and came from another angle.

I'd lost them for now, but that didn't mean I could stop and take a break.

My throat ached from lack of water. My legs burned. How long had it been since I'd done a sprint like this? I couldn't remember. Not that it mattered. I would run until my legs turned to Jell-O.

I gasped for air as I trudged through the jungle, my pace slowing only slightly. The gunshots continued to fade. I no longer heard the men shouting.

The most dangerous of things crept into my mind—hope. I was going to make it. I had to make it. If for no other reason than to reach the police and tell them what happened with... with Amy.

The thought of my dead wife sent a hammer blow into my chest. *Were the pictures real? Had she truly been having an affair? If so, was that the only one?*

My entire world had been wrecked in a single night. Everything I'd ever worked for and built was gone. But I could make it right. I could get back to Guadalajara and then the States. Once there, the American authorities would send in the cavalry and take out Carrillo.

At least that's how I thought it worked.

I could figure that out later. I just had to get back to civilization.

I thought I heard a sound to my right and froze, nearly tripping over my own feet in the process. Something rustled in the darkness, and I didn't know if I should run or stay still. There was no sign of Carrillo and his men, so the only thing I could think of was that there must be an animal lurking in the jungle.

I just hoped it wasn't the—

That fleeting thought was interrupted by a familiar growl.

Then I saw the eyes. They gleamed like yellowish-green jewels in the light of the rising sun. There was a macabre beauty in them, like staring into the eyes of the angel of death—mesmerizing and sinister.

I trembled at the sight. There was nowhere to run now. The beast had me right where it wanted me. If it hadn't gotten enough from the appetizer it mauled at the camp, perhaps I was the main course.

"Good kitty," I said in the softest, most disarming tone I could muster. "Sweet kitty."

The beast crept forward, leading with its right paw, then the left.

I retreated a step. The creature matched with one of its own.

"Why don't you go back to the camp? There's plenty to eat there. You don't want me. I'll taste like fast food." It didn't seem like anything I said was having any effect on the beast.

It stalked forward another step.

Then everything paused. At the top of the trees, a golden ray of light streaked across the lush green canopy over the jaguar.

All of a sudden, the big cat growled as if about to pounce. I staggered backward with a start and felt my heel strike a root. The impact threw me off balance. I waved my arms around to steady myself, but gravity won, and I felt the absence of earth beneath me as I fell backward.

I expected to hit the ground but instead found myself tumbling backward. I looked up at my feet over my head, and for a split second saw a blinding flash of golden light. Then I was in utter darkness, falling for what felt like an eternity.

I didn't scream. I was too panicked and confused to do that. Instead, I resigned myself to my fate, falling to my death in some pit or off a cliff in the Mexican jungle.

Something hit my back. Then my leg. Then my back again.

The objects slapped painfully against my body, and I instinctively reached my hands back to cover my skull. More of the objects continued hitting me, and I realized my speed was slowing. Then I hit the ground, or what I assumed was the ground, with a heavy thump.

The landing hurt, jarring me in a dozen places and sending an immediate surge of pain from my tailbone all the way up to the back of my head. I didn't lose my breath, though, and somehow, I wasn't dead. At least I didn't think I was.

I rolled over onto my side and looked around.

The dim light of sunrise overhead was gone, and I found myself in total darkness.

I sat up, unable to see anything around me. My hand crossed something dry and familiar. I rubbed my fingers on it, hoping it wasn't something else like a venomous snake, or worse if that was possible.

It felt like a vine, and as I pulled on it, I discovered that assessment to be correct.

Sitting there on the ground, I wasn't sure if I should stand up or stay where I was. The good news was that Carrillo and his men were gone, and I seriously doubted they would find me down here. Wherever here was.

Eventually, though, I was going to need to find a way out of whatever this was. I knew I hadn't fallen off a cliff because there was no sign of the sky overhead and no light whatsoever. The next thing that hit me was the abject silence. The sounds of the jungle no longer rang in my ears, and I suddenly found myself missing them.

I forced myself to stand up carefully with my hands out wide. For all I knew, there could be another drop nearby. Had I fallen into a vertical cave? It's the only thing that made sense. Surprisingly, despite feeling a little sore from the landing, it didn't appear I'd broken any bones.

I reached out my right hand and felt around, hoping to find a wall or something. The smell of the air reminded me of a cave, and the temperature only reinforced that sense.

My fingers brushed against something, and I realized it was another vine hanging from above. For a second, I considered the crazy idea of using the vines to climb back up, but I quickly decided against it. I had no idea how far I'd fallen, and I didn't feel like seeing if the vines would break my fall a second time.

"The wolf will rise," a voice hissed in the darkness.

A chill ran across my skin, and I nearly fell to my knees again in fear. "Who's there? Where am I?"

"Arise, Gideon Wolf. And take your rightful place as a guardian of the innocent."

My head snapped around, but I saw no one. Nothing. Only the blackest darkness. The voice spoke to me in English. The accent, however, was one I could not place. It sounded foreign but not like any Mexican accent I'd heard. There was something to it, something native perhaps.

"Who are you?"

A torch flamed to life on the wall ahead. More just like it lit in quick succession along the wall, illuminating the room around me. I could see the thick tangles of vines over my head, and the ones that slowed my fall scattered on the floor.

As I surveyed the room, one thing became poignantly clear. This was no cave. It was the hidden temple.

8

I stood there for several seconds, which felt more like hours, taking in the temple interior with disbelieving eyes.

"This is impossible," I muttered.

"And yet here you are."

I snapped my head to the left but saw nothing. The voice didn't sound threatening. Rather, it was almost soothing in a stern, grandfatherly kind of way.

"What is this place?" I asked, still uncertain what or who I was talking to.

"You know what it is, Gideon."

I choked on the realization. "The ancient temple. The one Pizarro was looking for."

"This is the temple of Xolotl."

"The dog god." The snarky part of my brain lingered on the palindrome for a second.

"A common misconception. Xolotl is not a god. It is a power. And it is time for that power to rise again."

More torches flamed to life straight ahead, illuminating a passage leading out of the circular chamber.

"So, I guess I'm supposed to follow the light then?"

No response.

"Okay. Clearly, I'm hallucinating or dreaming. Or I died, and this is the entrance to the afterlife. No big deal. I'll just wake up any second."

Some of the torches behind me started flickering and then died. Two more began to wane immediately after, as if whatever strange being controlling this place was trying to herd me forward.

"Fine. I'm going. Jeez." Unwilling to stand there in the dark again, I moved ahead into the passage.

Torches continued to flare in front of me, casting their eerie glow deeper into the corridor.

The stone walls looked as if they'd been laid thousands of years ago. No mortar bound them together. Each had been cut with laser precision and placed one on top of the other. It reminded me of the construction techniques used at Cusco and Machu Picchu.

The passage opened up again. The torches continued to light all the way around a giant new chamber. The ceilings rose at an angle to meet at the top, forming the shape of a pyramid.

Then I saw the creatures. I stopped, freezing in my tracks at the sight of the beasts. Most towered over the floor, though a few of them appeared to be my height, even shorter. My fears shrank when I realized the figures were only statues, sculptures of bizarre half-human, half-animal beings. Some were combinations of animals, like so many mythical creatures from the Old World.

These, however, were none I recognized. There was no sign of Apollo or Zeus, or the pantheons they commanded. One or two looked similar to a few of the Egyptian deities but nothing purely from that mythology.

"What is this?" I wondered out loud, only half expecting an answer.

The combined torchlight reflected off the white stone ceiling, casting a bright, radiant glow throughout the room.

Pedestals, columns, and giant foundation stones lay strewn around on the floor. The statues, by stark contrast, nearly looked brand new, as though time or natural disasters had only wreaked havoc on their surroundings.

In the center of the chamber, an altar stood about five feet high, made from the same stacked stones that built the rest of the temple. I cocked my head to the side at the sight of something on top of the altar.

An obsidian box rested on top of the stone table. I took a step closer, narrowing the gap between myself and the unusual plinth. The container seemed to almost absorb all light from the torches and their reflections, as if sucking it in like a miniature black hole.

I felt drawn to it, and not just in a poetic sense. Something tangible tugged on my chest, as if a string was hooked to my heart and being reeled in by the box.

"What is this place?" I asked out loud to the flaky voice. I had no idea if I would get an answer or not.

"Go to it." This time, the voice wasn't one voice but many, all speaking in unison. I snapped my head around, eyeing the statues. I had to be hallucinating. The voices seemed to come from the sculptures. But they hadn't moved, and there was no sign of life from them.

"To the box?" I asked for clarification.

The voice—or in the most recent instance, voices—didn't answer.

"Fine," I said. "Whatever you are or whoever you are, you're really good at being vague."

I waited, but nothing happened.

I shook my head and sighed, continuing forward.

The smell of burned fuel filled the room, or at least I thought that's what it was. The acrid scent tingled my nostrils. I fought off the urge to sneeze and stopped close to the altar, a few steps away.

I marveled at the black box. There was no lid and no seams on any side. It was a perfect square. Now that I looked closer, I saw the reflections of the torches in the glossy obsidian. What really threw me off was that even the torches behind me reflected in the stone. I looked back over my shoulder and then again at the box. It was as if I wasn't even there, or the light was going straight through me.

"Open it."

"How?" I asked. "There's no lid."

No answer.

"Could I get a hint, at least?"

I exhaled in frustration. "This is a weird dream. That's all I'm saying."

I took the final two steps to the altar and stood next to it, staring into the box. *Wait, how was I staring into it? That made no sense.* The thing was solid, and yet it seemed to be alive. I gazed into it, and the torch reflections began to melt and swirl. I frowned at the sight but found myself drawn to it—leaning closer and closer until I hovered right over the top of the thing.

Something told me to reach out and touch it, but I felt a wave of fear and uncertainty wash over me. I didn't know what this box was. For all I knew, it could be radioactive. I'd seen hundreds, maybe thousands of artifacts in my career and during my education, but I had never beheld anything like this.

Unconsciously, both hands reached out toward the sides of the box, and I felt a sort of energy pulling my fingers closer. I tried to pull away, but I couldn't.

"What is this?" I asked, a panicked tremble in my voice.

I frantically attempted to withdraw my hands, but there was no going back. The force tugging on my fingertips was too strong. And now I felt my entire body being sucked into the obsidian cube.

The voices returned, though distant this time, and not in sync. I couldn't make out a distinct message in the mishmash of words, but the rhythm... it felt contagious. Their cadence started slow at first, then continued to speed up and swell as if chanting an ancient incantation.

With every pulse, I drew ever nearer to the box.

Then, my fingers touched the surface—the strange, fluid, warm surface. In that instant, the voices hushed. All the torches snuffed at once, too, and I found myself in utter darkness once again.

But this darkness felt different. The air wasn't cool anymore. It was hot and thick, and it seemed to crawl over my skin like it was alive.

I narrowed my eyes to focus my attention straight ahead, fighting a wave of nausea that suddenly gripped me.

I tried to speak, to ask the voices what was happening, but my vocal cords failed, and only air escaped my lips. Panic flooded my mind. *What is happening? I have to be dead. Right?*

"You are not dead, Gideon Wolf," the first voice said. This time, however, it sounded like it was coming from inside my head.

"What do you want from me? Where am I?"

"You are within the sanctum of Xolotl."

"That isn't helpful."

"This is a plane between dimensions, Gideon, where realities overlap."

"Okay," I said, hesitantly. "Where realities overlap." I tried to sound like I was playing along, while at the same time I pinched my left forearm to try to wake up from whatever hellish nightmare I'd stumbled into.

"His unbelief is strong," another voice said. This one sounded feminine and petulant.

"Yes," a third hissed. It was the tone I imagined a snake would have if serpents could speak. "He cannot be the one. Too much doubt does he retain. And look at him. He's weak and frail."

"Was Manoah's son any different?"

No response came, and the first voice had effectively silenced the critics. Even though I agreed with them.

"I don't understand any of this," I said, feeling more than a little crazy talking to a void.

A bright light streaked down from above, like a beam from the sun. As quickly as it appeared, it was gone, and in front of me, several paces away, a silver medallion hung in the air. Two red gems stared out at me set within the eyes of a wolf's head carved from the metal.

"The amulet," I muttered. "That's the necklace Carrillo was looking for."

"Is," the ethereal voice corrected. "He will not stop. And you must never let someone like him gain access to the amulet. A power like that cannot fall into the wrong hands."

"Power?" I asked. Everything Carrillo said to me was a touch foggy at this point, but it seemed like he'd mentioned the medallion possessed a power of some kind. What that meant, I had no idea. "What kind of power?"

"The shaman will guide you."

"Shaman? I'm sorry, but I don't do the whole witch doctor thing. Forces of darkness and all that. I don't dabble with those things."

"The shaman will guide you," the voice repeated. There was no irritation in the tone, but it did carry more weight the second time.

"Got it. Shaman. Am I supposed to find this guy, or will he find me? Or is it a woman? I don't want to be sexist. Anyone can become a witch doctor, right?"

"He makes jokes," the serpentine voice hissed. "We should kill him now and find another."

"Silence," the first voice boomed. "The burden belongs to the wolf. Only through the blood of the wolf can Xolotl reach his full power."

"I'm sorry," I interrupted. "I'm just a little foggy as to what all this means?"

Then the medallion flew at me. I instinctively put up my hands to keep it from hitting me in the face. The second the amulet touched my fingers, the darkness vanished in a blink.

I opened my eyes groggily and tried to take in my surroundings. Moonlight illuminated the jungle around me in a dim, pale glow. I'd expected to find myself in the temple interior, but there was no sign of the ancient place.

I stood up, immediately remembering that Carrillo and his men were still out there in the jungle somewhere, hunting for me.

The second thing I noticed was that I felt surprisingly good. A kind of energy coursed through me, and I felt like I could lift a truck. My senses of smell and hearing were almost overpowering. I heard everything in the jungle, or at least it seemed that way—even tiny insects on nearby plants. The scent of bark, leaves, and dirt assaulted my nostrils.

I raised my hands to cover my ears, and that's when I knew something was wrong. Instead of my normal human hands, they'd been replaced by larger, half paw, half hands covered in dark brown fur on the top.

"What the—?"

I felt a tidal wave of nausea smash into me, and I fell back onto my tailbone. I barely felt the ground when I hit it and continued to stare at my paw-like hands. Amid the confusion and fear, I managed to ask, "What is happening to me?"

But the voices were gone. I was alone again. And something was very wrong.

9

"What happened to me?"

I stared down at my mutated hands for minutes. I realized my clothes had ripped to shreds, and there was virtually nothing left of my shoes. My now-furry legs were huge and muscular.

I looked like... some kind of massive dog. I heard the sound of water flowing nearby and wondered if it was actually close or if I was hearing something a few miles away.

I stood up and surveyed the forest around me. I pinpointed the source of the sound and started toward it.

At least I can still walk upright, I thought.

Deep down, I hoped all of this was just a crazy dream. Or that I had accidentally ingested some ayahuasca or a magic mushroom.

I shook my heavy head. Then ran my hands—er, paws—over my ears. I let out an exhale at the touch of pointed, furry ears.

"This is insane. It's just a dream." I racked my brain trying to remember what words Dorothy had used to get home, but I was all out of shiny red shoes.

The sound of the stream grew louder in my head. I was close now and hurried my pace as much as I could with my huge, doglike feet.

As I prowled toward the source of noise, I wondered what became of the morning. The last thing I remembered before falling into that... place was the sun peeking over the horizon. By all accounts, it should have been morning. Maybe late morning, depending on how long I was in the temple.

What time is it?

I instinctively looked down at my wrist, but my watch was gone. I tried to recall if Carrillo had taken it. Not that it mattered. My wrist was at least double its previous size, and whatever strange transformation had happened to me would have snapped the band in two as my body mutated.

I reached the little brook and looked down at it from above. The stream ran through a deep ditch that dropped down about ten feet to the bottom. To my left, the water pooled in an area where the liquid didn't move as much. I quickly slid down the embankment and stumbled over to the poolside, where I hovered over the water and stared into the reflection the morning sky provided.

The face that stared back was not my own. In its place, the face and head of a doglike creature sat atop a matching body.

A dizzying barrage of emotions tackled me, and I lost my balance. I fell back onto the rocks behind me and gasped. I felt like throwing up but managed to keep the bile down—for the moment, anyway.

"What is going on with me? What is this? Why do I look like some big... dog-man?"

My answer came in the form of a rustling of leaves and snapping sticks. My ears twitched, and I perked up, as if aroused by thousands of years of instinct.

Was the jaguar back? Or was it Carrillo's men?

Then I heard the whisper that confirmed the answer.

"He has to be around here somewhere," the voice said in Spanish. "Keep looking."

It wasn't Carrillo, but it was definitely one of his men.

Early morning daylight continued to creep across the jungle.

I searched the immediate area for a place to hide. The voice came from just beyond the other side of the creek, which meant the second the guy saw me, he would open fire. But I could take cover against the embankment over there, and the gunman might not see me down below.

The decision made, I waded through the cool water, and when I reached the embankment, I pressed my back into the dirt and waited.

The clumsy gunman approached without regard to all the noise he was making. Or maybe these monster ears I had made it seem louder than normal. My hearing had certainly increased dramatically.

As the man drew near, I could even hear his breathing, and worse, I smelled the cheap cologne on his skin, mixing with sweat and alcohol.

It was a noxious combination, and I almost lost control of my impulses to vomit. Fighting off my own bodily protests, I pushed my back hard into the bank.

I waited, holding my breath, certain I would be found. But after several seconds, I heard the man start to move away, heading upstream.

Suddenly, my foot slipped on a loose stone and sent a rock skittering across the others. The loud rattling sound echoed around the immediate area, and the gunman froze. He whipped his submachine gun around and looked in my direction, but in the shadows of the bank, he didn't see me. Or I didn't think he did.

He looked right at me, then back down to the water, then began retracing his steps until he'd reached the edge of the bank. He swept his weapon left to right and back again. For a second, I thought he might keep going and write off the sound to random chance, or perhaps a jungle animal slipping on the stones.

That hope faded when he bent down and set a foot onto the embankment.

He was coming down, and within seconds, he'd see me. Without a weapon, I would be dead.

Or was I without a weapon?

I felt saliva dripping down my teeth. Except they weren't my normal human teeth. They were long, sharp fangs that hung down over my gums. I risked reaching up and touching one of the teeth, and my suspicion was confirmed. And there was something else.

I was struck with the overwhelming feeling—no, desire—to kill the gunman. It was unlike anything I'd ever felt before, and maybe it was simply fight-or-flight kicking in. But that instinct felt real and tangible, like the most natural urge I've ever felt in my life.

The gunman slid on the loose dirt and rocks and nearly landed on his backside as he skidded down the embankment.

He first looked to his right, then swept the gun around toward me.

The whites of his eyes expanded in sheer terror, and he fumbled the gun in his hands as he tried to raise it.

I stepped out of the shadows and snarled. *I snarled?* I let the question go, and lunged toward him, baring my fangs in midair.

The panic on his face swelled. He managed to get one shot off before I pounced, smashing into him with superhuman power. The man crumbled under my new weight like a flower under a bulldozer. Without thinking, I bit hard into his neck, twisting my jaw with a quick snap. I felt warm liquid gush over my tongue and mouth. The resistance from the gunman immediately turned into unconscious twitching as he died.

I stood up again and looked down at my handiwork, staring in disbelief at the bloody mess I'd made. The man's legs kicked for a few more seconds before he went still.

I breathed hard but didn't feel tired. It must have been from the adrenaline pumping through me. I'd never killed anyone before. I had always imagined I would feel guilt or pain or regret or a million different negative emotions. Now, however, all I felt was satisfaction. And there was something else.

Up until that moment, whenever I had tasted blood, it had a metal flavor to it, like drinking water from a rusty pipe. This blood didn't taste like that at all. It was sweet and... refreshing?

How was that possible?

Beyond that, I suddenly felt energized and stronger. It was as if the man's blood had given me more power.

But I wasn't a vampire. That much I knew. I didn't believe in vampires, but beyond that, I'd never seen one that looked like me.

I shook off the thought and stumbled back over to the water's edge, looking into the still pool once more.

I still looked like the dog-man from before, but now there was something different. In the dark, clear water, my eyes glowed red like blazing rubies.

I needed answers but didn't know where to turn. Then I remembered. The shaman. The voice in the temple, whether real or dreamed, had told me to find a shaman. Would have been nice if he'd given me a little direction. Maybe the name of the village or town where this witch doctor lived. As it was, I would have to roam the country trying to locate this person.

Another voice touched my ears. It wasn't close, maybe fifty yards away. Perhaps a little more. It was another one of Carrillo's men.

I took one more look at the monster in the reflection and flashed a toothy, monstrous grin. I'd find the shaman. After I took out Carrillo.

10

The power surging through me was unlike anything I'd ever experienced. I'd experimented with a few mild drugs in college: some pot, a 'shroom one time that didn't do much other than make it seem like things moved more than they really were. That one had been a disappointment. I'd gone in expecting to cross a dimensional plane or something. Turns out, to do that I had to fall into some ethereal ancient Aztec temple.

No, I countered myself. *This is a dream. Just play along, and you'll wake up.*

It didn't matter how many times I told myself that. I had a feeling I wasn't going to be waking up from this. No matter how unrealistic or outrageous it might have seemed.

More questions filled my mind as I stalked through the jungle. I looked down at the necklace dangling around my upper chest. The medallion had been shiny and silver in the temple, but out here, in the dark of the forest, it seemed to retreat from the light, as if camouflaging itself.

One thing was certain. I needed to relearn everything I thought I ever knew about Xolotl.

"Yes."

I twisted my head at the word. It hadn't come from anywhere around me. It came from within me. That made no sense, and yet it was the only way I could explain it. As if another conscience was in my head.

I hoped quietly that this wouldn't be a regular occurrence. I had enough to think about. I didn't need another voice chirping in my ear.

I waited for a second, and after no more voices, I kept going.

The scent of too much cologne, and a hint of sweat, filled the air and rippled its way through my nostrils. Twisting my head to the left, I heard the sound of something creeping amid the underbrush. It was too light to be the jaguar from before. Which meant it was either one of Carrillo's men or another creature I'd yet to encounter.

Either way, I had to check it out.

I walked toward where the sound originated. Then I crouched down on all fours and prowled like an animal. The move, to my surprise, felt natural and normal. It was as though I obeyed an instinct that, while not controlling my actions entirely, definitely had a strong sway over what I did.

I don't know if I'm going to get used to this.

Still, stalking through the jungle as an animal-monster, whatever I was, seemed to have its advantages. I could stay low and out of sight, using the foliage and infinite trees for cover as I hunted my prey.

My paws didn't make a sound, even when I touched dry leaves or sticks.

The quarry's scent grew stronger with every step, and I found myself letting my ears and nose lead me, rather than only my eyes.

My other senses pulled on me, tugging me toward the man who believed he was hunting a helpless archaeologist.

He had another thing coming.

I rounded a huge tree trunk, and the gunman came into view. My eyes widened, and I felt the same strange urge pulsing through my veins. I grinned, brandishing my teeth again. Then I crouched down on my back feet and prepared to spring.

The gunman swept his firearm to the right, left, and back again. I sensed something else from him that wasn't a smell or a sound. It was something intangible, except I definitely knew it was there. I listened harder, trying to determine what this sensation could be.

As the man twisted to the right again, nearly turning all the way around, I saw his face in the pale radiance of the dawn. This hardened killer, a man who'd probably whacked any number of people as part of his daily routine, looked terrified.

Tattooed, muscled, and fierce, this cartel hit man bore the fear of a six-year-old-boy left in the dark by himself.

My grin widened.

I was definitely going to mess with this one before he died.

I didn't know where Carrillo was, or the man who'd killed Amy, but they could wait for now. *Always take the low-hanging meat... er, fruit.*

Had I just called this guy meat? Or was it the other voice?

"No," I whispered. *I'm the only one allowed in this head.*

I retreated behind the tree, raised up on my hind legs, and let out the loudest howl I could muster.

To my surprise, my voice boomed powerfully through the trees. It echoed off a hillside somewhere in the distance. A few birds resting in the treetops took flight, their wings flapping wildly among the leaves as they punched through the canopy to the safety of the night sky.

I peeked around the tree and spotted the gunman. The man was freaking out, waving his gun around wildly in random directions. He looked like a frightened deer, but one that didn't know if they should run and hide or try to stay put in hopes that the threat would somehow magically disappear.

I spied another tree of similar size about thirty feet away and decided to flank the gunman. I took off, intending to sprint to the next spot, but as quickly as I had the thought, I was there. I hadn't teleported, but I'd moved faster than I could have ever believed possible. For anyone or anything.

"Señor Wolf?" The gunman's voice trembled with fear. "It's okay to come out. I'm not going to hurt you. Señor Carrillo only wants your help. We're not going to hurt you. He did you a favor killing your wife. You're a free man now. And with the money he's going to pay you, you'll be able to do whatever you want. Move to another country. Buy your own island. The world is yours."

I remembered the line from *Scarface*. But it barely registered. All I could think about was what he said regarding my wife's murder. This guy was acting like Carrillo had done me a favor, that he'd opened up a whole world of opportunities by killing an innocent woman.

I felt rage course through me. My breathing grew deeper, more deliberate. "She didn't deserve to die." I said the words loud enough for the man to hear, but he still didn't see me. He snapped the gun around in my general direction, but all he saw were the endless trees that evaporated into a ghostly mist.

"She cheated on you, gringo."

I didn't give the man a chance to say anything else. I surged from my hiding place and sprinted toward him.

He saw movement, reacted, and fired.

I was too fast, and before I knew it, I was behind another tree as the goon ripped off several shots from his automatic weapon.

Pausing behind the tree trunk, I waited until he stopped shooting. I'd run across a wide clearing at a dead sprint, covering the distance in an extraordinarily short amount of time. I mean in mere seconds. Not quite teleporting, but I was booking it. What was more, I hadn't even broken a sweat. My breath came in a calm, even rhythm.

I needed to learn more about these bizarre powers and how to hone them, but I'd figure that out later.

Meanwhile, I heard the gunman's heart pounding in his chest. I heard his rapid, fear-riddled breathing.

"El diablo," he muttered.

I smiled to myself.

"Better the devil you know," I said back, loud enough that I knew he heard me.

"What are you?"

Ironic. He's asking the same question I asked the voice in the temple.

I replied, but it didn't feel like me. "I am the incarnation of Xolotl, and I have come to defend those who cannot defend themselves."

"Xo... lotl?" The man's trembling voice sounded like he was sitting in one of those vibrating chairs.

"Yes. And I have also come to escort the unworthy to the land of the dead."

I forcibly stopped myself from talking and bit my dog lip. What was I saying? Or rather, who was saying these things?

I didn't have to ask the question. I had a sneaking, fear-stricken suspicion that I already knew. This Xolotl thing had possessed me. And I wasn't down with that kind of deal. At the time, I didn't think I could negotiate that.

"You cannot."

"Okay, stop that," I said out loud to the voice in my head.

"What?" the gunman shouted back.

"Where is Carrillo?" I answered. "Tell me where he is, and I won't kill you."

"Dr. Wolf. Is that you? Come out from behind the tree. You look different. I thought it was a wild animal or something. Just come out and we can discuss this."

"Yeah right," I countered. "You just tried to shoot me."

"That's because I thought you were the jaguar from before. I can understand why you ran away. But the animal is gone now. So, just come out, and we'll head back to the camp. No worries. Señor Carrillo will be glad I found you."

"I'm sure he would be. Tell you what. Put down your gun, and I'll think about it."

"Doesn't work like that, amigo."

I heard something else in the jungle. The movement was subtle, and if I hadn't had these unusual canine senses, I doubted I would have detected it. But I did sense it, and I knew immediately it was no animal. Carrillo, or one of his men, was circling around to flank me.

"This is your last chance," I warned. "Put down your gun, and tell me where Carrillo is, and I'll let you live. For now, anyway." I couldn't promise him I wouldn't kill him eventually. After all, he was one of the men responsible for Amy's death.

The thought of my wife's murder renewed the rage pumping

through me, but I suppressed it, waiting and listening for the enemy's next move.

"Okay, Dr. Wolf. I'm putting my gun down. Just come out from behind there, and we can go back to the camp."

I leaned around the tree and saw the man lowering his weapon to the ground. Then he put up his hands in a show of good faith that he was no longer armed. Which I believed for about two seconds. Even if he had relinquished his weapons, I knew it was only because the other gunman was closing in on my position.

I heard a crunch about forty feet away from behind a thicket of underbrush and immediately darted to my right. I barely felt the ground under my feet as I ran to another tree and took cover. Looking around the trunk, I located the sneaking gunman. He was looking toward the little clearing where his partner stood, and apparently believed I was still in that area.

He only looked my direction in the last second as I flew toward him, my legs, all four of them, pumping at supernatural speed.

The gunman shrieked and managed one shot from his gun before I sank my teeth into his neck. I snapped my head to the side, ripping through flesh. The man's screams vanished an instant before his muscles went limp.

I let the body drop to the ground in a heap and wiped my jaw with my forearm. That's when I felt the stinging pain in my left side.

I looked down, touching the wound with my fingers. Thick blood, so dark it was nearly black, oozed from a gash in my side. I winced at the pain, but it wasn't as bad as I imagined a bullet could be.

Then, in amazement, as I examined the injury, I saw my flesh slowly begin to close the wound. Within seconds, the blood was gone, and the wound was healed.

"What the—?" I sputtered.

Did my body just heal itself? I looked down on the ground and saw the mashed bullet lying on the dirt.

"Did you get him?" The voice of the other gunman echoed through the jungle.

The goon took a step forward, collected his gun, and looped the strap over his shoulder. He wore a look of fear that seemed out of place on someone whose job hinged on being a stone-cold killer.

He walked forward toward where the dead man lay in the mist, hidden in the undergrowth.

"I'm sure you must be hungry," the gunman said. "And thirsty. You're lucky you're still alive, Dr. Wolf. Being out here for nearly two days. I'm surprised that jaguar didn't get you. Or something else."

What did he just say? Two days? I've been gone nearly two days? How is that possible?

"What are you talking about?" I asked. Then I zipped away from the body, stopping fifteen yards away behind another tree, watching as the man stalked toward his fallen comrade.

The gunman paused, looking around as if he'd heard something, then took another wary step forward. "You must be hallucinating. Did you fall and hurt yourself? Señor Carrillo can help you. He has doctors. You won't even have to go to a hospital. Just come out here in the open, and we can get you back to camp. I bet a good meal could make you feel better in no time."

He never saw me flash through the jungle, circling around behind him in a blur. I moved so fast I was nothing more than a shadow in the dark. Standing three feet behind him, I growled, "I've already eaten."

He spun around clumsily, the gun going off in his hand and firing errant rounds into the jungle. I grabbed his trigger hand with a long paw and snapped the man's arm backward with an audible crack.

He screamed at the pain scorching his arm. The gun clattered onto the ground. He tried to reach for a knife on his left hip, but I grabbed his other arm and broke it in a similar fashion, sending him spiraling into the depths of agony. He dropped to his knees, still yelling. Then I wrapped my fingers around his throat and squeezed.

"Where is Carrillo?"

The look in the man's eyes was a mixture of fear and pain.

"El Chupacabra," he whispered, as if in disbelief.

"What did you say?"

"El diablo. Jesus Christo. Por favor, mi dío."

"I'm not the devil," I corrected, squeezing tighter. His eyes bulged. "What was the first thing you said?"

He looked confused for a second, then repeated: "Chupacabra?" His arms dangled at his sides.

I frowned at the word. "What does that mean?"

Tears welled in the man's eyes, another curious contradiction in terms.

"El diablo," was all he said. I saw the color leaving his face. Shock was setting in, and with it came the loss of rational thought. His words slurred into a string of absentminded prayers he barely remembered, probably from a childhood of attending mass.

"Where is the camp?" I pressed. "Where is Carrillo?"

He only continued muttering the incoherent words, as if they could somehow save his blackened soul.

"You killed my wife," I said. "Carrillo ordered it. Tell me where he is, and I won't make you suffer."

That seemed to connect with the distant look in the man's eyes. He looked up at me, staring at the monster in his face. Then he glanced to the left. It was the only signal he gave, and all I needed.

I followed his gaze for a few seconds and then looked back at him. "Thank you," I said. I picked him up with one arm, holding him up over my head with a powerful grip. My mind wondered how this was possible. How could I hold up a grown man with one arm, and do it with almost no effort? An incredible strength flowed through me. My muscles rippled as I held the cartel thug aloft. Then, I twisted my torso and smashed his head into the ground until his body sagged.

I exhaled and dropped him to the ground, his face and skull battered and bloody from the beating.

Looking to the west, where the dead man had indicated, I found a nearby tree and started climbing.

With my animal body, I found scaling the trunk much easier than if I were still human. As I continued to climb, that thought haunted me. *Would I be this creature permanently? Or is there a time limit on it?* It still felt like I was walking through a dream or some kind of alternate reality. This defied everything I knew about science. And I was still curious about the word that last gunman had used.

"Chupacabra," I said as I neared the top of the tree. The limbs were thinner at the top, and less stable, but I managed to reach the clear sky above while hanging on to another branch from a separate tree.

There, at the pinnacle of the forest, I kept my eyes west. I spotted the smoke from Carrillo's camp rising into the night, trickling by the moon like a churning gray river.

"There you are," I said. "Time to pay for your sins, Carrillo."

11

I woke up with my face in the dirt and a pounding headache in the back of my skull. It felt like I'd gone on five all-night benders in one terrible evening.

A dense fog hung around me, cutting my visibility to almost nothing, save for the jungle around me.

The jungle. I realized where I was. But what happened? I looked around, hoping one of Carrillo's men hadn't gotten lucky and happened upon where I was lying in the dirt. Then there was the matter of the jaguar that was still on the loose—as far as I knew.

I sat up, continuing to scan my surroundings.

That's when I realized it.

My hands were human hands. I quickly looked over my body and realized that I'd changed back into my human form. The medallion, however, still hung around my neck, dangling at the top of my chest. Unlike other metals, though, it felt warm against my skin instead of cold and lifeless. This thing seemed to have a life of its own.

I hurriedly reached to remove it, but it grew hotter, and I nearly burned my fingers before I let go of it and allowed it to fall back to my chest, where it, oddly, returned instantly to merely warm.

"What is going on?" I asked. My pants hung loosely around my waist. The belt had been shorn long ago, and the button and zipper were pretty much useless. I was surprised the pants had managed to stay on, even though they were shredded at the bottom and along the waist. The shirt I had on barely clung to my torso, hanging loosely off my shoulders, tattered and ripped.

I got up and surveyed the area again, and that's when I saw it. Something stuck out from behind a tree close to the trail. I cocked my head to the side and took a cautious step toward it.

Then I realized what it was. A foot jutted out from underneath huge green leaves.

My eyes widened at the sight of the dead man lying just off the side of the path. Then everything from the night before flashed in my mind.

I remembered chasing the man down, hunting him like a wild animal. I could see the entire chase play out. I ran through the jungle, catching up to him in no time. I pounced on him, pinned him down, and...

"Ah, my head." I clutched at the base of my skull. The headache was killing me. I tried to refocus my energy and attention on the medallion, the night before, and finding some answers.

The memory of the night's final interrogation returned in a flash. I was there, holding the last of Carrillo's men down. I asked him where I could find the cartel don. *What was it he'd said?*

My mind locked in on the moment, and I could feel it as though I was right there. The man's fear had oozed from every pore.

"Where is Carrillo?" I asked again.

"He has a place. Outside the city. Everyone knows it. But the cops won't do anything. They're too afraid."

No lie occupied his eyes.

I told him to get up and leave, to run, but he got stupid. The memory ran through my head like a 4-D movie, one where I could sense everything playing out before me. As I turned to make my way down the trail, he raised a pistol and shot me in the back.

After I bit his arm off, he took longer than the others to die. I made sure of that.

I exhaled after reliving the events. The mist around me was rising into the sky now, and I could see the trail more clearly than before.

With the sun rising to the east, I figured that was as good a place as any to go. But I needed clothes. I didn't want to roam into some village looking like a vagrant who'd been lost in the jungle for days or weeks. I looked back at the dead man on the ground and noted the size of his pants. They were still fairly clean. At least they didn't have bloodstains, which was more than I could say for the guy's shirt.

I'd have to figure out the shirt thing later on.

I winced at the notion of pulling the man's pants off and wearing them, but I didn't have a choice. So, with a large degree of trepidation, I removed the trousers and slipped them on. As I suspected, they fit, albeit a touch loosely. Still, with the belt, they were better than my previous option.

I took off down the trail, hoping I'd seen the last of Carrillo's men. For now, anyway. I still couldn't come to grips with all that had happened the night before. It still felt like a bizarre dream, but I knew that wasn't the case. The pants covering my legs were proof. Unless I was still in the dream.

"This is maddening," I mumbled.

"It won't be for long, Gideon." I whipped my head around but saw nothing and no one.

"The voice in my head again, huh?" I asked.

No answer.

"Fine." I kept walking. "So, I'm trying to understand all this. Can you explain what's going on? You know, so I have at least a frame of reference?"

More silence.

I sighed, frustrated, but kept going anyway, attempting to sort through the insanity of the last... What was it? Two nights? Three?

I shook my head to clear the cobwebs but only succeeded in hurting the back of my skull. I closed my eyes for a second, willing the pain away. Strangely, it melted within seconds, and my head didn't hurt anymore.

"So, I can just heal myself like that?"

"Yes," the voice answered in my mind.

"You'll answer that one but not the others?"

I got the response I expected, which was nothing.

"You're annoying. Whatever you are."

The trail bent and weaved through the jungle, and as the fog continued to rise, I could see deeper into the vegetation surrounding me. I hiked uphill for what seemed like forever, and I had no idea if I was going the right way or not. Something inside me told me I was, although I didn't fully trust my instincts right now for the simple reason that they weren't entirely my own. Something else was there now—a new, more primal awareness—and I didn't know how to absorb that.

I stopped at the top of the ridge, amazed at how fresh my muscles still felt, and looked back down the trail. Turning to my left, I saw the true magnitude of the mountain I'd just climbed. I also spotted something far more important.

Smoke rose in multiple pillars from a village in the valley below. A dirt road ran through it, and there were a few cars and trucks parked along the main street—if it could be called a street. The vehicles appeared to be very old, rusting everywhere and covered in dried mud, some permanently canted to one side, all the headlights long since busted out. The villagers milled around a few of the buildings, but there was very little foot traffic generally.

The homes were little more than huts, or pueblos, constructed from mud and wood from the surrounding jungle.

The place didn't look promising, but without any better options, it was the only choice I had. Maybe one of the old trucks still had a working motor and I could hitch a ride back to Guadalajara. From there, I could find a doctor, perhaps learn what was going on with me. Then again, I probably needed a psychiatrist.

I shook my head again, still grappling with the disbelief of everything that transpired over the last few days. *Was Amy really dead?*

That one continued haunting me. It all happened so fast, so abruptly; none of it seemed real.

Yet here I was, traipsing through the Mexican jungle, trying to find—

What was I looking for again?

"The shaman."

"Stop it," I warned.

And the voice said nothing else.

I picked my way through the jungle, heading down the hill toward the village. The journey down the steep hillside took a good fifteen minutes, and I slipped more than once, nearly busting my tail along the way.

At the bottom of the mountain, I lingered at the forest edge, looking for a building that I thought might house the person who had keys to the trucks.

Upon closer inspection, I noticed that one of the vehicles had a flat tire. The other—a 1985 Chevy Silverado pickup—featured an image of a mountain range on the back window and a rusty tailgate that looked like it was about to fall off. The tires appeared to be in working order, though, and that gave me a semblance of hope.

I started toward the middle of the village but stopped within three steps. It felt like I'd walked into an invisible wall. One of my cousins did that once at a family gathering. After loading his plate with food, he started for the back porch and walked straight into the screen door.

In this instance, however, there was no door.

"What is this?" I put out my hand and reached forward. Nothing. I took a step in that direction and again met the same resistance.

I stepped to the left, hoping to go around the invisible wall, but I bumped into the same barrier again. When I stepped to the right, however, nothing stopped me.

Ahead, off to the right of the village and sitting on its own, was a small pueblo in a meadow. I hadn't noticed the humble dwelling before, and for a second, I wondered if I was imagining the structure.

I took a step toward it, and still nothing blocked my path. I continued ahead until I arrived at a firepit built of stacked stones. The remnants of the previous evening's fire still smoldered in the black coals and ash. Three wooden benches cut from logs surrounded the fire circle.

I looked to the pueblo's door and saw that it hung open. *Was it open a second ago?*

It seemed like I'd seen the door closed, but now it was open.

"This is getting creepier by the minute," I whispered.

A gush of air blew through the clearing, and it felt like the wind came straight from the door of the little hut.

I frowned at the notion. The smoke from the fire swirled around me.

The voice in my head urged me to go inside, though this time there were no words. It felt more like a need, an instinctual drive.

I rolled my eyes and trudged toward the pueblo. I stopped near the door and waited for a few seconds before sticking my head inside.

"Hello?" I called.

"Come in," a rickety voice said.

The interior of the place was pitch black, or so I thought. It had to be my eyes playing tricks on me, possibly after the brightness of day.

"Your eyes will adjust," the voice added, as if reading my thoughts.

I took one last look around outside and then stepped in.

The second I set foot in the humble abode, the wooden door slammed shut behind me.

12

I stopped near the outskirts of the camp and counted the men circling the perimeter. They were spaced out evenly, and there were more than I recalled from my previous visit when I escaped.

He must have called in reinforcements.

I still wondered if the last guy I killed was telling the truth about how much time had passed since I disappeared. *Was I really in that temple for a full day and change?* It seemed like no time had passed, perhaps minutes or maybe an hour at most.

That didn't matter now. I needed to finish this, to take out Carrillo and his thugs. I'd figure the rest out later.

Thoughts of what the voice said in the temple still lingered in my mind. "Find the shaman," it had said.

Whatever that meant.

I looked down at the medallion clinging tightly to my neck. The necklace that had felt longer on my human form was much tighter against my... whatever-I-was form. It almost seemed like it was a part of me, as if we'd become one.

I finished counting the men surrounding the camp and grinned with a sort of wicked pleasure. Twenty gunmen stood guard, all facing out into the darkness of the jungle.

They had no idea what was about to hit them.

I stood behind a tree trunk along the path that wound directly into the camp. Five tents like the one I'd been kept in stood in a circle around a central bonfire. The flames roared high into the darkness, casting the flickering shadows onto the forest surrounding the camp.

A light in the largest tent glowed under the flaps, and I figured that had to be the one where Carrillo was hiding. He would, of course, save the biggest and most comfortable tent for himself.

Two men stood on the path just outside the encampment. They stared right toward me without detecting my presence. One of them reached into his pocket and drew a pack of cigarettes. He took a lighter out of the same pocket, tapped the bottom of the pack, then pulled a white stick out. He fit the cigarette between his lips, held the lighter to the tip, and flicked it with his thumb.

The flame illuminated the gunman's face with a yellow glow. And it lit up my dog face, too, only a few inches away.

My movements were so fast, by the time he saw the red glowing eyes, it was already too late. He tried to react, but I grabbed him by his throat and whipped him into the man next to him before either knew what happened. The men tumbled to the ground in a pile, dazed by the impact.

They couldn't muster a defense as I stepped over them before biting hard into their necks, first one, then the other. The two men died in short order, bleeding out quickly onto the jungle soil.

I looked ahead into the camp at the bonfire and then to the right at the next man in line. Moving back into the shadows, I crept around the perimeter. I brandished a claw with the first man and swept it across his throat as I passed. He gurgled as his skin split, opening the floodgates for his life's blood to spill out. Falling to his knees, he twitched his trigger finger, and the submachine gun in his hand rattled. Bullets spewed into the night, random and harmlessly sailing everywhere but my direction.

Shouts from around the camp filled the air. The dying man's

gunfire had sounded the alarm, but that wouldn't save Carrillo and his men.

The next man in the perimeter came into view, his weapon pointed vaguely in my direction. He held the gun waist high, eyes narrowed as he peered into the darkness.

I sprinted hard toward him. He saw me, or at least a glimpse of me, and opened fire. The gun spat hot metal around me, but he couldn't keep the aim true as I circled around and disappeared behind another tree. Bullets cracked the air, some zipping by, others smashing into the trees and earth close by.

I waited until I heard his gun click empty, and then I sprang from my hiding place. I ran hard at him, covering the distance in seconds. The man was ejecting the empty magazine and loading a new one when he saw me coming. Fear streaked the whites of his eyes, and he desperately tried to chamber the first round of the new magazine.

His hand slipped, and he raised the weapon, pulling the trigger again without effect. The round never made it into the pipe. I crashed into the gunman.

He yelled as I picked him up mid-tackle and drove him toward a broad tree trunk with several broken, jagged branches jutting out.

The man kicked his legs and tried to swing fists, but it did him no good as I plowed him into the tree, sinking the sharp branches into his back and through his torso.

I swatted the gun out of his hands. Leaving him hanging there against the tree, I moved on to the next guard.

One by one, I sliced and swatted my way through Carrillo's forces. The men came one by one at first, each attempting to rally and aid the others. Then they realized that they could put up a better fight if they did it in numbers. With only ten men left, the remaining forces gathered around the fire in the camp's center, and waited.

I circled around the perimeter, bounding between cover in the darkness, watching Carrillo's guards stare out in fear of the demon haunting their night.

"Where is he?" I howled. "Where is your master? I want Carrillo."

The men started at the terrifying sound of the monstrous voice booming through the forest.

They twitched and snapped, looking around for the source of the voice. But none of them said a thing.

"He doesn't care about you," I warned. "You're all expendable. Which is why you're out here, and he's..." I stopped, knowing that if Carrillo really was in the big tent, he no longer had any men between me and him.

I glided through the night, unseen by the guards, and stopped at the backside of Carrillo's tent.

I stood there for a second, out of sight, waiting. The man responsible for my wife's death was inside, just beyond these fabric walls. He was probably cowering in there with a gun, waiting, hoping I didn't find him. I wondered if he felt the same fear as all his men. I could smell it on them, like a rotting stench of filth spilling from the sewers.

I decided I was going to make Carrillo suffer for what he'd done.

I lifted the side of the tent and stepped into the light flung around the room by a lantern in the corner. I took in the interior in an instant, and a terrible realization hit me like a brick to the skull.

Carrillo wasn't here.

I retreated back out of the tent and circled around to the next. I checked under the wall. Empty, just like the first one. I moved on to the next, and the next, finding every tent the same—vacant.

I roared in frustration from the darkness, and the men surrounding the fire all spun around my way. I stood in the open now, and I wondered if they could see the same red eyes I noticed before when I was by the water's edge.

Every gunman took aim at me, and I knew they had spotted me.

They opened fire in unison, filling the night air with the sound of gunfire. Bullets streaked around me, cutting leaves and branches from trees and bushes. The birds above had long since evacuated the war zone, leaving nothing but empty jungle around me.

I leaped high into the air, soaring thirty feet up to a tree limb high above the forest floor. It was then I found myself breathing heavily. It wasn't from the jump. It felt like panic, panic from the uncertainty around Carrillo's disappearance. Where had he gone?

I knew deep down the coward had run away, probably back to the city or his fortress estate. He wouldn't stand and fight. He'd pay these sheep to do his bidding for him, and send them to me like lambs to the slaughter.

I winced at the thought.

That wasn't me thinking those words. It was the voice again, the Xolotl or whatever, that had somehow melded with my mind or soul or spirit or however all this worked.

"Something like that." The voice spoke to me for the first time in a while. I hadn't missed it.

"Kill them all," it said to me.

I shook off the command. I wanted to end them, all of them. They deserved it. Each man down below worked for the side of evil. How many lives had they ruined? How many innocent people like my wife had they brutally murdered in cold blood?

There wasn't an innocent among them.

As I stared at the cluster of gunmen reloading their weapons and firming their positions, I noticed something I hadn't seen, or realized I'd seen, before. Each one of them appeared to have a muddy aura around them, dull colors of red, green, and brown, all blending together. It was barely noticeable, but now that I'd seen it, I couldn't unsee it.

I watched them for a minute as they tried to reorganize. And I wondered what the odd glow around their figures meant.

I needed to know where Carrillo was, which meant I needed a prisoner.

I searched the faces of the men around the fire, and found one who looked far more afraid than the others. *That's your patsy.*

Again with the annoying voice in my head.

I let out a howl that would have peeled the rotting skin off a zombie, and watched as the men all jumped and moved. The one I'd picked out suddenly turned and started running in the opposite direction, sprinting down the path away from the camp.

Nine left.

I felt a ravenous urge consume me. It told me to leap and destroy, and so I did.

I jumped from my perch, dropping into the midst of the enemy even as they searched the jungle for their hunter.

I slashed one across the neck, tearing through flesh with a jagged claw. The man on the other side spun as if to fire but was too slow. I backhanded him and sent him flying into the middle of the fire. His horrific screams pierced the night as I whooshed over to the next in line, then the one after him, and so on, ripping through them in a blinding flurry of righteous rage.

Guns fired. Men screamed. They all died.

The last one gave the best effort. He fired his weapon, hitting me square in the chest. I looked down at the bullet wound as if curious, then up at the shooter. The man fired again and again, unloading the entire magazine. Most of the bullets pounded into my chest. One hit me in the forehead. That one really hurt.

The gunman stood there with his weapon extended, the magazine empty, and a trickle of smoke seeping out of the muzzle.

I staggered backward, grimacing at the pain. I fell onto my back and looked up at the man standing there with his gun, watching me.

The pain subsided, and as before, the bullets popped out of my body and the skin healed itself.

A powerful energy coursed through me, and I sprang from the ground, launching myself at the shooter before he could muster another attack.

I snapped at his head and jerked to the side. The man's neck popped, and he fell to the ground, dead.

The jungle fell silent, aside from the crackling of the fire and... something else. *Yes. There it is.* The sound of feet hitting the ground and heavy breathing filled my ears. I turned toward where the frightened thug had run and took off after him.

13

I rounded toward the entrance and considered making a break for it, but the door closed on its own, as if by magic.

"There is no need to flee," the voice said. The tone, while scratchy and old, also carried a sense of calm with it—grandfatherly in a way.

I spun around again, and when I did, the entire home was alight with candles burning on sconces, a fire in the hearth, and several lamps on the kitchen counter and the wooden dining table.

The floor in the pueblo was made of wood, sanded down by time and foot traffic. No pictures adorned the walls. Only a sage clipping dangled from each of the corners, and from the header over the door.

"Who are you?" I asked, looking across the room at an older man sitting in a rocking chair by the fire.

"You know who I am," he said. He didn't smile or frown. His face remained in a perfect state of non-emotion. Black hair dangled in braids around his tanned, wrinkled features. He wore a brown tunic and gray trousers. His bare feet remained planted on the floor, twitching subtly to keep him rocking back and forth in the same, monotonous cadence.

I wondered how a man who looked so old could have such jet-black hair, but I kept the question to myself.

"Things are not always what they appear on the outside, Gideon."

"You know my name," I blurted.

A thin smile spread across his face. "Of course. You are the one I've been waiting for."

"What's that supposed to mean?"

"Sit down," he said, motioning to an uncomfortable-looking chair to his right. "And I will tell you everything you need to know."

I heard him speaking in perfect English. The accent wasn't Spanish. Much like the voice in the temple, it was some other kind of sound—something from another culture long since gone.

I hesitated, and he noticed. He passed me a disarming grin and then turned toward the flame in the hearth. He stared at it, waiting for me to take my seat. I watched him closely for several seconds, and when he didn't move or speak, I ventured forward across the room and sat down.

The chair felt cold and impersonal and hard in an unwelcoming way. I adjusted my position to get as comfortable as possible then sat there looking awkwardly at the man across from me.

Multiple colors of beads hung from earrings in his lobes. I wondered if the adornments had some kind of spiritual meaning or if they were merely accessories.

"Each one has meaning," the man said.

I nearly fell over backward in my seat. "How did you—?"

"Your thoughts are easy to read, Gideon Wolf. A man so full of questions and emotions always is."

"Oh? And what is it I'm thinking now?"

The man smiled, which was a strange look for a guy who appeared as though life had rolled him through the dryer.

"You're wondering if I'm the shaman you were meant to see, along with a great many other questions."

"Well?" I asked. "Are you?"

"The shaman?" He laughed. "If I'm not, I should probably look into a different wardrobe." He tugged on his ragged tunic.

"Fair enough," I said. "Who are you? And what is going on with me?"

The man stared at the medallion around my neck, his eyes unwilling to let go.

"I am the shaman, as you said. I've been known by many names over the years, but usually people just call me that."

"Get a lot of visitors, do you?" I asked, panning the unimpressive room.

"Not so many," he admitted. "Every few centuries, someone like you comes along. The in-between can get a bit boring, although I've taken up some hobbies that help pass the time."

I furrowed my brow at the man's unusual comment. "I'm sorry. Did you—"

"Yes, centuries. I know. Hard to believe, isn't it? I don't look a day over nine hundred."

I swallowed back the disbelief in my throat. "Nine... hundred. You're nine hundred years old?"

"Oh no. Don't be silly, Gideon. I'm much older than that." He waved a dismissive hand at me, blowing off my absurd question. "I'm a guide. And a guide is not always needed."

"A guide?"

He nodded, and his braids bounced like black ropes hanging from his head. "For guardians. Like you."

"Guardian?" I wondered, my frown deepening.

"And now we come to the part where you receive the answers you've been looking for." He raised his left hand and looked at a watch on his wrist. It clung to his skin with a black leather strap, and I half wondered if the thing was real.

Suddenly, the flames flickered and nearly died, slowing to nothing but a single tongue in the hearth. The lanterns and candles also dimmed, casting the room into darkness.

Then a light appeared before me in the shape of an orb, like a hologram I'd seen in science fiction movies.

"At the dawn of time on Earth, many eons ago, we were a feeble, weak race."

Were?

"That's a fair question," the shaman said.

I rolled my eyes at him reading my mind again and then allowed myself to wonder if he was the voice I'd been hearing.

"I'm not," the man confessed. "Now, moving on." He pointed at the sphere. Within it, beasts took shape, and some of them looked familiar—though I couldn't place why.

"When the Creator shaped this place, and put people on it to rule the land, they quickly fell to the temptations of evil. When that happened, the Creator cut them off, and so they fell into darkness, spiritually and mentally. But the One who made them didn't leave them to fend for themselves, not entirely. Humans were given guardians to teach them and protect them from the forces of evil, from the demons who dwell in the shadows and lead the hearts of men to stray until they are forever lost."

"Okay," I said, not fully believing what I was hearing. "And what are these guardians? What do they do?"

"Guardians are a power, a force that can inhabit the body of a person in order to fight injustice or exact revenge, if necessary. They fight for the innocent and are the executioners of the wicked. You have been chosen by Xolotl, which is a difficult, and powerful, spirit. It is the power of the dog guardian. I've long wondered when you would arrive, the wolf that would become the chupacabra. That prophecy always perplexed me."

"Why did you say that? Prophecy? What prophecy? About a wolf? My last name is Wolf. It's just a name." I thought about the voice I'd heard in the temple, telling me that I was the wolf there to join the dog or something. It hadn't made sense then, and the shaman wasn't clearing up much at the moment.

"Your name *Wolf* is by no accident, Gideon. You come from a long lineage of guardian squires. Yours is the House of Claw and Fang."

"What?" My jaw hung slack, and I did nothing to close it.

"Squires? Oh yes. After mankind was cut off, no longer allowed to interact directly with the Creator, they were given one last gift before the separation. Seven houses, or families, were chosen and granted crests, and they were each assigned a guardian spirit that would come to their aid when they needed it most. Sometimes, the need was a personal one. Other times, the guardians were called upon in moments of national distress."

I thought about what he said, trying to connect the information to something I already knew—a fact or tidbit locked away in the deep recesses of my memory.

"I heard a story once," I said absently. "Ogier the Dane. It was Ogier the Dane."

The shaman merely smiled at me, not confirming or denying my assertion.

"It was said that Ogier slept until the nation of Denmark needed him again. Then he would rise to defend her people." I looked over at the man by the fire. "Was Ogier a guardian?"

"Yes," the shaman said. "He was. Of the wolf clan. Same as you."

"Wait. You're saying that I'm a descendant of Ogier the Dane?" The idea was insane.

"I didn't say it. You did." He raised a bony finger and extended it toward me. "The seven clans were each given medallions, talismans of great power. When the one who claims it dies, it is returned to its hiding place until the next guardian comes."

"How long is that?"

"It depends. There are forces of evil who seek the seven medallions. They would use the amulets for wickedness, and the world would be plunged into the blackest of nights."

"Seven medallions?" I pinched the one around my neck and held it up to examine it more closely. "Where are the others?"

"I don't know," the shaman said. "I am only permitted to know the location of this one. It was the one assigned to me. Each medallion has a guide. And each guide a medallion. Each one is different, just like each guide is different."

I took a deep breath, trying not to disparage everything the man was telling me. But he was saying he was centuries old and that there were seven magical amulets that could turn people into—

"I understand your doubts, Gideon. But you must have worked

through those to some degree when the transformation happened. Yes?"

I didn't answer immediately, so he went on.

"You put on the medallion. You experienced the change. It is a part of you now, until you die. It is your burden, your curse, and your righteous purpose."

"Purpose? I'm an archaeologist. That's my purpose." I stood up, a sudden rush of anger pulsing through me. "I am not some vigilante. I'm not a hero." Tears broke through the corners of my eyes. "I just want all this to go away. I want to go back to my life, back to Amy. I want our life back. Okay? I don't know what any of this is or what it means. And I don't care. I'm not here to be some kind of superhero." I stared down at the medallion, one thought pulsing through my mind. "I will use this thing," I held it up, "to take out Carrillo for what he did to my wife. After that, I'm done."

The shaman stared at me. His kind expression never changed, but I did feel like he was gazing at me as he might have a rare animal in the wild.

"Will killing Carrillo get your wife back?" he asked.

I glowered at him for even daring to go there. This stranger, a man I'd just met and who believed he was maybe thousands of years old, just had the cojones to ask if killing a cartel kingpin would get my wife back.

"That's a cliché thing to ask a man," I spat through gritted teeth.

"We both know the answer. Killing Carrillo won't give you your wife, or your life, back. The life you knew, the way you lived, is a thing of the past, Gideon. You can either embrace the gift you've been given, despite the fact that it looks like a punishment, or you can try to ignore your true purpose. The decision is yours. Whether you choose to serve mankind, defending and avenging those who cannot for themselves, is entirely up to you. I think you'll find, though, that this path will lead to a better future. Not just for those you help but for yourself, too."

My breathing calmed, and I felt a wave of peace wash over me. A tear trickled down my cheek and onto the floor by my feet. "They shot her," I said, remembering the execution of my wife with glaring detail. "We'd been at a party for an exhibit we opened. Went back to the room. They came in and killed her right there in front of me."

The shaman only listened, though a spark of pity flickered in his eyes.

Somehow, I fell back into my seat with a thud. "I couldn't stop them. They put the gun to her head and fired. There was so much more blood than I would have ever thought." I felt like retching, but I kept my wits and forced my stomach to behave. "They told me she cheated on me with someone we know, a man we've worked with before."

The shaman's nose twitched but otherwise showed no signs of emotion.

"I didn't believe them. Maybe a part of me did. I don't know. What I do know is that Carrillo had her killed. And I need to take him out, along with everyone who works for him. Will it bring my wife back?" I shrugged and huffed a cynical laugh. "I know it won't. But at least that man won't be able to hurt anyone else again. No more wives or mothers or children will suffer because of him. And if this thing"—I pinched the medallion again—"can help make that happen, then that's what I want. After that, I don't care what happens to me. Let someone else have this thing. I'll send it back to the temple."

He blinked slowly as if to appease me and then said, "I've told you how the rules work. The medallion will only be returned to the temple when you're dead. Of course, it can be taken from you."

I frowned. "What happens if someone takes it from me?"

"They will inherit the power. You don't want that, at least, not from an enemy."

No. He was right. In the wrong hands, this power could be used for all sorts of bad. Then it hit me.

"Carrillo is looking for the same thing." I looked down at the heavy silver around my neck. The red eyes set inside the wolf's face—or dog's face; I couldn't decide—seemed to stare back at me as if alive. "He was looking for a temple." I shifted my view to the old man in the rocking chair.

"The temple you visited."

"Yes," I said, knowing that had to be the truth. I looked down at the floor and then up again. "The temple. It vanished. I wandered through the jungle, but I never saw it again."

"Nor will you."

I compressed all the information the man was giving me, trying to make sense of it. "The beasts in the temple. They were in a chamber where I found this."

"The seven powers. Along with their first squires."

"And the voice in my head?" That was the one I wished the shaman could answer more than any. Well, maybe second. How to get rid of it was the most important thing at the moment.

"Xolotl dwells within you. It gives you incredible strength and speed."

"No kidding."

"The voice you hear will begin to meld with your own until you don't even notice it anymore. He will act as your animal self until you can learn to control it."

That explained why I felt almost unconscious as I tore through Carrillo's men. It felt like I was obeying something deep, strings that were controlling me but allowing me to believe I was still running the show.

"I can see you're still trying to work through much of this," the shaman said. "So, I will let you go for now. You have much to do, and your adversary will be hunting for you."

"Wait," I begged, not wanting the man to go just yet. The truth was I didn't want to be alone again yet, either. No one else would understand any of this, and I wanted as many details as I could gather.

"Why did I change back?" I asked.

"What do you mean?" He tilted his head at an angle to display genuine curiosity.

"Why did I change back to a human? I woke up this morning facedown in the dirt, and I was a human again."

"Oh that. Yes. You will only remain in the Xolotl form in the dark. In daylight, you will appear to be a man."

That didn't sound like the answer I was looking for. "Wait, you're saying I'll automatically turn into a freak when the sun goes down?"

He laughed. "No. That's not what I'm saying. In the light, you will always look like a human. And the same in the dark. In the darkness, however, Xolotl may be unleashed. You may choose when, though at first I suspect it may take a little practice. It usually does for any new guardian."

"So, I do what? Say a little prayer or something? Do a special dance? Maybe chant some kind of spell?" I had no idea what he meant when he said that Xolotl could be unleashed.

"When the moment comes, you'll know what to do."

"That isn't helpful."

"Isn't it?" His playful and somewhat irritating grin remained intact as his head twitched to the opposite angle.

"Okay, fine. Am I like a werewolf or something now? I can't be killed except with a silver bullet?"

"Yes. A silver bullet is the only thing that can kill you."

My head retreated a few inches. "What? Seriously?"

"No. Not seriously." He shook his head in disappointment. "Your body has incredible healing properties now."

That's an understatement.

"That power will always be present, even in your human form. It will heal itself of any injuries except one."

"And what's that?" I wondered.

"Let's just say, don't lose your head."

I pressed my lips together and then nodded. "So, no decapitation. That's it? The only way I die is through decapitation?"

"No, but the other ways involve things like falling into a volcano or something along those lines. Perhaps a vat of acid." He pressed a finger to his cheek and looked up at the ceiling, considering the methods. "I haven't thought of that one before. If the medallion is taken from you, you become mortal. As I believe I may have mentioned. Beyond that, if your body is destroyed, it cannot house the power of Xolotl, and so it will return to the temple."

"Okay, so it sounds like aside from a pretty gruesome ending, I'll be okay."

"Basically. Yes."

I sighed and stood up again, then paced to the other side of the room. "So, what am I supposed to do? Roam the countryside like some kind of freak, handing out justice to those who have hurt others, and defending those who can't defend themselves? I don't mean to sound rude, but all of this is a little crazy. Right?"

I spun around and found, to my astonishment, that I was standing in the clearing just outside the village. The pueblo was gone, and night had fallen in the valley.

I looked around the meadow and over to the village. Smoke ascended from several chimneys.

The shaman and his home had simply disappeared. I was standing there one second, inside the man's home, and then it was gone. Literally in the blink of an eye.

How was that possible?

No answers came. Not from the field or the village or the hillsides around me. And not from in my own mind.

"Finally decided to shut up, huh?" I asked.

I only received silence.

"That figures." I inhaled the wet air. I would need to find a way back to the city, and from the looks of it, my best bet was the rickety-looking vehicle on the dirt street.

More questions bounced around in my head. I found myself wondering about the other animal families the shaman had mentioned. And I never got the man's name. He said that I was part of an ancient collective, from the wolf family. But what other families were there? And were they all based on—

Then it hit me.

I recalled my studies of ancient indigenous tribes, and the way some of them viewed animals, spirits, guides, and the ancient world.

The pieces came together in my brain, as if something was

shoving them into the forefront of my thoughts. I wondered if the legends and myths I'd studied were actually true, especially regarding ancient religions. Were the gods from the Greek mythologies actually these guardians the shaman told me about? That question applied to all of them, from Roman to Babylonian and all points in between.

I had time to think about that stuff on my way back to Guadalajara. First, I needed to find some proper clothes that hadn't belonged to a dead guy. Then I would track down Carrillo, and make him pay for what he'd done.

Someone could tell me where Carrillo was. And I would burn through everyone in his little army until I found him.

14

I ambled into the village like a defeated cowboy in the most depressing spaghetti western ever made—one of those scenes where the people are sitting or standing outside their shops, staring through vapid eyes at a newcomer venturing into their town.

I just hoped they didn't think I was going to be any trouble.

I noticed a sign for a cantina halfway down the main street and decided that was as good as any place to find out where I was, and if I could get a ride back into the city.

Out of habit, I looked to my wrist but was quickly reminded my watch was gone. I'd have to get a new one, or maybe not. If this shape-shifting thing continued, what would be the point?

A girl on a porch made eye contact with me. She couldn't have been more than seven, maybe eight. I wondered briefly why she wasn't in school. Then I remembered I was out in the Middle of Nowhere, Mexico, and maybe there wasn't a decent school nearby. I knew about the history, not the current state of education in this foreign land.

The girl watched me closely even after I'd stopped looking at her. I could feel her stare as I passed, making my way to the entrance of the cantina. I figured she was gawking due to my tattered clothes, and maybe possibly at the sight of the first gringo she'd seen here in a while. Either way, I didn't want to stop and leave too much of an impression.

Carrillo was still out there, and despite taking out a small contingent of his forces, I knew the man surely had plenty more in reserve —potentially in this town. The thought sent a shiver across my skin, and I stole a quick look around before walking through the open cantina door.

Inside, the place reminded me of a Mississippi juke joint from sixty years ago. Old metal signs hung from the walls advertising Mexican beer, tequilas, and various soccer—football in these parts —teams.

I found a clock hanging over the bar in the back and noted the time was just after eleven o'clock.

A young woman with thick black hair, a white shirt with three buttons—two of them undone—and a charcoal-gray skirt stood behind the counter hanging beer mugs from hooks above a mirror along the back wall.

"We just opened," she said in Spanish. "If you want something to drink, you'll have to wait a few minutes."

"I'm not in a hurry," I lied, responding in fluent Spanish. I caught myself, realizing that my command of the foreign language felt easier, effortless. Before, I had labored through it, learning it to the level some would call fluent, but I never felt like it was natural—a part of me.

The barkeep looked over her shoulder and caught me staring. I couldn't help myself. She was... well, breathtaking. A jewel in a wasteland.

She scowled at me, though I wasn't sure if it was because I was looking at her or if it was due to my appearance. I got my answer a second later.

"If you don't have money, you can leave. I'm running a business here." She issued the warning and continued hanging the clean mugs.

I found my way over to a seat in the corner and sat down, keeping the door to my left and the bar directly ahead.

"Please, excuse my appearance," I offered. "I'm not a beggar. I was just going to see if I could get a ride back to Guadalajara."

Her frown deepened, and I could tell she'd already had enough of me. "Does this look like a taxi service?"

"No," I admitted. "Does this town have one of those?"

The question caught her off guard. She paused, then answered, "No." Then she finished hanging the last of the mugs.

I nodded, looking down at the table as if the glossy surface would have an answer to my plight.

Here I was with ancient powers bestowed on me that made me stronger, faster, and virtually immortal, but without a fistful of pesos, I couldn't get anywhere.

I unconsciously fingered the medallion around my neck. Apparently, it was a new nervous tick I'd picked up in the last twenty-four insane hours.

"Nice necklace," the girl behind the counter said.

"Oh." I suddenly realized I'd been absently playing with the thing. "It's a family heirloom." After I made the comment, I also remembered that it wasn't a lie.

I tucked the medallion back into the shredded fabric of my shirt.

"Are you going to buy something?" She asked the question bluntly. There was something cute about the no-BS way she carried herself.

"I'm sorry," I said, standing up. "No. I don't have any money, and as you said, you're running a business."

She didn't need to hear the whole story of why I didn't have my wallet, ID, or anything else except some shredded clothes. The part about the cartel would probably frighten her. I doubted she wanted to have anything to do with them. And the last thing I wanted to do was bring trouble into her cantina.

I shuffled to the door and was about to leave when she stopped me.

"Hey," she said.

I froze and looked back at her.

She sighed. "You look like you could use a warm meal and a cold drink."

My stomach growled on cue. I felt a strange sense of gratitude for not thirsting for blood. But as the shaman, or my guide, said, I wasn't a vampire.

I nodded. "I appreciate the offer, but I don't have anything to give you in return."

She tilted her head to the side, crossing her arms over her chest. "We've established that. But you look like you're in good shape."

I blushed.

"Don't get any ideas, gringo. I was just thinking maybe you could help me with a few things here in the cantina."

She's going to make me wash dishes. I just know it.

"My cook isn't here yet. This is the second day this week he hasn't shown up on time."

I looked around the empty cantina, wondering if the cook not being there was really a problem.

I arched an eyebrow at her, and she caught my drift.

"Look, do you want something to eat or not?" she pressed.

My empty stomach said yes despite my pride screaming no. But pride didn't make the hunger go away. So, I nodded. "Sure. Just show me what to do."

"We'll need to get you out of those clothes," she said, eyeing me from head to toe. She realized how that sounded, then quickly added, "There's some extra cook clothes in the back. They should probably fit you."

"Thanks," I said, blushing slightly at the initial insinuation. "Um, my name is Gideon."

"I'm Veronica. My friends call me Vero."

She led me to the back of the cantina through a narrow hallway, past a couple of dingy bathrooms, to an office in the very rear of the building. The room was smaller than my master bathroom back home, with only enough space for an old metal desk like teachers in public schools had in the '80s and '90s. A single chair sat off to the side of one corner of the desk, its vinyl upholstery cracked and peeling in multiple places.

Vero walked over to a folding closet door and pulled it open. Pants and a white button-up shirt hung inside. Old stains splotched the shirt and one of the pant legs.

"Sorry about the stains," she said. "But it's been washed."

"Does it look like I really care?" I chuffed.

She looked at me and chuckled, quickly recovering and painting a stoic look back on her face. "You can change in here. Come back out front when you're done."

I noticed the safe in the far corner. It was one of those jobs that had been built into the wall. Paperwork festooned the desk's surface. Apparently, Vero's strong point wasn't organization. Or maybe she preferred to work with the "pile method."

"Thank you," I said, keeping my voice as low as I felt in that moment.

"Don't mess with my stuff, okay? If I come back here and anything's missing, I'll feed you to the cartel myself."

The word sent a dagger of fear into my belly. *The cartel? Does she work for them? Maybe she could help me find Carrillo?*

"I won't steal anything. I'm not a thief. And if I am, it doesn't appear that I'm a very good one."

Her lips cracked a smile again, against her will. "See you out front, and I'll show you what to do. The lunch crowd is about to come in."

Lunch crowd? How much of a crowd could this two-horse town have?

She disappeared through the door, leaving it cracked as she left. Maybe she didn't fully trust me. She shouldn't; I knew that much. Random derelict wanders into a bar. Young girl gives him a job, few questions asked? Either she was way too trusting, way too desperate, or some amalgamation of both.

I slipped out of the stringy remains of my clothes and slipped into the spare cook's outfit from the closet. The trousers were a little big, but the shirt fit okay. And with the belt, the pants stayed up better than the ones I had on, although I wondered why any cook or chef would want to don white in the kitchen with sauces flying around.

Once I had the new clothes on, I stepped out into the corridor and walked back to the front.

It felt weird, and I couldn't tell what was stranger—the fact that I was about to try to work my way into a ride back to Guadalajara or that I was now some kind of ancient shapeshifter, sent to protect mankind from the wicked.

Okay, the latter was still weirder, but the cook thing took second place. For now.

She bobbed her head upon seeing me round the corner. It took effort for her not to laugh, and I imagined I looked pretty pathetic.

I stiffened my spine with what little pride I had left and raised my hands. "So, what do you want me to do first?"

Vero ran me through the short list of offerings her cantina had available for lunch that day—mostly tacos and tortas. She showed me the different meats and vegetables, the sauces, how to prepare everything, and all within a fifteen-minute training session.

"You think you got it, gringo?" she asked.

I wanted to say if I could earn a couple of degrees in ancient history and archaeology, I could surely handle sizzling some steak and chicken on a griddle, but I knew that would sound terrible. And even thinking it made me feel snobbish.

"Yes, ma'am,' I said instead. "I can handle it."

"I hope so. They'll be here in a few minutes." She looked me up and down, doubt oozing from her eyes. "What are you doing in this town, anyway?"

I let out a tired laugh. "This town? I don't even know where I am right now."

"Santa Rojo," she said.

"Interesting name."

"Yes. It comes from an old legend."

Those words spiked my attention. "Old... legend?"

"About a man who purged the region of evil. They called him a saint, even though he wasn't Catholic."

"I see." I felt suddenly uncomfortable with the conversation. I shifted nervously, hoping the medallion concealed in my cook's shirt didn't catch her attention again. "This... saint, you said. How exactly did he... um, drive away the—"

"Evil?" She finished my sentence, looking at me like I had worms crawling out of my nose. "I don't know. It's just an old legend. I don't know why I even remember that. Not many people around here talk about it much after childhood. It's just an old kids' story they tell."

"Like a ghost story."

"Yeah. Or the chupacabra."

I froze again, and this time I felt sure she noticed. "Oh? I don't know much about that. Was that some kind of monster or something?"

She rolled her eyes and started removing Coke bottles from an ice bin under the counter. She set them up on the bar, lining the bottles up evenly, with about six inches between each.

"You need to get back there and start cooking. Our customers will be here soon."

So now they're our customers?

"Of course. I'm sorry."

I wandered back into the kitchen and started cooking the various meats, seasoning them the way Vero had shown me.

I enjoyed cooking and usually was the one to make the meals back at our home in the States. *My home*, I corrected in my mind. There was no *our* anymore. My heart stung at the thought, and the memory of Amy being shot in front of me replayed over and over.

The sizzling carne asada brought my mind back and forced me to focus. I flipped the meat over, then turned the chicken. The steak took on a nice brown color, and the aromas filled my nostrils, twisting my stomach into knots.

I could have scooped all of it up and eaten it in one go.

Vero appeared in a little window that allowed me to see from the kitchen all the way out to the front door.

"We'll need six steak tortas and ten chicken tacos."

I raised my eyebrows, wondering who came in and ordered all that food.

I shifted the meat on the grill, splashed a little oil on it, and tossed in some onions and peppers. The veggies sizzled and squealed, pounding my senses with more aromas.

The blades in my hands worked fast, much like the hibachi chefs I enjoyed watching at my favorite Japanese place back home. I'd always loved how they could move so fast, so fluidly, and wondered if I could do the same thing, or how much practice it took to get to that level.

Evidently, it took *some* practice. My moves weren't as smooth as theirs, but I got the job done.

I picked out the buns for the tortas and stuffed them with meat, lettuce, tomato slices, and the special sauce Vero showed me in a metal container at the end of the grill. I didn't know what was in the mixture, but it looked appetizing. Then again, a car tire looked appetizing to me at that moment.

I finished the first set of sandwiches and tossed more meat onto the grill. Then I flipped the chicken again, checked it to make sure it was cooked through, and gave it another minute before pressing it down and then dumping it onto some corn tortillas. I topped the tacos with a little cabbage relish Vero made, I guessed from scratch, and a little white cheese. With the first plates ready, I placed them onto the window's landing and said, "Order up," in English.

She looked at me, slightly surprised to hear the words, smiled, and took the first two plates. I watched her for a second and saw her setting the plates on the counter. Then I heard the voices over the sputtering sizzle of the steak on the griddle.

They were children's voices, cackling and screaming.

Then the kids were there. They poured through the open front door into the cantina, yelling at the top of their lungs with looks of joy on their faces.

"Those other tortas ready yet?" Vero asked.

"Coming right up," I half lied, snapping back to my job. I spun around and flipped the steak, mashed it down with the spatula, and added the onions and peppers to a new splotch of oil.

I waited thirty seconds to let the onions melt a little and then shoveled the steak over top of the veggies, tossed the mixture around, then loaded up the remainder of the sandwiches.

I slid the plates onto the landing, and Vero took them, placing them next to the remaining bottles of Coke.

Three more kids grabbed the plates, smiling and thanking Vero for the meal.

I leaned into the window and watched the gaggle of kids motor through the sandwiches and tacos. They eagerly gulped down the cola while talking to each other at a million miles an hour.

Vero leaned over the bar and watched with her elbows planted on the surface. I accidentally caught myself looking down at her legs and quickly averted my eyes. My wife had just died. Something felt wrong about checking out another woman.

I'd always prided myself on being respectful in that regard, never letting my eyes or desires stray. Now, though, I felt different, something instinctive... animal.

She turned around, fortunately after I had already looked the other way.

"You can make yourself something to eat now if you want," she said. She wore a smile, muted and distant, but satisfied.

"Who are they?" I asked.

Vero turned her head, her dark brown eyes panning over the little horde. "Kids from the neighborhood," she answered. "Every Sunday after they leave mass, I give them free lunch."

"Where are their parents?"

Vero shrugged. "This group?" The smile vanished. "They're orphans. The church takes care of them."

"Oh. I'm sorry. I didn't—"

"How could you have known?" The smile returned but this time forced, sadder. "Most of them lost their families to the cartel wars. Collateral damage, the police called it. That's why they're here, in Santa Rojo. There's less cartel activity here. Sure, they come through, make us pay them for protection, but there isn't much violence this far outside the cities."

I nodded, feeling terrible for even bringing it up.

"Get some food. When you're done, we'll see about getting you a ride back into Guadalajara, Gideon."

15

I stared down at the little break table in the back corner of the kitchen as I ate the last of the steak and chicken piled together in a torta. I'd been right about the sauce. I had no idea what Vero put in it, but the stuff was excellent. It reminded me of a garlic aioli, with a hint of cilantro and some cayenne, maybe a dash of smoked paprika.

When the children left and the noise died down out in the cantina, Vero appeared in the kitchen doorway.

"Good?" she asked.

I nodded, unable to speak with a mouthful of meat and bread.

"Good." She walked into the kitchen, switched off the griddle, and leaned against the wall next to the window.

"That sauce is terrific," I said.

"That's my personal recipe. Compliments the other flavors."

"I'll say." I sounded like a kid from a 1950s television show. What would I say next, "Jeepers, lady?"

She took a scraper hanging off the side of the grill and started running the blade over the metal surface, removing the burned grease and remnants of charred meat.

"I have to ask," she said as she worked, "what's an American like you doing homeless in Mexico? Are you one of those banditos who robbed a bank and crossed the border to escape the police?"

I nearly choked at the insinuation. "No," I laughed. "I'm not homeless. I live in the United States."

"What's with the clothes, then?" Vero looked over her shoulder at me with blatant skepticism.

I nodded, knowing that one was coming. "I had... an accident."

Her right eyebrow lifted, and I knew she didn't buy that for a second. "With what? A jaguar? You looked like a wild animal ravaged you, except they only ruined your clothes."

I choked again. After forcing down the piece of steak, I nodded. "I can see why you'd say that."

"So, what was it?"

I took a deep breath, considering the answer. "Honestly?" I exhaled. "I don't really know what happened. I'm still trying to figure that out."

She picked up a rag and held it for a second. "There's got to be a story behind that."

I shrugged, took a swig of Coke, and set down the bottle. "I'm an archaeologist. Okay? I have a home back in the States. I live in Nashville. My wife—" I cut myself off. "We came to Guadalajara for an exhibit, to show the world a history of Mexico previously unseen."

"That sounds important. And you wore those clothes?" She laughed at her own joke.

"They didn't look like that before. I assure you." I looked around nervously, then checked the window. "I... don't think I should talk about it."

She turned her head slightly, analyzing my body language with those probing dark eyes. "The cartel did this to you?"

I was in the middle of taking the last bite of sandwich when she asked the question, and I coughed, spitting out the first bit of it.

"I'm sorry," she said. "I've just never seen them tear up someone's clothes and leave them alive."

"They didn't tear my clothes." I lowered my voice, and my eyes. "I don't want to talk about it."

She moved over to the little table and sat down across from me, putting her arms on top of the chairback. "Did you cause trouble with the cartels? Which one? Because if you did, I don't need that kind of heat." She raised a finger in warning. "You hear me?"

"No. I know. I mean, I didn't cause trouble with them. They caused trouble with me."

"What do you mean?"

I shook my head and finished the sandwich. As I chewed, I said, "I just need to get back to Guadalajara. From there, I can—" I cut myself off as the epiphany, the sickening realization, blew away any thoughts I had of returning to my former life.

"You can what?"

All of a sudden, I felt lost, like an airplane pilot who just lost all his instruments while flying through a thunderstorm.

"I can't go back," I muttered.

"Why not?"

I sighed. *What do I have to lose by telling this bar owner what happened?* "Vicente Carrillo killed my wife. It happened in the city. I guess a few nights ago. I woke up in the middle of the jungle earlier today and wandered into town. To be honest, it all feels like one big, horrible nightmare."

Her gaze bore into me, testing to see if I was lying—as best I could figure. Then, pity stretched out from the corners of her eyes, wrinkling the otherwise perfect skin.

"You're serious, aren't you?"

"I think so. Honestly, I don't know if it's real or not. It's all... very confusing."

She exhaled, her pity melting into a concerned expression. "How do you know it was Carrillo? Did one of his men tell you that? Or witnesses?"

"There were no witnesses, Vero. They shot her in our hotel room. I know it was him because he was there. He ordered her execution." I spat out the last few words with as much disdain as I could mine from my burning heart. "I watched her die."

I realized I was spilling a lot of emotional, deeply personal information to a stranger I'd only met a half hour ago, so I fought off the feelings ravaging me and said, "It's none of your concern. I'm sorry. I shouldn't have said anything. I just met you, and... well, you seem like a good person. You take care of those orphans." I don't know why I said the next part, but it felt truer than anything I'd ever sensed in a person. "You have a good heart. I can see that in you."

"I'm not that good," she deflected.

"Well, anyone who feeds orphans for free probably gets a free pass through the pearly gates. That's all I'm saying."

She smiled, humbly lowering her head. "Guadalajara is a few hours from here. When we close down this afternoon, I'll give you a ride over there."

"Don't you have to run your cantina?"

Vero chuckled at that. "José will be here. He can handle it. Not like we get a ton of business in here anyway."

"How do you stay open?"

She shrugged. "We get enough visitors and locals to keep things running, but it's hard. Especially with the cartel taking money from us. Some of the other businesses..." Her voice wandered for a second. "They weren't so lucky."

I'd seen a few of the shops with boards over the windows and doors on my way into the village.

I tried to resist but had to ask. "Which cartel?" I wasn't sure if I wanted to hear the answer or not.

Vero's eyes locked with mine. "Carrillo's cartel. They run most of this region."

Hearing the name sparked a flame in my mind. Anger burned in my veins. "Do you know where I can find him?"

"Carrillo? Look, I understand he killed your wife, but going to look for that man... It's suicide."

"Maybe," I hedged.

"Maybe? No offense, but you think you can just walk into Carrillo's mansion like some kind of superhero and take him out?"

"Something like that."

She shook her head. "You're loco, amigo," she said in Spanglish. "And you'll get yourself killed. It's not worth it."

I'd been thinking while I ate, and now things were clearer than ever. "I appreciate the offer, taking me back to the city and all. But I can't go back there."

"Why?"

"I have nothing to go back to. My things are in the hotel, but if I go there, the cops will wonder what happened to me. They'll think I killed her." The words stuck a spear through my chest. "And if they don't think I killed her, how do I know I can trust the cops?"

She seemed to pick up on the problems. I made it hard not to.

"Just because you can't go back to the hotel doesn't mean you have to try to find Carrillo. You can go to the American embassy. They'll help you figure out what to do. They can get you a new passport, help arrange for transportation back to the States."

Vero was right. The smart thing to do was go to the American embassy. Maybe I would do that. The other issue was I did need to get my passport and other belongings. I had no money, no ID, and no plane ticket home.

Then again, all of those things were in the hotel room. I was certain Carrillo and his men had stolen that stuff, but there was a chance they hadn't. Moreover, if Carrillo was smart and believed that I'd escaped, the first place he would expect me to go would be back to Guadalajara, and to the hotel.

"Yes. You're right," I said. "I should go to the embassy. They can help me with everything I need."

She nodded. "Now you're making sense, gringo. When José gets here, I'll get my car and give you a ride back into the city."

"You're very kind to do that," I said. "I'll pay you."

"I'm not worried about money."

Considering she was sitting in the kitchen talking to me and not out at the bar, worried about customers, I knew she meant it. Though I still couldn't figure out how she paid the bills.

Part of me wondered if she was one of Carrillo's distributors. She seemed to know a lot about the guy, though I shouldn't have held that against her. Such tyrannical figures often spread their fame far and wide. It helped with their image. A picture of fear and obedience they wished to imprint on the minds of those they would rule. It was the reason for the grotesque display of dismembered bodies, and of corpses hanging from bridges or walls that the American news media seemed to love painting all over television screens and digital devices.

I'd never felt unsafe in Mexico. Not until I met Carrillo.

And now that I had an advantage on my side, I had no reason to feel unsafe.

Ever. Again.

16

José showed up thirty minutes after I finished eating.

Veronica gave him a mild scolding for being so late, but I got the feeling it wasn't the first time and it wouldn't be the last. I'd learned, and grown to appreciate, the fact that Mexican people didn't worry as much about time. They were laid back, relaxed, and to Americans that could feel strange. It certainly had to me at first. But over time, ironically, I saw the beauty in taking things slower, spending more time with those around you than on a phone.

It was a pace of life I could get used to. I was accustomed to doing things the slow way. As an archaeologist, almost nothing ever happened quickly.

Once José had his marching orders, Vero led me to the back of the cantina again, and through a different door that opened to a small parking area. There were only three spots for cars to park, and hers was the lone vehicle sitting idle atop the gravel.

Her modest car didn't offer any luxuries. The sedan looked to be ten, maybe twelve years old. The black paint had faded in spots. The tires were worn. And there was a dent in the front-right quarter panel.

"It isn't much," she said, catching my disapproving stare. "But it gets me where I need to go. And it never breaks down."

I looked for a piece of wood to knock on. Knowing my luck, today would be the day it broke down.

She walked over to the driver's side and unlocked the door. I stopped at the passenger door and waited for her to unlock it. When she did, I climbed inside.

An overpowering smell filled the vehicle, like cheap air fresheners you get from the car wash. I noted one lying on the floor at my feet.

Well, that explains it.

Vero inserted the keys into the ignition and paused, staring at the dashboard. "One second," she said. "I have to run back inside."

"Forget your driver's license?"

"Actually, yes. And credit cards, money." She opened the door and stepped out. "I'll be right back. Don't go anywhere."

I laughed quietly at the order. Something about her telling me what to do felt good. It left questions on the wayside. Amy had always bossed me around, but never in a cute way, the way Vero just did. She'd done it with a wink and a smirk.

This girl was way too trusting. Then again, she looked like maybe she was in her late twenties, more than experienced enough to have seen how rotten the world could be sometimes. She wasn't naïve. Heck, she ran a bar.

I watched her disappear back through the rear door and sat quietly in the car, waiting. After a minute of sitting there, another vehicle pulled up in the parking spot two spaces over.

The white SUV's dark-tinted windows didn't allow me to see who was inside. Based on the make and model, I didn't figure the driver was anyone from this little village. I didn't see any other high-end SUVs driving around the area.

Then it hit me.

A sense of dread crept into my gut, and I turned my head the other direction just as the first guy on the passenger side got out of the SUV.

He wore wire-frame sunglasses and a silvery suit with black button-up shirt and no tie. I kept my head down and turned to the side, watching as much as possible with my peripheral vision.

The men didn't seem to be paying any attention to me and walked brazenly in through the back door. The driver wore a black shirt and gray pants, and his head was shaved, same as the other.

What bothered me the most about the two guys wasn't their menacing appearance. It was the red mist that followed them as they approached the rear door. Even out of my chupacabra form, the mist —it seemed—still appeared around the wicked.

I watched the two disappear into the cantina, and I knew from their tattoos that these two were some of Carrillo's goons. If not Carrillo, some other cartel. Either way, they were bad news, and neither of them tried to hide the pistols hanging from their belts. The one with the jacket let it flap in the breeze as he walked inside, all too happy to let others know he was armed—probably for the fear effect.

What were they doing here? Looking for me? Or had they come to roll Vero for more money?

I glanced over at the keys dangling in the ignition. I could take her car, drive back to Guadalajara, do what I needed, and bring it back to her. Heck, I could buy her a new car.

I knew those weren't options.

If the guys were here for me, maybe they could give me some answers. But it wasn't night. I didn't have my secret weapon in the daylight. But the shaman... er, guide said that my healing ability would still be there at all times.

I ran through the scenarios in my head, and none of them looked appetizing. But with every passing second Vero failed to return to the car, I knew something wasn't right.

I sighed and stepped out of the sedan, eased the door shut, and started for the back door.

After a short pause to make sure I was doing the right thing, I reached out and pulled on the little handle and yanked the door open.

Immediately, I heard the sound of Vero's voice. She was begging the men to leave.

"You already got your money last week. Tell Vicente he can wait until next month to get it."

"We'll leave when we want to," one of them said.

I saw José run out the front door and dash to the left, vanishing from sight. He must have been scared. Then again, it was a cowardly look.

Normally, I might have been running, too. I'd never been courageous, but now, there was less fear in me than I ever remembered. I worried, mostly because I knew I was about to face two stone-cold killers, but I didn't feel afraid.

I continued down the corridor, hearing the voices coming from the kitchen to the right.

"And we collect whenever we want to," one of the voices added.

"Please. Just get out of here. I don't have any more money right now. Vicente knows my cantina doesn't bring in many people."

"Then maybe you shouldn't be in a business."

"Look, if you guys want a few beers, maybe some tequila, help yourselves."

"No," the other man declined. "If you haven't seen the American, and you don't have our money, we'll just take our payment some other way."

A chill shivered through me, both at hearing him refer to me and at the disgusting insinuation.

Chupacabra or not, I wasn't going to allow this to happen.

A splinter of rage burned in my chest as I rounded the corner into the kitchen doorway.

Inside, I saw Vero cornered by the two men. The one with the blazer was taking it off and hanging it on the chair I'd sat in earlier. The other encroached closer to her. Vero was defenseless, unarmed.

I noticed the waves of heat rippling up through the air from the griddle, sans meat.

When the guy without the jacket took one step too close to her, reaching up his hand as if to stroke her neck, I'd seen enough.

"Leave her alone," I growled.

The two men snapped their heads around, casting scowls at me like I'd opened their birthday presents.

"You better leave while you can, gringo," the driver said. "This doesn't concern you."

I cocked my head to the side. "Actually," I paused, "I think it does."

The goons looked to each other, searching for answers.

I rolled my eyes. "Um, the American archaeologist you're looking for? About my height? Same hair and eye color? Ring a bell?"

Their eyes widened when they realized I was who they were there for.

The two reached for their pistols, but I was already moving. I lunged toward the one on the right, grabbing his wrist before he could draw the weapon. The two were much stronger than me, which I suspected was a result of hours in prison gyms. The gunman twisted his arm up, but my grip held firm, much to my surprise.

I jerked him around in front of the other gunman as he drew his pistol and leveled it at me. Using his partner as a human shield, I shoved my hostage toward the other guy and sent them crashing into each other.

A clear path to the door opened up for Vero.

"Get out of here. Now. I'll meet you outside."

She looked at me with fear and uncertainty in her eyes but did as I said and darted out the door while the two gangsters untangled.

They both raised their pistols and aimed them at my chest.

The medallion warmed against my skin. I hoped what the shaman told me was right, and I had a feeling I was about to find out.

"Señor Carrillo has put out a big bounty on your head, gringo," the driver said, tilting his weapon to the side the way thugs like him always seemed to do. It was a total disregard for accuracy. I wasn't even a big gun aficionado, and I knew that.

"Dead or alive?" I asked, though it didn't feel like me asking the question.

"Either," the passenger answered. "But I'm thinking you'll be less trouble dead."

"Yes, but Vicente said he would pay more if we brought him in alive."

The passenger nodded. "True. I think he wants to kill you himself, gringo. And I have a feeling he's going to make it hurt."

"Well," I said, raising my hands, "I guess you'd better take me in."

The men both narrowed their eyes. Suspicion dripped from their pupils, as if approaching a venomous snake coiled in the leaves.

The driver took the first step toward me. "Keep your hands up. I am just as happy to shoot you right now."

"Understood."

Within arm's reach, he snatched out his free hand to grab my right wrist. Instead, I snapped my hand down and grabbed his, spinning him around to face his partner again. The passenger fired his pistol, filling the tiny kitchen with deafening thunder.

The rounds sank into my human shield's chest and belly. The man yelled at the mortal wounds just before I shoved him toward the shooter.

The passenger squeezed off two more rounds, effectively killing his partner before the man staggered onto him, hands out in a desperate attempt to keep from falling.

As the unwounded gunman tried to shrug off his dying partner, I surged forward, grabbing the weapon as he fired two more times.

I twisted the pistol in his hand. Another shot erupted.

Then I wrenched the weapon from the man's hand, nearly breaking his thumb. I tossed the weapon to the floor, grabbed him by the wrinkled skin on the back of his head, and shoved him across the tiny kitchen to the griddle.

He put out his hands to brace himself and instantly regretted it. His palms landed on the hot steel surface. A horrible sizzle filled the air, along with the smell of burning flesh.

The thug screamed in agony, yanking his hands away from the hot surface. His pain was just beginning.

I grabbed the back of his head again and shoved it down toward the scalding grill. He resisted, kicking out with his feet, jamming his elbows backward, but he was shorter than me, and I used my reach to keep out of danger, all the while lowering his face closer to the scorching steel.

"Where is Carrillo?" I asked.

"I don't know!" the man yelled.

"Oh, you don't know? That's funny. Because a minute ago, you and your dead friend over there were talking about taking me to Carrillo. Now you don't know where he is? Which is it?"

The goon let out a profane slur.

"I know what you just said," I told him. "And that isn't polite."

I shoved his face within two inches of the griddle. "Last chance, cholo."

"He's looking for you. I swear. Last we saw him was in the jungle. He has his whole army after you. You're going to die, gringo. There is nowhere in Mexico you can hide that he won't find you."

"That's cool," I said. "But it doesn't really help me out. Let me clarify." I shoved his right cheek onto the griddle.

He squealed in agony as his face fried on steel.

I pulled his head up away from the heat. "Oh, that's gotta hurt. Right? Now, it will hurt just as bad on the other side. And then we go for the nose, the ears, until your own family won't recognize you."

He replied with another string of obscenities.

I inhaled and then exhaled, exasperated. "No. No. No. Maybe there's something lost in translation. You tell me where Carrillo is, or I will keep torturing you." I stopped and twitched my nose. "Do you smell hot dogs? I think I smell hot dogs."

More profanity.

"Fine."

I smashed the other side of his face into the griddle. He screamed louder this time. I wondered if anyone else in the town was hearing this because with the front door open, I doubted the people at the closest shops or any random person walking by would miss it.

I didn't care. These men killed Amy. And they were there to kill me.

I pulled his melted face away from the steel again and turned his eyes toward me. His eyes filled with the pain his skin felt.

"Still stubborn, huh?" I asked.

His eyes dropped to my chest, and I instinctively followed his gaze.

Blood soaked my cook's shirt in two places where bullets had torn holes in the fabric. I hadn't felt the rounds when they struck. Immediately, I figured it was due to adrenaline, the fight-or-flight response from my body.

I let the goon go and stumbled backward, putting an index finger through one of the holes in the shirt.

I felt the pain then, the burning sensation from being shot.

I grimaced, but it wasn't as bad as I'd thought it would be. Breathing hard, I leaned against the wall near the window looking out into the cantina.

The gunman evened his breath, staring at me like the first steak he'd seen in a decade. He bent down and picked up his gun, raised it high, and aimed for my head.

"Time to die, gringo."

His finger tensed, and a loud pop boomed through the kitchen.

17

The right side of the gunman's head spewed a red mist onto the wall. He dropped sideways, hitting the side of the griddle with his jaw before falling next to his partner.

Dazed for a second, I could only stare at the two dead men before I pried my eyes away and turned to the door.

Vero stood there holding a 9mm pistol, a thin stream of smoke trailing out of the muzzle.

She trembled for a few seconds, then lowered the weapon.

"Are you okay?" she asked, rounding to face me. Then she saw the bloody shirt.

"I'll be fine," I grunted. "Sorry about your shirt."

"You're shot. And bleeding. We need to get you to a hospital."

I shook my head. "No. No hospitals. I'll be okay. Just need to rest for a second."

I slumped down onto the floor against the wall and swallowed.

She knelt next to me and put her hand on my shoulder, assessing the damage with worried eyes.

"I'm going to take the shirt off you," she said.

I coughed a laugh. "We haven't even gone out on a real date."

She shook her head at the joke and pulled up on the fabric. I squinted against the pain, but it already hurt less than a few seconds before.

Vero finished tugging the shirt up over my head and looked at my bloody chest. But her look of fear quickly morphed into curiosity, and then disbelief.

"That's not possible."

I looked down at the wounds. The blackish-red holes closed on their own, spitting out the flattened metal rounds before sealing. Within seconds, blood no longer leaked from my body.

Vero searched my face for answers. She retreated a few inches.

"What?" I asked. "I mean, other than the magical healing thing?"

She couldn't tear her eyes from mine. "Your... eyes. They're red."

Then her gaze fell to the medallion around my neck. "Just like the eyes on that thing."

I checked the amulet, and sure enough, the dog's eyes glowed bright red.

"Oh that. I can explain."

"Vero?" A man's voice interrupted us.

She popped up, hiding the pistol behind her back, and leaned out through the window.

"Yes?" she answered.

A squat, balding older man stood in the doorway just beyond the threshold. The belt buckle at his waist shone nearly as bright as the sun off the top of his head.

"Is everything okay in here? I thought I heard... something that sounded like gunshots."

"Gunshots?" She shook her head. "No, I'm sorry. I dropped a bunch of pots and pans. I'm so clumsy. I knew it was loud, but I didn't think it sounded like gunshots."

The man puzzled at her response. "You sure everything is fine?"

"Yes. I'm sure. Thank you for checking on me."

No way the guy would buy it. Pots and pans? Come on. No one was that gullible.

"All right, then. Sorry to bother you. Do you need any help cleaning up?"

"Nope. I got it. Almost done."

"Okay, Vero. Have a good day. I'll be by later for a beer."

"See you then, Pedro."

She watched the man leave, and when he was gone, knelt down next to me.

"What is this thing?" she asked, holding up the medallion. "Why were your eyes glowing? And how did those wounds just heal themselves in seconds? You should be dead."

"Glad to hear you're happy I'm not," I groused, pushing myself up off the ground. I felt good. Oddly good. Borderline invigorated.

"I'm not kidding, Gideon. Is that even your real name?"

I nodded absently. "Yes. But we should probably get out of here. Carrillo might wonder where his two puppies went and why they aren't checking in."

She heard me say the words, but they went in one ear and out the other. "How are you still alive, Gideon? What's going on here?"

I walked over to the dead men and sifted through the driver's pockets. I removed the keys from one pocket and a fistful of cash from the other. The second guy had money, too, but nothing else. I scooped up their guns, stuffed them in the back of my pants like I'd seen people do on television or in movies, and then put on the jacket hanging on the back of the chair.

It felt weird to wear it without a shirt underneath, but I'd find a shirt later.

Vero watched me with a fearful sort of awe as I worked. With the jacket on, I looked back at her.

"Okay. Let's go."

"What are you?"

I stepped close to her and slowly removed the pistol from her hand, worried she might turn it on me out of irrational, or slightly rational, fear.

"Let's take this with us," I said in the most soothing voice I could find. "And I will explain everything on the way."

She still resisted without saying anything.

"Also, you should probably close your cantina. I have a feeling José isn't coming back for the rest of his shift."

"No," she agreed. "Probably not."

After Vero shut the front doors and flipped the open sign to the closed side, we hurried out the rear and into the parking lot. She started to get in her car, but I made for the SUV.

"What are you doing?" she demanded.

I jiggled the dead man's keys from a finger and thumb. "We take their truck."

"Are you crazy? That's one of Carrillo's rides."

"We just killed two of his enforcers. I'd say we're beyond pissing him off at this point. Besides, if he comes around and finds your car here, he'll assume you were kidnapped by the guy—me—who took out his goons. You get plausible deniability."

She processed the idea quickly, then nodded her assent. "Okay, fine. But I drive."

"Obviously. I don't know my way around here."

I tossed her the keys and climbed into the passenger seat. She hopped in behind the wheel, adjusted the seat, and revved the engine.

A minute later, dust kicked up out from behind the rear wheels as we sped away from Santa Rojo toward the main highway.

For I don't know how long, neither of us said a thing. I rolled down the window and breathed the fresh air slowly, watching the dense forests pass by. Occasionally we passed a farm or another tiny village.

Finally, when Vero merged onto the highway, she rolled up my window and turned on the air conditioning.

"It's too loud with the window open," she explained. "And I want you to tell me what is going on. Who are you really, Gideon?"

It was the question I knew was coming, and I was glad I had a little while to consider the answer. I could tell her the truth, but she'd think me crazy. I could lie, but she'd probably see through that. I'd never been a good liar, and I didn't want to start trying now.

"Are you going to answer me? What was that back there? Why did your body heal like that? You should be dead."

"You sound pretty busted up about that," I joked.

She twisted her head and lashed out at me with a fiery glare.

"You're right. This is no time to be joking. I apologize."

"What are you? Some kind of alien?" The words blew out of her mouth like a fire hose. Her fingers moved and tapped on the steering wheel. To say she was nervous and confused would have been an understatement.

"I'm not an alien. Okay. I'm just a man."

Her head tossed back and forth. "No. I have never seen anything like that before. What are you, Gideon? Be straight with me."

"I will. If you'll listen for a second."

She looked over at me, then turned her eyes back to the road. "Okay."

"I didn't lie to you. I'm an archaeologist." I sighed. "I don't know exactly how many days I've been gone."

"Gone?"

I cast a sidelong glance that reminded her it was time for her to listen.

"Sorry. Go on," she said.

"Look. This is a lot weirder for me than it is for you. However many nights ago, we had a big gala for the new exhibit. Vicente Carrillo approached me about finding an amulet. He showed me some documents that he claimed proved this thing existed." I held up the medallion for her to see.

She glanced at it then focused on the road.

"So he was right?" she asked.

"I guess. That night my wife and I went back to the hotel." Reliving her murder over and over wasn't helping. Every time, it felt like cutting a wound just before it healed. "They showed me pictures of her with other men. One man in particular. He's a guy we've known a while."

"She was cheating on you?" The nervousness was gone from Vero's voice, replaced with a delicate sort of pity.

"Yes. No." I struggled with the truth. "I don't know. The man who told me was Carrillo. Not exactly the most trustworthy source."

"But you saw pictures."

"Yeah," I relinquished. I guess I'd been holding on to false hope the last... however many days I'd been gone. "I wanted to believe that wasn't true," I confessed. I looked out the window at the passing hills in the Mexican countryside. "Maybe we'd grown apart the last few years. Both always working on projects. I thought this one would sort of bring us back together, rekindle the excitement we had when we first met."

My voice trailed off along with my thoughts.

"That's got to be so difficult. All at once, finding that out, then watching her—" Vero stopped herself before she crossed a line she didn't want to.

"Yeah," I agreed in a faint sound. I cleared my throat and went on. "Carrillo drugged me after that. Next thing I knew, I was waking up in a tent in the jungle." It all seemed like a blur as I recalled everything that happened. "Carrillo told me again that he wanted me to find the medallion. He didn't give me a choice. Fortunately, I managed to escape."

I stopped talking for a second to examine the amulet around my neck, remembering the voices that spoke to me that night. "I ran as fast as I could to get away from the camp. Fortunately, a jaguar attacked some of Carrillo's men. So that helped."

"A jaguar?"

"Yeah," I laughed. "Like I said, I was lucky. Also lucky not to have been tracked down by the big cat. I don't know how many of Carrillo's men that animal took out, but it bought me enough time to get away."

Vero wore a frown that told me she was trying to process the story, or maybe piece something together.

"You know," she said, "jaguars were sacred to the people who lived here long ago."

Her comment piqued my attention. "That's true. Ruler of the underworld. A powerful creature, admired for its ferocity and aggressiveness. People took them as a sign to face their fears."

"Yes. And they were also guardians."

My head snapped instinctively in her direction. "What did you just say?"

She kept her head forward but allowed her eyes to shift my way for a second. "Guardians? They were one of the guardians of the underworld. But also could serve as guides to wandering souls."

"Guide?" I breathed.

"Yes. Like a spirit guide."

I felt my heart pounding in my chest, and a sudden weakness gripped me.

"A spirit guide." I nodded absently.

"You okay? You don't look well." She took her eyes from the road and really looked at me.

"Yeah. I... Anyway, the temple that this thing was in could only be seen at dawn, and only for a few moments. Apparently, I ran right into it at just the right time. Weird coincidence, I guess."

She laughed.

"What? What's so funny?" I wondered.

Her head turned back and forth. "No such thing as coincidences, Gideon. Surprised I have to tell you that."

"Oh." I thought about that, looking out the window at the landscape passing by. "Anyway, I fell into a hole and found myself in an ancient temple. It was weird, like the place was alive or something. And it spoke to me. Or someone spoke to me."

"Yep. Now it's getting weird."

"I know. It sounds crazy."

She snickered. "I just saw two bullet holes in your body just miraculously heal themselves. I think we passed crazy earlier."

I liked the way she talked, the way she saw things. I wondered if anyone else would have been so accommodating, and her comment about coincidences reinforced itself as I pondered that question.

"When I took the medallion, I... I changed into something. A creature." I paused and took a breath. To her credit, she didn't interrupt, waiting patiently for me to finish. "The amulet turned me into the chupacabra."

I waited for her reaction, unsure where it would go.

Then she broke out laughing. "The goat sucker? The medallion turned you into a dog monster that drinks goat blood?"

I joined in the laughter, unable to control myself. "When you put it that way, it does sound ridiculous. But no, it would seem the legend of the chupacabra has been... changed over the years. Anyway, the temple disappeared, and I found myself in the jungle again. Carrillo's men were hunting for me. I... killed them. Then I woke up outside the village."

I didn't know if I should tell her about the shaman. It had to be impossible to believe anything else I said, although she'd seen the bullet wounds heal themselves. I'd like to think she saw some kind of superhuman power in the way I'd taken out Carrillo's goons, but I'd never changed. Then again, I hadn't been in a fight since high school, and even then it wasn't much of one.

Where had I learned those moves? And where had that strength come from?

The same answer kept throttling my consciousness. *Your ancestors were strong. Their strength is yours.*

"Hey," Vero interrupted the voices in my head. "You okay?"

I looked over at her. She genuinely cared. I could see it on her face and in her eyes as they shifted between the road ahead and me.

"Yeah," I said, breaking away to look outside once more. "I'll be okay. It's just... disorienting, to say the least."

"I would say so. And if I hadn't seen what happened for myself, I would say you're crazy." She paused for a few breaths. "But I know you're not."

"This power, Vero. I... It has a history. My family has apparently been a part of it for I don't know how many hundreds or thousands of years. We were guardians of humanity. Legendary figures who fought for the innocent against the wicked."

Her eyes lingered on the amulet for a second. "And now that responsibility is yours."

"I don't know. It's all so confusing. I just—"

"Wish your life could go back to normal?"

I nodded reluctantly.

"Yeah, well, life doesn't always go that way. Sometimes, we're given a bad hand. All we can do is play it." She turned on the blinker, merged into the lane to the left to pass a produce truck, then returned to the right-hand side. "This power you have, you could do a lot of good in the world. There are evil people doing horrible things. Maybe you're the one who can stand up for the innocent."

I shook it off. "I'm not a hero."

"Perhaps," she said. "Or maybe the hero people need to face their monsters is a monster, too."

18

Her comment silenced me for nearly the rest of the drive into Guadalajara. When we reached the city limits, she woke me from my daydreams.

"Hey, Gideon. The consulate isn't far from here. You'll be able to figure out a way back into the States from there. I imagine a renowned archaeologist shouldn't have any trouble getting moved to the front of the line."

After shaking my head back to the present, I realized how long I'd been off in my own mind. I snorted at her words. "I'm not renowned by man. I know that."

"You had a big exhibit here in Guadalajara. You must be some kind of a big deal."

I sensed she thought that was possible and yet hoped it wasn't true.

I was getting a lot of new senses lately, ever since I found this medallion.

Vero had turned out to be more than just a local barkeep, or even a small business owner. There was something about her. I couldn't place it. So I brought it up.

"You seem to know a little about history," I eased into it. "Do I detect a history buff over there?"

She smiled without looking over at me. "Maybe. I enjoy learning about it." Vero stopped the SUV at the next light.

I allowed that. "Earlier, you mentioned the story behind the name of your village. Santa Rojo."

"Yes. A strange tale."

"And yet, maybe not so strange?"

She kept her face forward, unwilling to give up the goods yet. When the light changed, she turned left.

"The story is about me, isn't it? The chupacabra." I didn't want to force it, but I needed to know.

"The medallion around your neck," she began, "I recognized it. When you first came in the cantina, I noticed that necklace. The legend says that the saint who purged the wicked wore the medallion of the dog—and that the hero was a descendant of the wolf."

Now it made sense. Well, it started to. She'd been keeping that from me, and for good reason. A sensible person would have called her crazy if she'd started relating wild stories about a dog-man who drew his power from a magical amulet. Had I not experienced it for myself, I would have happily been that sensible person telling her how insane she was for passing along an old urban legend.

"Is there anything else the legend says that I should know about?" I asked.

Her shoulders lifted and dropped. "I know that whoever created the story didn't call such a person the goat sucker. That must have gotten changed along the way."

"It happens more than you might think," I offered, recollecting on the way societies changed the stories of what really happened. History, it's said, is written by the victors. The original fake news, I called it. "Oftentimes throughout history, the past has been rewritten to vilify certain people, places, or entire civilizations. It's possible the goat sucker was concocted to make it seem like a ridiculous legend."

The embassy appeared ahead on the right. The stars and stripes of the American flag flapped in the afternoon breeze like a giant welcome sign to my eyes.

And yet I didn't feel convinced that going home was the right thing to do now. I reminded myself that I could, and probably should, be dead.

Did that mean I could turn my back on something I felt pressed, more and more, to do?

Vero stopped the car by the gate and reached out to shake my hand. "It was nice to meet you, Gideon..."

"Wolf" I finished, realizing she was asking for my last name without saying a word. I shook her hand, and when I opened my palm found a piece of paper with a number on it.

"In case you need a good torta the next time you're in Santa Rojo." Vero smiled through her discontent. "I wish you luck, Gideon Wolf," she said. "It was nice to meet you."

I felt compelled to stay in the car, to tell her to turn around and head back to Santa Rojo. Instead, I shook her hand and thanked her for her hospitality.

"If you give me your information, I'll send you some money for bringing me back into the city."

"I already told you," she said, shaking her head, "I don't need your money."

Again, something told me there was more to this young woman's story than I was getting on the surface. I didn't press her, though, and climbed out of the car. I took one of the guns out of my belt and laid it on the seat. "You might need this."

"I hope not," she said, eyeing it suspiciously.

"So, you'll head back to Santa Rojo?" I asked, as if the nebulous question would keep her around a few minutes longer.

"Yes. After I ditch this SUV somewhere."

I nodded. Then caught myself. "Wait. What?"

"This vehicle belongs to Carrillo. You don't think after his men fail to report in that he won't try to track it down? Especially when he gets word that they're dead?"

She was right. How could I not have thought of it?

"I'm sorry," I offered. "I should have considered that."

Vero shrugged. "No, it's okay. Better to bring their ride here to Guadalajara and dump it somewhere. Maybe Carrillo won't think I had anything to do with it."

"Except the two dead guys in your kitchen."

"True. But no one will notice since we closed the place down. Although I will have to figure out what to do with those when I get back."

I grimaced at the grisly task I'd burdened her with.

"Don't say it," she stopped me. "I know. You're sorry. You apologize a lot, Gideon. I'll figure it out. I'm a big girl."

"Thanks again, Vero," I said. "I really appreciate your help."

"You're welcome." She faced forward and stepped on the gas before I could say anything else.

I couldn't help but feel as if she were mad at me for some reason, but I wasn't the best at picking up on those things, especially from women. Apparently, I'd been missing signals from Amy for a long time.

She'd been unhappy or, at the very least, unfulfilled in our marriage. I started wondering if that was my fault. And the more I considered that, the more plausible it felt in my mind.

I turned away from the street and walked toward the front of the building with the American flag hanging from light-brown brick walls. A high fence with a green façade attached to it wrapped around the consulate. I kept moving, circling the facility, until I found a white outbuilding that served as the point of entry.

The fence ran out of both sides of the checkpoint. Dark-tinted windows allowed those inside to see out. I couldn't tell who was inside, or how many.

I stopped at the gate and waved a hand to the camera. A guard in a military uniform stood off to the side of the guard house, or whatever it was.

I was going to tell the guard I was an American, that my things had been stolen—including my money and passport—and that a cartel had killed my wife. But something stopped me.

A feeling deep down kept me from saying anything. Instead, I kept walking, moving down the sidewalk until I reached the next corner and then ducked out of sight.

"This is crazy," I said to myself. "What are you doing, Gideon?"

I continued down the sidewalk until I found an electronics store. It wasn't exactly Best Buy, but it would do. They sold phones, and that was what I needed at the moment.

I went inside, purchased a prepaid device with the money I pulled off the dead men, and returned to the street. I'd planned on leaving some of the cash in the floor of the SUV when Vero left, a sort of gift to say thank you for bringing me into the city. After I found out she was going to ditch the ride, I had to abort that plan.

I'd repay her. That truth resounded in my head. But first, I need to find out what was going on.

I looked up the number of the hotel and called the front desk. I didn't know the city that well, but I figured it was probably fifteen to thirty minutes away at most.

The receptionist answered and asked how she could be of service.

"Yes," I answered. "I'm sorry to bother you. I'm trying to remember my checkout date, and I was wondering if you could help me with that. My name is Gideon Wolf."

"Not a problem, Mr. Wolf. Do you have your confirmation number?"

Of course I don't have my confirmation number. "I'm afraid I don't recall it." But I did remember the room number. I told her the room, and that seemed to do the trick.

"Yes, sir. It looks like we have you here until Tuesday."

"Okay, that's what I thought," I said quickly. I'd originally booked the room for a week. Based on what Vero told me regarding the orphans and mass, I figured today was Sunday.

"Will you be needing anything in your room, sir?"

"Uh, no. No, thank you. We're good. Have a nice day."

"You as well, sir."

I ended the call and stuffed the phone into my pants. Then I realized, rather abruptly, I was still wearing the white pants from Vero's kitchen, and a blazer with no shirt underneath.

Based on the brief phone conversation, I surmised that the staff was unaware of the murder in my room a few nights before. That meant Carrillo had...

I doubled over right there on the sidewalk and threw up on a patch of grass next to the concrete.

Everything hit me then. My wife's murder. My abduction and unlikely escape. And the way my life had been flipped upside down. It was too much to take.

My brain swirled in a fog. And after I finished retching, I slumped down against a wall like a homeless person, out of ideas about what to do next and out of motivation to take another step.

I don't know how long I sat there. It was less than an hour but more than five minutes. I watched as cars drove by and occasional pedestrians walked down the sidewalk. Most of the people ignored me. None of them offered any help.

Not that I blamed them. I probably would have ignored me, too. I must have looked like I belonged in an asylum.

After I'd wallowed long enough, I dusted myself off, straightened my cartel blazer, and pulled out the rest of the cash in my pocket. I had more than enough for a ride back to the hotel and a dinner at one of the best restaurants in the area. The gunmen had been carrying a small fortune, more cash than I ever cared to have on me —present excluded.

I stood on the curb and watched for a taxi. When one finally appeared, I flagged the driver down and climbed in the back.

He was a gruff-looking guy, with a rim of thin hair around a bald scalp and thick fat rolls on the back of his neck.

"You pay first," he said in crappy English.

"I have the money," I said, savvy to the scam. I showed him the cash. "And I'll tip you if you get me where I want to go quickly."

"Where you headed?"

I told him the name of the hotel. He nodded, tripped the meter, and drove away.

If my things were still there at the hotel, I could get a proper change of clothes, my ID, and everything else, and I would head back to Santa Rojo.

Something told me none of it would be that simple.

19

The cab driver pulled up just outside the entrance to the hotel. One of the valets walked over and opened the door for me, then stood back as if disgusted by my appearance.

I straightened my jacket with as much dignity as I could muster, then made a show of how much money I gave the driver—partly to teach the doorman not to read a book by its cover and partly because the driver had done me a solid in getting there so fast. There were a few minutes when I actually thought he might get stopped for speeding. Then I remembered the cops here had more pressing matters to worry about than a cab going ten miles per hour over the speed limit.

After entering the hotel, I strode across the lobby, again with as much dignity as I could scrounge, and stopped at the concierge desk, thankful there wasn't a line.

The young woman behind the counter looked at me like my head was on fire, but I ignored it and straightened my posture.

"Hello. I seem to have lost my key. My name is Gideon Wolf."

"Of course, Mr. Wolf," she replied. "Not to worry. This happens all the time. Room number, please?"

I gave her the number, and within a minute she produced a new key for me.

I thanked her and wandered over to the elevators, scanning the room as I proceeded. I didn't see anyone that warranted concern, but then again, I wasn't a secret agent or a special operator. I could pick out suspicious characters, or people I thought could be suspicious, but that didn't mean anything.

I pressed the button next to the elevators and waited three seconds before one of them dinged and the up arrow appeared over the metal doors.

I stepped on and pressed the button for my floor, then moved to the back of the lift to wait for the doors to close.

Footsteps clicked on the black marble tile just outside, and I saw the reflection of someone hurrying to catch the elevator before the doors closed.

I instinctively started to reach over and press the button to hold the door but then thought better of it. *What if it's one of Carrillo's men?*

I hadn't seen anyone that looked like they worked for him.

The man caught the lift just before the doors closed, stepped on, and pressed the button for the fourth floor.

He wore an expensive suit and carried a bottle of champagne in one hand.

He gave a thankful nod, assuming—apparently—that I'd been responsible for him luckily getting to the door in time. I reciprocated, only to be polite. He didn't need to know I had nothing to do with it.

The elevator stopped at the fourth floor, the man got off, and the doors closed again. The lift moved fast, taking me up to my floor. When the doors opened, I hesitated, leaning my head out for a second to make sure no ambush was laid. The vacant elevator alcove gave no threat, and I stepped out into the open.

Around the corner, I checked again, but the corridor remained empty in both directions. Only a few empty plates and wine glasses sat outside a couple of doors along the wall, waiting for maids to pick them up in the morning.

I made my way toward the room, fighting off a sickening feeling with every single step. I fidgeted with the card, and second thoughts began rattling in my brain.

What if Amy's body is still in there? What if Carrillo followed me here? What if he stationed men here in case I tried to come back?

None of that mattered. If his men were inside, I had no reason to be afraid. I'd already killed... I forget how many. But more than I would have ever believed possible.

With the sun setting in the next hour, I knew I'd soon be able to summon the power of the medallion if I needed it. And even if I couldn't, anything short of them beheading me would end badly for them. Unfortunately, the cartels down here were kind of known for doing that to their victims.

I shuddered at the thought and refocused.

"No one is here," I said, more hopeful than actually believing it.

Staring at the door, I didn't know if I had the fortitude to go in. The questions still lingered, haunting me with visions of the past.

With a deep breath, I scanned the key card. The lock clicked, and I grasped the handle. I turned it so it wouldn't lock again, but I didn't open the door yet. I hesitated again at the thought of what waited on the other side.

Like ripping off a Band-Aid, I finally flung the door open and stepped in, quickly closing the door behind me in case someone happened to walk by and see... something horrible in my room.

I stared at the inside surface of the door, still not looking over at the window, beyond the bed.

"Just collect your things and get out of here," I mumbled.

I spun around and faced the room. To my surprise, it was almost as I'd left it. Except for a glaring omission. There was no trace of Amy's body. No blood on the wall or floor, as far as I could tell. My suitcase, laptop bag, clothes in the closet, hygiene kit, all just where I'd placed them before.

Slightly relieved but still on edge, I hurried over to the suitcase and unzipped the top pouch. Upon sliding my fingers inside, I felt the familiar, smooth, flat booklet. I pulled out the passport and set it on the bed.

Did I dare risk taking a shower? *No, idiot. Change into some normal clothes and get out of here.*

Carrillo's men weren't here. They had no way of knowing I came back. And it had been a few days since I showered. The more I thought about it, the more self-conscious I got. Vero hadn't said anything, which made her kind of a saint in my mind.

My mind made up, I turned on the shower and returned to the room while the water heated up.

I set out the clothes I'd wear, found my wallet, keys, and everything else from my old life. Everything except my wife.

The chair she'd been executed in sat ten feet away near the window. I saw the whole horrific event happen all over again in my mind. This time, though, as I saw the pleading in her eyes, I wondered.

Carrillo's words, the pictures he'd shown me, all of it ripped through my senses like a banshee howling in the night.

I lowered my head for a second, then noticed something on the desk. My wife's black leather clutch still sat where she'd left it.

Apparently, Carrillo and his men only cared about getting rid of the body, not stealing our personal belongings. Then again, what did they care about our low-limit credit cards? They carried wads of cash. Plus, stealing our cards would have been traceable by the authorities.

They'd taken nothing but my life and everything I'd thought normal.

My eyes remained fixed on Amy's clutch as I processed all of it. If I wanted the truth, at least about her, maybe I would find it in that little leather pouch.

I'd never been a jealous husband, or even the slightest bit paranoid. My wife's loyalty didn't come into question. Being suspicious wasn't my thing. I trusted her. I trusted most people. Maybe that trust had been misplaced.

The water continued running in the shower.

I paced over to the desk and stared at the clutch, debating whether to open it. But the fact I'd already come this far told me I wasn't going to stop now.

I unzipped the pouch and pulled out her phone. I wasn't sure I wanted to know what it contained. Then again, maybe I wouldn't know the passcode.

When I pressed the power button on the side, the screen bloomed to life. My heart sank as the first text preview popped up onto the screen. It was from Garcia. The lewd words sent a knife point into my gut.

I pressed the message, and the passcode request appeared. It was only four numbers, and I knew my wife liked to keep things simple.

I tried her birth date, but that didn't work.

I thought for a couple of breaths and then tried the last four of her Social Security number. The device clicked, and the text app opened on the screen.

A wave of nausea crashed into me as I pored over the flirting, the nude photos, the outright betrayal in the descriptive words of what they'd experienced together, and their desires.

My fingers trembled as I scrolled through the thread. I nearly dropped the phone. I couldn't believe it. Carrillo had been telling the truth. Amy cheated on me with Garcia, and from the looks of it, this infidelity had been going on for quite some time.

Months, at the very least.

I sucked in a long breath, turned off the phone, and stuffed it back in the clutch. Tears brimmed in the corners of my eyes, but they never came. They only teased me. Amy betrayed me, in frequent and gratuitous ways. There was no telling how long this had been going on. My brain went to a dark place, wondering how many others she kept from me.

The temptation to look at her phone again bubbled to the surface, but I resisted this time. A hunt like that wouldn't result in anything good. I'd start questioning everything that happened since we'd been married, maybe even before. I couldn't deal with it. And I didn't want to.

The sound of the shower running reminded me to hurry and get cleaned up. Hanging around here for too long was only asking for trouble.

I undressed, set the pistol I'd kept on the bathroom counter, and stepped into the shower, letting the hot water soak over me. I momentarily forgot about the medallion around my neck, and when I remembered, considered removing it. Then I thought better of it. The shaman had made it sound like I needed to keep it on me at all times. It wasn't as though the thing bothered me. It wasn't heavy, and I'd quickly grown accustomed to having it on.

I only stayed in the shower for seven minutes, just long enough to wash off and relax in the warm embrace of the water. The steam filled my nostrils and cleansed my mind. By the time I got out, I felt much better. Not quite like a new man, but sadness and betrayal no longer dragged on me.

Once I dried off, I slipped into the clothes I'd laid out and grabbed two other sets of clothes from my big luggage, then stuffed them into the laptop bag.

I'd buy more clothes. I knew I'd have to, especially if I shape-shifted again. Turning into the chupacabra essentially destroyed my other garments. The same thing would happen to these. I was fooling myself by saying "if."

The shifting would happen again. I'd need the monster to take down Carrillo.

Vero's words lingered in my mind. "A monster to take out a monster," I whispered. There was something about that young woman. *She was attractive, sure. Was that it? Just some carnal desire, fueled by some kind of vengeful sentiment because of what happened with my wife and Garcia?*

I shook it off. Vero was on her way back to Santa Rojo. I'd return there and thank her, after I took out Carrillo and his organization.

At least that's what I told myself. Part of me wondered if she'd want me to return. I'd brought trouble to her doorstep, and the guilt slithering through my veins begged me to simply leave her alone.

After I'd collected everything I thought I'd need and put it in my laptop bag, I slung it over my shoulders and made my way over to the door.

I was about to open it when I saw a shadow pass by underneath the bottom edge. The figure stopped and stood there. Goosebumps ran across my skin.

It still wasn't dark out yet. The sun wouldn't set for another hour. But that hadn't stopped me from taking out two of Carrillo's men before.

I looked through the peephole and held my breath. I exhaled when I saw the person on the other side.

A man looking very much like the two I'd killed earlier stood outside. He wore a black jacket over a black button-up shirt, and black pants. And I could tell from the bulge in his blazer that he carried a gun.

20

He looked both ways, then produced a key card just like the one I'd used to get in. *Had he gotten that from the concierge? Was hotel management in Carrillo's back pocket, too? Or when they were here the other night, had they taken one of our keys?*

The second question immediately proved incorrect as I considered it. They'd gotten in when Amy and I were already here. That meant the first possibility was the more likely. The hotel concierge, or manager, or both were in with Carrillo. At the very least, they were on the take.

The assassin standing outside looked both directions, and then swiped the card over the black panel to unlock the door.

Panic tried to take over me, but something else forced it away. A strange feeling of confidence I'd never really had before pulsed through me, almost wanting the hit man to enter.

I looked down and saw a red fog forming around the floor, seeping in and out of the crack at the bottom of the door.

The mist, I thought. I wondered briefly if Vero had seen the same crimson fog forming around the two men we took out in Santa Rojo.

The name of the town hung in my conscious mind. *Did the red-*

saint thing have any overlap with that color being so prominent in my new role—or whatever this was?

I didn't have time to think about that. The assassin eased the door open and started to step through.

Instinct took over.

I shoved the door back into him, smashing the surface into his forehead. He staggered back, momentarily stunned. I knew that wouldn't last and flung the door open as he retreated a step, grabbed him by the collar, and yanked him out of the hallway and into my room.

He frowned in protest but found himself helpless as I dragged him through the door and slammed him against the closest wall.

The door closed to our right with a loud slam.

He started to reach for his gun, but I squeezed his neck, causing his face to darken almost instantly. His eyes bulged from their sockets. He kept feeling for the pistol I could now see hanging from a shoulder holster. A small suppressor poked through the bottom where the barrel seated.

I used my left hand and pulled the weapon from its nest, then pressed it to his temple. The red fog was intense in color and mass, swirling around us as if thirsty for blood.

Fear rippled through the man's eyes. This hardened killer, sent to take me out, felt a haunting dread that his life was about to end.

"Where is Carrillo?" I asked plainly.

He shook his head. "El Diablo. El Diablo."

I shook my head. "I'm neither. I'll ask you again," I said in Spanish. "Where is Vicente Carrillo?"

His face jiggled as he shook his head harder. "I don't know. He's not here. Could be—" He tried to swallow, but my grip on his throat made that endeavor exceedingly difficult.

"What was that?" I encouraged.

"He could be in his estate. It's about an hour from here."

"Or?"

The man's lips quivered. For a guy about five feet ten and 190 pounds of muscle, he felt weak. More than that, he was terrified. This guy who was paid to hurt, kill, and probably torture others melted like a bully in the school yard when another kid finally stood up to him.

"He has a boat. A yacht on the gulf." He struggled to find the words. They barely made it through his lips. The struggle to breathe overwhelmed speaking in terms of importance.

"Where does it make port?" I asked.

He shook his head. "I don't... I don't know."

"Well, there are so many ports. Would be nice if you could"—I squeezed tighter, and his face continued to darken—"narrow it down for me."

The mist around his legs thickened, as if consuming him from the floor up.

"Grand Tortuga Marina," he managed.

"Grand Tortuga Marina?" I clarified.

He nodded.

"Good boy," I said. I eased my grip on his neck so he could take a breath, then tightened again. The temporary relief I saw in his eyes vanished.

"And the estate? Where might I find that?"

Another swallow against my tightening grip.

"Not far. I can show you where it is."

"Yes. I'm sure you can."

I wasn't about to get in a car with this hoodlum, but I needed to know where Carrillo called home. With the name of the marina, I could find that spot.

Suddenly, he jerked his left hand up to break my death grip on his neck. The move startled me, and the finger on the trigger twitched impulsively.

The back-left side of his head exploded to the sound of a click. Immediately, gravity pulled the man toward the floor.

I let go of his neck as the mist swirling around him subsided. I felt a wave of shock. It hadn't been my intention to execute the guy that way, at least not before I'd figured out where his employer was. I cursed myself for my panicked reaction in shooting him.

Fortunately, the suppressor on the weapon kept the gunshot to the faintest sound possible. But now there was a mess in my hotel room. I had no way of cleaning something like this. Blood on the wall, the mirror, and now the floor would require a sort of sanitation I had no experience using.

My brain raced, trying to figure out what to do.

I realized I was still holding the weapon and briefly considered tucking it in the dead man's hand to make it look like he killed himself.

That would fool no one except maybe the maid.

Carrillo sent the man here to kill me. Or perhaps to abduct me again. Either way, the guy wasn't going to show up on a job and then decide to off himself. It might buy me time, but I would find myself in the same situation as before—on the run in a foreign land. Except this time, I wasn't running from anyone. I was running to them.

I looked at the pistol. No serial number. That meant it was untraceable, not that the cartels were running around with a bunch of guns the government was tracking. Or maybe they were. I didn't know how things worked in that regard down here in Mexico.

The man's shoulder holster hung out of his jacket. It had places for two weapons. I'd left one in the console of the SUV for Vero before getting out. Two holsters for two guns seemed like a good coincidence. Vero's statement about those reentered my memory.

I bent down and removed the holster from the dead assassin, looped it over my shoulders, and stuffed the pistol into the right holster pocket. Then I searched his pants and jacket. Like the two guys before, I found a roll of cash that equated to a few thousand American dollars. I also removed his phone and stuffed it into my left pocket. His keys I shoved into my right. The man didn't carry any identification, same as the other two. I wondered what these guys did if they were ever pulled over by a cop, but then realized the thick wad of cash probably served as his ID.

"Nothing like a picture of Benjamin Franklin to make a cop forget they saw you," a friend of mine loved to say.

I didn't know if Ben would work down here, but the other pictures on the pesos would probably do just as well.

I returned to the bathroom, picked up the other pistol, and stuffed it in the left holster. Then I opened the closet door and slipped on a navy-blue blazer over my white button-up shirt.

Looking at myself in the mirror with a dead body at my feet felt strange, but I was trying to make sure I didn't look like a man who'd just killed someone in their hotel room.

With a long exhale, I picked up my bag again, scanned the room one last time to make sure I wasn't leaving anything behind, and then went to the door.

I grasped the latch and twisted, then turned to look over my shoulder again. This room had changed everything. Then again, I didn't want to remember what happened here. I wanted to move forward with my life.

The pain and blame I'd felt over Amy's death only remained at a fraction of the level as before. The text message with Garcia had forever altered the way I saw her. I wondered if I'd ever really known the woman.

I wanted to believe I did, at least partially.

We'd been friends at first. Our love of history and archaeology brought us closer together.

We had our problems, just like anyone else, but I had never considered she would leave me for another man. Maybe I hadn't been attentive enough, or romantic enough, or... No, that was a dark road to walk down, and I wouldn't do it.

The world was full of men and women who blamed themselves for this kind of thing when, in reality, blame was a two-way street.

It took two people to build a marriage, and two to bring it down.

I wasn't glad Amy was gone. And I knew that over the coming days, weeks, months, maybe years, I would face memories that squeezed tears from my eyes and caused me to question everything all over again. For now, I had other things to occupy my mind.

I had a mission. A purpose.

I would find Vicente Carrillo.

21

I left the room and marched down the corridor toward the elevators. The guns shifted slightly with every step, and I felt certain other people would notice them or at least the awkward bulges sticking out of my ribcage.

When I stopped at the elevators to wait for the next lift, I fixed the top two buttons on my jacket so the guns wouldn't be directly visible to anyone I walked past.

The door to my right dinged, and the red down arrow illuminated over the doors a second before they opened.

I stepped in, joining a Mexican family with a young girl. I guessed she was around five or six. Since I'd never had kids, I wasn't as good at guessing their ages as my friends who were parents.

I tried not to make eye contact with the girl, but she kept staring up at me. I wanted to smile or be polite, but I couldn't get over the sense that she knew I was carrying a couple of guns or that I'd just killed a guy, or....

The paranoia subsided with a deep breath and the ding of the elevator as it reached the lobby.

I motioned for the family to exit first and then followed them out.

I was being nice, but I also wanted to use their bodies to keep me hidden from the concierge. If the girl behind the front desk, or anyone else, had called Carrillo, the sight of me would produce another call.

I saw the girl I'd gotten my spare key from earlier. She was all the way across the lobby, a good hundred feet away. Maybe more. Fortunately, she was helping another patron, so I broke away from the family ahead of me and strolled toward the side door with my bag slung over one shoulder.

Keeping my eyes on the door, I didn't dare turn my head for fear she'd recognize me. There was no telling what kind of hell would break loose if that happened. An insanely implausible scenario of a gunfight with dozens of cartel thugs played through my imagination in the span of seconds.

The idea vanished as quickly as it appeared, and I went through the side door and out into the warm, late afternoon air.

I finally exhaled after what seemed like minutes and looked down both sides of the street. I shoved my hand in the pocket where I'd put the assassin's car key and looked at the fob.

"Land Rover, huh?" I said. "Shouldn't be too hard to find."

A look to the left produced nothing. Neither did a glance to the right.

He must have parked out front, on the main street.

Cars busily drove by in a steady stream on the street to the right. And pedestrians walked by intermittently but also at a fairly consistent rate.

The hotel's location was prime and in one of the safest areas in the city. Some called it the Beverly Hills of Mexico. That wasn't too far off. I'd seen a Lamborghini dealership, even ones for Ferrari, Porsche, Maserati, and Aston Martin all within a mile or two of the hotel.

This area, it seemed, attracted Mexico's money.

With no sign of the assassin's car, I made my way down the sidewalk to the front of the building. I paused at the corner and checked to the right and left. Down the street, parked against the curb about a half block away, I spotted the white SUV.

When the traffic light changed, I crossed the intersection and stalked toward the vehicle. From about eight car lengths away, I pressed on the unlock button and saw the front lights blink once.

Yep. That's his ride.

I picked up the pace and trotted down the sidewalk to the vehicle. After a quick look around, and no one paying attention to me, I opened the driver's side door and climbed in. When I closed the door, I stared at the wheel for a second. My mind stuck on Vero. I was worried about her. I'd told her to dump the vehicle somewhere in the city. I had no idea how she was going to get home, but Santa Rojo didn't seem like a place with a lot of inbound buses or cabs. And certainly no planes. I hadn't even noticed a train nearby when I was there.

I sighed, knowing what I had to do.

Before I realized it, the phone was against my ear, and I listened to it ringing.

"Buena," Vero answered.

"Hey. It's me. Don't hang up."

"Gideon? Is this your number?"

"Yes. I mean, no. It's a burner phone. Prepaid. I lost my phone when I was abducted. It's probably still in the jungle somewhere."

"Oh." A silent pause took over. "What are you doing? Did you forget something?"

"No," I said, watching the traffic pass by to my left. "I didn't forget anything." I exhaled, trying to find the right words without sounding weird. *How could anything I said now come off as weird?* I was a freak of nature. And she'd listened to the entire thing, even witnessed some of it. "I'm coming back to Santa Rojo. Are you still in Guadalajara?"

"Um, yes. I'm still in the city. Actually, I was going to get a room here and stay the night before heading back in the morning."

"Oh. Okay. I didn't mean to suggest—"

"But if you are offering me a ride, I would be happy to leave now. I haven't checked into a hotel yet."

I smiled. "Where are you? I'll come get you."

After the call ended, I pulled the SUV out of the curbside parking spot and out into traffic. Vero was at a hotel about twenty minutes away. She said she left the enforcers' vehicle in a mall parking lot where it would blend in. It was a smart move, and I'd happily told her as much.

A place like that had lots of people and cars. It would be much easier to blend in, and with so many witnesses around, the potential for trouble was significantly lower. Even the baddest dudes in the world would hesitate to try anything with too many people close by. The secret to getting away with a crime, as any criminal would say, is not getting caught.

Ten minutes after I'd left the hotel, I sat at a stop light behind three other cars waiting for the light to turn green. I glanced down at the phone I'd pulled off the dead man in my room, wondering if Carrillo would call. I suspected he was waiting for his assassin to call first since risking an outbound call could set off the killer's phone in the middle of the job. Nothing like a vibrating or ringing phone to alert a victim and give them a chance to escape.

It had been a while, though, and I kept wondering how long the boss would give his dog before demanding an update. Carrillo, I'd learned, was not a patient man.

The light changed, and I steered the car through the intersection, making my way through the city toward another hotel where Vero waited.

Five more minutes passed, and I noted the time left on the navigation screen. It told me the current route would take an additional six minutes. Not too bad.

Suddenly, the phone started dancing in the center console. It jiggled and vibrated, rattling the leather and plastic around it. At first, I considered not answering, but I knew that would be just as bad as picking up the call. Or would it?

I weighed the consequences in my head. If I answered the call pretending to be the assassin, perhaps I could buy some time. Maybe a day or two at most. But that would still give me a head start. For what, I had no idea.

If I didn't answer, Carrillo would assume something was wrong and probably send out his goons to scour the city.

Then again, in answering the phone, I would have to sound like the assassin. I figured I could pull off an authentic enough Mexican accent, but would I sound like the guy Carrillo sent to kill me?

The concierge or whoever the cartel don had working for him in the hotel hadn't seen me leave, at least not to my knowledge. It was possible I'd been spotted on a camera and that was the reason for this call.

I shook it off. "No," I said. "I have to answer."

I picked up the phone, resolved to do my best impression of the dead man in my room.

"Yes, sir," I said in perfect, gruff Spanish.

"Is it done?"

"Yes. He's dead."

"Good," Carrillo said.

I recognized the man's voice instantly, and it tickled my spine like a hundred spiders crawling across my skin.

"Where are you now?"

"Still in the city."

"Perfect. Return to the compound." Carrillo's voice darkened.

"Whatever you say, sir," I said.

Silence filled the earpiece, interrupted only by the man's breathing on the other end. "Are you unwell, Antonio? You don't sound like yourself."

A voice deep inside my head told me not to answer, to hang up the phone and keep driving. He was onto me. I knew it.

"Sorry," I said, breaking up my voice to make it sound as spotty as possible. "I think... connection... hello? Sir?"

I hit the red button on the screen and ended the call. The last thing I needed was to stay on the line a second longer. I didn't know the name of the device's owner. And I wasn't going to slip up and let Carrillo have an easy one. He used the name Antonio, but the way he said it sounded like a ruse. The man wasn't stupid. The phone may well have belonged to someone named Carlos or Juan or Pedro or any other name common to this part of the world.

I wasn't falling for it.

Ending the call left Carrillo in a state of uncertainty. Which is exactly where I wanted him.

22

I wasn't sure if I'd fooled him or not, but an uncomfortable feeling knotted in my stomach and continued turning and flipping the remaining five minutes of the drive.

When I pulled into the hotel lot, I spotted Vero sitting on a bench outside the lobby. I picked up my phone again and dialed her number.

"I'm in the Land Rover," I said when she answered. "You see me?"

"Yes. I see you. Nice ride. Where did you get that?"

"I'll explain later. Be ready to hop in. We have to move."

"What?"

"Again, I'll explain in a minute."

I steered the vehicle around the lot, following white arrows painted on the blacktop. I looped by the end of a row of cars, then guided the SUV to the front, where Veronica now stood by the curb.

When I stopped, I unlocked the door and reached over to pull the handle. The door popped open, and she climbed in. She looked at me in confusion.

"What happened?" she began "I thought you were going to the consulate to get your stuff worked out."

"I did. I mean, I was," I corrected. "I walked up to the front gate, but it didn't feel right. I couldn't do it."

"Couldn't go get your life back?"

"Well," I said, spinning the steering wheel as we drove out from under the hotel awning, "I don't think there is ever going to be any getting that life back. The life I knew is gone now. And there is nothing I can do to bring it back."

"Sounds familiar," she said, crossing her arms and glowering at me with an *I told you so* look her face.

"Yes. I know."

I drove down the street, leaving the hotel amid the thousands of other buildings behind us.

"You okay?" Vero asked after letting a minute or two pass.

I didn't answer immediately. "Am I okay?" I said it introspectively. "I don't know if anyone could really be okay having been through what I have this week. I was approached by one of the most dangerous men in the Western Hemisphere, told he wanted me to help him find this artifact." I looked down at the necklace for a half second. "Then I get out of the shower to find him and his men in my hotel room with a gun to my wife's head. They tell me she's been cheating on me, kill her in front of me, and I end up in some jungle with a necklace that turns me into some kind of crime-fighting monster." I glanced over at Vero. "So, yeah, considering all that, I'm actually doing okay. As okay as I can, anyway."

"I'm sorry. I shouldn't have said it that way."

"No. You're good. I'm glad you asked. And I know what you meant. I'm alive. And I'm trying to figure out what I should do next." I took a deep breath. "I'm sorry I wasted your day. You brought me all the way to the city to drop me off at the consulate, and..." I faltered, trying to think of the most rational way to say it. "But I couldn't leave. Carrillo is still out there. He will kill others. And if he thinks that you had something to do with the dead men in your kitchen—"

"Which he will."

"Right," I agreed. "There's no other conclusion he could reach. That means you could be in danger. And I'm not okay with that." I emphasized the word she'd chosen to jump-start this part of our conversation.

"So, if you didn't go into the consulate, where did you go? And where did you get this ride? Rental?"

My lips pinched together so tight, a business card would have bent in half trying to get through the seam.

"I went back to the hotel."

"What? You went back? That's exactly what Carrillo would expect you to do." The insanity of what I'd done was painted all over her face.

"I know," I conceded. "You're right. It is what he'd expect. And what he did expect."

More concern. "What?"

"Look, I didn't want to go back in there, to the room where I was abducted and my wife was murdered. You think that was easy? It wasn't." I didn't sound angry, just matter-of-fact. "I wasn't sure if the consulate would help. For all I know, they could be looking for me right now with the local police, thinking that maybe I murdered my wife."

"And yet somehow, going back to the hotel wouldn't play into that either?"

She made a good point. "You're right. Okay. I'm sorry. But I had to get a few things. Like clothes, for one. My passport was there, too. And something else."

Her concern melted. "What else?"

"Is this where I turn to get us back to the highway?" I asked, momentarily changing the course of the conversation.

"Yes. Turn right here. Then another right and you're there."

"Thanks." I switched on the turn signal and followed her directions. When I saw the signs for the highway, I resumed talking. "My wife's phone was still there. I've never done this before. I never had reason to." I felt like I was confessing my sins to a priest.

"Done what?" Vero pressed.

"I... looked through her phone. I figured out the passcode in two tries. She... she'd been texting with Garcia a lot. The man Carrillo said she'd been..." I faltered. The words had been hard enough to get out, but when it came to that part, the images, the messages they'd sent to each other, it stung all over again.

"Oh, Gideon. I'm so sorry." Sincere sadness filled her eyes.

This woman who'd only met me earlier that day and seen me at my rock-bottom worst, was genuinely sorry for everything I'd been through in the last few days.

"Thanks," I managed. "Look, I don't mean to put any of this on you, Vero. You've been so kind to me, giving me food, some clothes even though they were just those nasty cook clothes."

"Hey," she faked being hurt, finishing with a wry smile.

"And you brought me all the way into the city. Me, a total stranger with an even more bizarre story. I really appreciate everything you've done."

"You needed help. I try to help people who need it."

She did. I saw it with the kids from town that she fed after mass. She could have been terrified of me. Probably should have been and kicked me out of her cantina on sight.

"My parents died four years ago," she said. It was an awkward segue, but I allowed it, sensing she'd been wanting to talk to someone about it. "They were killed in a car accident. A drunk driver swerved into their lane. Dad steered the car off the road to avoid the other vehicle. He and Mom were killed almost instantly."

The story wrenched my heart. "Vero, I'm so sorry."

She shook her head. "It's okay. It's been four years. I've picked myself up and am still surviving."

Vero looked out the window to the west. The bottom edge of the sun touched the horizon, shimmering as it did just before setting.

"They left me enough money to start my own business in a new place, away from the troubles of the city. So, I bought the cantina. I make enough money to pay the bills, sometimes a little extra. But I'm never going to be rich. And that's okay. I don't need to be wealthy."

Something she said struck a chord with me, and I had to bring it up. "You said you're surviving. That's an interesting word choice."

"Oh?" She allowed a half laugh. "Why is that?"

"Because no one I know wants to simply survive. That's not what life is about. Making it long enough that the next in line can make it long enough so that the next in line—"

"I think I get your point," she said, laughing.

"Yeah, exactly. We're not here just to survive."

"Why are we here, Gideon?" She pried her way into my soul with her intense gaze.

"We're meant to live, for starters. The great masters of the past— the ones scriptures were written about, and stories were told about, religions formed around—they all told of making this life better for people, often through miracles. We've been told, at least in my religious background, that we should lay up our treasures in the afterlife. That this life doesn't matter. Well, I think it does. If it didn't, why would all those miracle workers across multiple religions have performed wonders that made people's temporary lives better?"

She hummed. "I guess I never really thought about it that way. I've studied several religions and the history around them."

I knew there was more to her than just being a bartender.

"We're not just meant to survive like animals. Yes, we're part of a delicate ecosystem, but our pursuit should be one of happiness and completion."

"Completion?"

I'd surprised myself with that word. "I guess what I mean is we need to figure out what our purpose is, and achieve that."

"What if your purpose is only to serve as a warning to others?" She raised both eyebrows.

I noticed the look and then merged into the middle lane on the highway to pass a slow-moving truck.

"That's actually a great question. And it could be. Then again, maybe we're surrounded by NPCs."

She burst out laughing. "Really? NPCs?"

"You know what those are?"

"Of course. I play video games. Non-player characters. The ones you interact with but aren't really people. Just bits of code designed to interact with the real players."

"I'm impressed," I said. "Well, other than people being NPCs, yes, it's possible some may serve as a warning to others. And that's sad."

She nodded, and the cabin silenced, only filled by the rumble of tires on asphalt and the steady purr of the engine.

The sun continued to dip behind us, nearly a quarter gone behind the hills to the west.

"I like your ideas, though," she said. "About purpose and living. I want to be happy and have more fun. I think part of my purpose is helping people, like the kids. But sometimes, I feel—maybe selfishly—that I wish I could have a turn at someone taking care of me. You know?"

"I do," I said.

The last several years of my life—all the years, actually, since I left my parents' home—no one had ever taken care of me. I'd always tried to be fairly independent. I didn't like having to rely on someone else.

But as I considered my relationship with Amy, I started to realize that she'd never made me feel like she would take care of me. More than that, she never made me feel like I was special. I guess early on she bought me a few things, some nice gifts, said all the right words.

The truth was I'd always felt like the lucky one.

"What are you thinking about?" Vero asked. "Seemed to lose you there for a second."

"Sorry. Yeah, I was just thinking about my marriage. She never took care of me either, and by that I mean I don't think I meant that much to her."

"Why's that?"

"Well, the obvious for starters. She cheated on me, and I don't know how many times or with how many men."

"You don't want to know those things," Vero cautioned.

"Oh, I know. You're right. That's a dark place to go, and no one leaves there happy. But Amy never made me feel like I mattered that much to her. We didn't fight much, almost never. I suppose I figured everything was great based on that fact alone. Turns out maybe it was because she really wasn't that invested in our marriage."

"She never made you feel special."

It was like Vero had reached into my brain and stolen those exact words I'd thought moments before.

"No. She didn't."

"You were surviving in your marriage," she added.

That one hit me like a sack of bricks. "Wow. I guess I was. And I never really saw that."

"And that, Gideon Wolf, is what we call ironic."

"Indeed."

As we increased distance from the city, driving farther into the countryside, fewer and fewer cars occupied the road.

Except for two, speeding toward us in the lane directly behind, and the one to the left of us.

I frowned when I noticed the twin luxury SUVs barreling down the highway at what I deemed—correctly—to be an unsafe speed.

"Um, Vero?"

"Yeah?"

"You see those two trucks behind us?"

She looked into the side mirror. "Are they racing? That's really dangerous."

"Yeah. It would be. Except I don't think they're racing. There's one more thing I meant to tell you about my trip to the hotel."

Her head twisted toward me, and she drilled into the side of my face with a questioning stare.

"What? Happened?"

23

I swerved left to dodge another slow-moving truck in the right lane, then quickly steered the SUV back to the right side. No more cars or trucks ahead of us gave me a clear run toward the coming darkness to the east, but that wouldn't mean much since two of Carrillo's vehicles were bearing down on us.

"When I went to the room, one of Carrillo's hit men showed up. I killed him."

"What?"

I realized how callously I'd made the confession. "Sorry. I'm just a little concerned about those two trucks coming for us." I glanced into the mirror and pushed the pedal to the floor. The SUV groaned, sending our heads back to the headrests as we accelerated.

"I know. It's crazy. He was there to kill me. Or bring me in. Either way, he had a gun. I didn't mean to kill him with it. The thing went off before I could finish questioning him."

"It... went off?" Vero clarified.

"I mean I took it from him and pointed it at the side of his head. But I wasn't intending to shoot him. I just wanted answers. Then he tried to get the gun back. It went off. I couldn't help it."

"Well, that's good. You took out one of his men. How many is that now?"

I left out the ones from the jungle, the men I'd killed in my animal form.

"Anyway, I took his money, and I found his keys in one of his pockets. So, I stole his car."

"This car. So Carrillo is tracking us."

"It's possible."

She glanced in the rearview mirror again. The trucks behind us were still closing in, though not nearly as fast as before. "Possible? I'd say it's happening."

"That or he may have realized I was here when he called earlier."

"Wait." She stared deadpan at me. "What do you mean, when he called earlier?"

"Yeah, so I also stole the assassin's phone. I figured it would be a good way to maybe get Carrillo's location. I didn't think he'd actually call."

She rolled her eyes and threw her right hand up in the air. "You didn't think that the guy he sent to kill you might be required to, oh, I don't know, report in at some point?"

It was the first time she'd scolded me for anything. It felt funny but not threatening. Of course, that might have been because there was an actual threat coming at us from the rear.

"I did think of that after the fact. Like when he was calling."

She laughed but wasn't enjoying it.

"So, he called," I continued hurriedly. "And I couldn't not answer because then he would know something was wrong."

One of the SUVs moved over into the far-left lane to allow the one on the right to merge to the center. They were fewer than sixty yards back now.

"You don't think an American answering the phone would tip him off?"

"I tried to use the killer's voice. I thought I was pretty good, actually."

I was surprised how cool I sounded considering I was driving at a high rate of speed with two vehicles behind us—their occupants intent on killing us.

"How in the world did you think that was a good idea?"

"It was that or let the phone ring."

"Let the phone ring!" she exclaimed, shaking her hands.

"If I let it ring, then Carrillo assumes something is wrong. Maybe he sends someone else to check it out. I figured I bought us a little time."

She looked out the back window, over at me, and back out the window again. "Doesn't seem like it worked. Got any other bright ideas?"

I checked the side mirror again and noted the SUV in the middle lane gaining ground to the left. They would be on us soon. How their engines were that much faster didn't compute. Unless they had an upgraded model or something.

"Gideon?"

I blinked back to attention, realizing my tangent-driven thought wasn't helping the current situation.

"Sorry. I'll handle it," I said, glancing back. "But I'm going to need you to drive."

"Wait. What?"

I looked into the rearview mirror, into the west behind us. Only a slice of the orange sun remained on the dazzling horizon. That wasn't all I saw.

A swirling red fog chased the other two SUVs, swirling around their tires as if to consume them. It would have made things a lot simpler if it worked that way. As far as I could tell, it didn't. But something itched in my mind, like an ancient question begging to be answered.

I'd have to come back to that later.

"Yes," I said to Vero. "I need you to take the wheel. I'll handle those guys. We'll have to slow down to make this work. And that's okay."

"Slow down? We need to speed up. They're going to catch us any second."

I looked into her eyes and nodded, hoping she could see that I wasn't concerned. Why I wasn't concerned still escaped me. This foreign confidence pulsed through my veins like a metal adrenaline, almost as if I was feeding off the possibility of another kill.

"Gideon?" Vero's expression mutated to one of fear.

Glancing into her eyes again, I knew why. My eyes reflected in hers, glowing blood red.

"It's okay." I said, turning to face the road. I realized I'd had my eyes off it for way too many seconds. "I won't hurt you. I promise." Behind us, the sun dipped lower. Only a dull orange cap remained. "Trust me."

She stared in semi-horror but nodded. "Okay, Gideon. I trust you."

I shifted, removing my seatbelt, and motioned for her to come over. I leaned the seat back as far as it would go. Vero climbed over the gear shift in the center, and in an awkward yet deft move, I pulled my foot off the gas pedal and held on to the wheel as she slid into my place. I let go of the wheel and scooted back.

"You can put the seat up now," I said. "Just keep this thing on the road."

I watched the SUVs behind us. They'd nearly caught up, and the fog around them pulsed bright, anticipating the bloodshed to come.

I leaned forward and pressed the button to open the sunroof, then double-checked the pistols in my belt. "By the way," I said, standing up on the back seat. I craned my neck forward so she could hear me with the wind overhead. "I should probably get some bigger clothes. Like monks' robes or something."

She frowned up at me in the mirror. "What are you talking about?"

"You'll see." I offered a disarming grin. Then I climbed up through the window as the sun disappeared over the horizon. The medallion's eyes glowed scarlet, and it felt warm against my skin. Power coursed through me, and I felt the change happen almost instantly.

I gripped the cargo rack on top and wedged my right shoe against the base to brace myself. Then I reached behind me and drew the two pistols and took aim at the SUV in the middle lane.

The driver slowed down upon seeing the threat. I fired five quick shots from the two pistols, hitting the hood with a single round that sparked off harmlessly.

My skin morphed; my muscles swelled.

Darkness had fallen.

"Time to play," I said.

The other SUV directly behind us risked a charge forward.

I fired again, and this time I hit the target three times. Two in the grill and one in the windshield. Based on the controlled braking by the driver, I assumed I hadn't killed him.

The other SUV caught up again on my right. This time, a gunman hung out of each passenger window with pistols aimed at me.

I wasn't worried about getting shot. It didn't feel good, but it wasn't going to kill me unless it was with a 105mm raining down hell metal from an AC-130 gunship. Unlikely these fools had anything like that.

Holding out the pistols at full extension, I aimed at the two SUVs —one with each gun—and emptied the contents of the magazines.

I dropped the guns back through the sunroof as my hands finished the change. My skin was covered with dark fur, and my fingers surrendered to paws.

The SUV on the right swerved hard to its left, glanced off the railing, and shot across the highway—narrowly missing their accompanying vehicle. The careening SUV flew off the road, hit a small hill, and flipped over as it twisted through the air.

For a few seconds, nothing happened. Then a fiery blaze shot up through the sky as the enemy vehicle erupted. I'd wondered if that sort of thing happened in real life. Then again, I was a dog-man. Who was I to question anything now?

I bared my fangs at the thought in a sort of sinister smile. Turning my attention to the remaining SUV, I roared into the night as the wind blew through my fur.

My moment of bravado evaporated when Vero jerked the wheel to the left and steered us into the middle lane.

For a second, I wondered what she was doing and considered asking—in a loud voice. Then I saw the antique station wagon pass by going maybe half our speed. At most. My irritation melted at the sight of the female driver spotting me, even though the momentum nearly sent me over the edge of the roof. Their reaction of awe and abject terror was borderline hilarious. So, I offered her a wink as if this was the sort of thing I did all the time.

She reacted by slamming on the brakes and nearly running her car into the guard rail to her left.

I clung to the roof rack before I flew over the side and hoisted myself back up to the top.

"Sorry!" Vero yelled.

I didn't reply, thinking the monster voice might be unsettling and cause another abrupt move from the driver.

I turned my attention back to the men chasing us and eased my way to the back of the vehicle.

Men stuck out from the three passenger windows and one from the sunroof. Three pistols and a submachine gun aimed at me from the corresponding openings. I couldn't risk letting them miss me and hit Vero.

Something inside me said something that both excited and unnerved me. "Jump."

I grinned, and without another thought leaped into the air. My muscles powered me high above the road, easily clearing twenty feet —maybe more. My animal senses fully active, I could see the looks on the gunmen's faces as they watched me soar into the night above them.

Astonished and terrified, they opened fire. The whole move took maybe three seconds, but it felt like a full minute as I twisted through the air and onto the roof of the cartel SUV.

The guy in the sunroof tried to turn around and fire, but I grabbed him by the neck and threw him thirty feet into the air. His body tumbled through the darkness before it hit the asphalt far behind the moving vehicle.

The gunman behind the driver fired a bullet through my left leg. The muscles screamed from the burning sting. He fired four more shots into my torso before I lashed out with my right paw. I felt a slight resistance against two claws, then nothing. The gunman's headless torso bobbed along for a second, and then fell out of the window onto the highway.

I winced and turned back to the other shooters, who'd recovered and turned to take aim. My body sealed the wounds and pushed two rounds out of my flesh, bouncing them off the truck's roof.

As the other gunmen fired their pistols, I swung down through the open window their compadre just vacated, and into the back seat. I snapped my jaws into the closest gunman's leg before he knew what happened. He lost his balance and fell backward through his open window—which I helped with shove from powerful paws.

The man hit the pavement headfirst and tumbled down the road, dead in an instant.

For a split second, I felt bad for the people who were going to have to work this macabre crime scene. Then I lunged for the driver's neck, sinking my fangs in deep until I felt warm liquid gushing over my gums. I snapped my powerful jaws to one side and felt a pop. Then the driver's hands fell limp from the steering wheel. I jumped out through the sunroof with the last gunman still hanging out the window, firing a few last desperate shots in my direction before the steering wheel jerked to the right.

The SUV's left tires bit into the asphalt and flipped the vehicle into the air, sending it side over side three times before it crashed down on top of the gunman, crushing him to death in an instant.

I landed on my paws and rolled to a stop as the SUV tumbled down the road ahead. I took off at a sprint, oddly unsurprised the leap from a speeding car had done nothing to me physically.

Straight in front of me, I watched Vero slow down and pull off on the side of the road. I guessed she'd seen the two vehicles crash. I probably should have told her to keep going and not stop until she got to Santa Rojo, but then I wouldn't have had a ride.

The red mist swirled around the crashed SUV as I sped by at a superhuman pace. It started evaporating immediately, and by the time I reached Vero, all traces of it were gone.

She opened the door and looked back as I charged toward her.

"Gideon?" she shouted back at me, confusion and fear crackling in her voice.

I slowed down to a trot and then stood up straight, towering over her. I nodded. "Yes. It's me."

Her fear melted right before my eyes. "They all dead?" She nodded over my shoulder.

I glanced back while nodding. The SUV that was on fire in the distance sent a black pillar of smoke into the orange-and-pink sunset.

"Yes. They're definitely dead."

She bobbed her head, looking at me like I was the star attraction in a traveling freak show. Which I was. I mean, come on. I would have looked at me the same way.

"Do... you want to...." She couldn't find the words to say.

"Head back to Santa Rojo? Yes. If that's okay. I know I look pretty scary right now."

"No. No, you're good. I..."

"Vero. It's okay. I know. We probably need to get going, though. Okay?"

Traffic on the other side of the interstate congealed as drivers began slowing down to see what happened. One driver had stopped his pickup truck and climbed out, presumably to cross the median to see if anyone needed help.

When he spotted me, his eyes widened, and I ducked my head to the side.

"I don't think other people will take the sight of me as coolly as you did."

"Yeah. You're probably right," she agreed.

I hurried around to the other side of the truck and climbed into the front. She got back behind the wheel and stomped on the gas.

We surged forward away from the carnage, and I took one last look back to make sure we weren't being followed. With no sign of trouble behind us, I slumped into the seat, nearly bumping my head on the roof.

"First of all," Vero said, doing her best to keep her eyes forward, "that was pretty amazing. How did you do that?"

I shrugged and felt my body sagging. With a glance at my paws, I realized they were changing back into their human shape.

"Weird," I muttered.

"What?" Vero asked. Then she saw me transforming back into Gideon the man.

"Nothing. I just don't really know when I'm going to change back."

She arched her right eyebrow, cocking her head in my direction. "You don't control it?"

I shrugged. "Not really. I think this time maybe I controlled changing into the chupacabra, or at least I felt like it was going to happen. The turning back..." I suddenly realized how shredded my clothes were and why Vero was desperately trying to keep her eyes on the road.

"Yeah," she said, "you were right earlier. We need to get you some kind of outfit that won't tear every time you turn into the animal."

I looked over at her, my eyebrows high with suspicion. "I hope you're not thinking of some kind of Superman suit or something."

She snorted—a little too loudly.

"No," she corrected. "Definitely not. I was thinking something else. Like you said before, a monk's robe." She stole a sidelong glance at my tattered clothes. "I think I may know someone who can make exactly what we need."

I didn't like the way she said it. Or the way she eyed me.

I took one more look out the back of the SUV. Nothing but darkness followed us, and a sporadic line of red taillights on the other side of the road.

24

For the remainder of the drive into Santa Rojo, my mind stayed fixed on a single issue: what to do about the cantina.

Two dead bodies in the kitchen were bad enough for business. And I'm sure back home in the States the health inspector wouldn't approve. The thought made me laugh, seeing the face of some imagined person in that thankless job walking in and finding a couple of corpses on the floor.

Vero steered the SUV down the road toward the tiny village near the edge of the jungle. When we reached the main street, she steered it to the right down another road.

"Where are we going?" I asked.

"To my secret place," she said. "It's a few minutes from here. And it's quiet."

"You think it will be safe?"

"I don't know," she said with a shrug. "I'm sure Carrillo knows where I live. But I own another piece of property with a small shipping-container home on it."

It was my turn to arch a questioning eyebrow. "Wait. This isn't your home we're going to? You have another property? In the same town?"

"I bought the land a few years ago to have a quiet place outside the village."

I wondered how loud she thought it really was. I'd seen only a handful of people there. Most of the area was rural or jungle forest.

"My house is inside town," she continued. "Out here, I can think and not be bothered." She looked out through the windshield, tilting her head to the side to get a better view of the night sky.

"The stars are beautiful out there," I said, noting her attention to them.

"Yes. We don't have the light pollution the cities have."

She continued down the road a little farther, then turned off on what was nothing more than a trail worn down by tires over time.

The SUV rocked and bounced along the rough road, and I wondered how often she brought her little sedan out here.

I instinctively looked back down the road again to see if anyone was behind us, but we were the only vehicle out, at least in the area.

Vero continued into a heavily forested area, and I quickly realized when she said she bought a place in the jungle, she really meant it was *in* the jungle.

"Do you get a lot of... um, wildlife out here?" I asked, somewhat uncomfortable.

"Present company excluded?"

"Hilarious."

I was salty, but I laughed when I said it. Vero was funny and kind of a smart aleck. I liked that.

"To answer your question, yes. I do see some interesting wildlife out here. Some big cats now and then. Snakes, obviously."

"Snakes?" I blurted out the concern.

"You don't like snakes?" she asked.

"No. No, I do not."

"I guess they're not for everyone. You just have to know which ones to avoid."

"All of them," I said, only half kidding. Maybe less than that.

She brought the SUV around a curve in the trail, and the canopy opened up above us, revealing a small clearing within the jungle.

A forty-foot-long gray shipping container rested on the ground, with two twenty footers on either end sticking out to create a U shape. One more container rested on top of the forty-foot one, providing a second floor with a balcony overlooking the jungle and the trail.

I looked over at her in surprise. "When you said a shipping container, I thought you just meant one. This place is huge."

She smiled. "Yes, originally I was only going to use the one big container. But I saw some cool ideas online and thought I would add onto it. Since it didn't cost much, I thought I might as well have the extra space, and if I wanted, I could rent it out on one of those sites or apps where people can rent their homes or apartments to travelers.

I nodded. Having used those apps multiple times, I was quite familiar.

"Smart," I said, although I wasn't sure how many travelers would be coming to this area. I wasn't going to say that. She had a good head on her shoulders, and certainly knew her region better than me.

She parked the SUV around behind the container home. Bulbs that simulated gas lanterns burned on either side of the wall at the top of a set of steps leading to a wide wooden deck. I'd noticed two more of those on the balcony.

"I have the same fake lanterns on my house back in the States," I said. "Always wanted to put in the real gas ones, but—" I stopped talking, recalling the argument with Amy about installing the gas lines. I'd always loved those kinds of lamps. I don't know what it was about them that made me feel relaxed or at home or like I was in a peaceful place, but that's why I liked them. Something about that flickering flame dancing in a glass box was cool to me. Amy would have none of it.

"But what?"

I blew it off with a roll of the shoulders. "Too expensive," I lied. "I mean, it would have cost quite a bit to run the gas line through the crawlspace and all that. Money better used somewhere else."

She nodded as if she believed me, but it felt like she didn't.

"Come on. Let's get inside."

She stepped out of the vehicle and slammed the door shut. After the sounds of the doors closing filtered through the jungle around us, we were immersed in the sounds of nature.

Exotic birds squawked in the night amid other chirps. Other sounds came from the trees, but I wasn't sure what those were and didn't feel like finding out. Even a chupacabra could get creeped out.

I followed Vero up the steps to the door and noted the security camera next to the lantern on the left.

"You aren't taking any chances," I said, indicating the camera with a nod.

"Nope. Not with Carrillo's men around." She unlocked the door and pushed it open.

"So, what? You take video and send it to the cops if something goes down?"

She turned to me as she crossed the threshold into the home. "No," Vero shook her head. "How many cops have you seen in Santa Rojo?"

"Good point," I conceded and stepped inside.

I closed the door after a quick look out into the darkness. If Carrillo's men had been following us, I would have detected it—a sound, a flash of light, even the smell of that pungent cologne all his men seemed to wear.

Even though I was in human form again, the animal senses felt stronger in the night than they had during daylight hours, as if the creature waited within me, ready at a moment's notice to reemerge.

I turned around and looked into the home Vero had created. Vintage lights dangled over a modest IKEA kitchen. A black heating stove sat idle in the far corner. An orange sofa rested to the left against the near wall, with a couple of black chairs positioned close to the stove.

I noticed the absence of a television. Instead, big windows occupied the front wall, giving a wide view into the jungle.

"Would you like a drink?" she asked, making her way over to the corner in the kitchen. She opened a cabinet door, revealing a treasure trove of tequila, bourbon, and rum within.

"Uh... yes, please."

"What's your poison, cowboy?"

I couldn't lie to myself. I liked the flirty way she looked at me, and the tone in her voice. It would be a long time before I could even consider anything with a woman, but Vero was cute. I had to give her that.

"Normally, bourbon. But I'll have what you're having."

"Risk taker, huh?" She flashed that flirty smile one more time before turning around and pulling a bottle from the middle shelf. I didn't recognize the brand, but based on the selection I could see none of it was going to be bad.

"Not in my past life. But now, what do I have to lose? Surprise me."

"Okay. I can do that. Make yourself comfortable."

I did as instructed, as much as possible, and walked over to one of the chairs near the stove. After I sat down, I felt the weight of everything slide off my shoulders. Even though the furniture was economical—and had probably been put together by Vero—it felt like the most comfortable seat I'd been in for a long time.

Vero popped the cork off the top of a bottle, and then I heard the familiar splashing sound of liquor pouring into a glass.

"That was crazy what you did back there," she said, pouring the second drink. "You're like some kind of super monster hero."

I shrugged. All the bullet wounds had healed while I was still on the highway. I recalled what the shaman had told me—about how with the blood of the wicked my powers would increase.

I wondered what else I could do. Flying seemed to be out of the question, but maybe it wasn't.

Vero turned around holding two tumblers half full of an amber liquid.

"Now that is a bartender pour right there," I said with a smile.

"I'm glad you approve," she replied. She stopped a few inches short of me and bent down to hand me the glass.

"Thank you." I accepted the drink with an appreciative nod.

"You're welcome. Salud." She raised the glass.

I copied her. "Salud. And thank you for helping me." The gravity of her actions smacked me in the conscience like a tree branch. "You took a lot of risk helping me. I can't tell you how grateful I am. Especially considering how homely I must have looked when you first saw me."

She nearly spit out her drink but managed to force it down with a hard swallow. "Yes, you did. And you still do. Which reminds me, we need to get you something to wear."

"I have some clothes in my bag. I picked them up at the hotel."

She chuckled. "Yeah, but those will be ripped to shreds, too, the next time you transform. You can't keep buying new outfits every time you change into the chupacabra."

"Yeah, you're right. I'll go broke at that rate." I had plenty of money in the bank. I wasn't a multimillionaire, but I'd managed to make a few good investments along the way and saved up in my short life so far.

"We'll go see my friend in the morning. She may have some ideas about what to make for you."

I considered the offer, but a question remained. "So, what are you going to tell her?"

Vero's lips creased. "That I need something for a shape-shifter, of course."

I laughed, but Vero took a somber drink from the glass, and I could tell immediately she wasn't kidding.

"Wait. What? You're going to tell someone?"

"Relax, Gideon," she soothed. "My friend Myra is very old. She believes in many of the ancient traditions. Myra is the one who told me the story about the saint of Santa Rojo."

"Oh," I said. "So, she's a believer in forgotten lore?"

"I guess so. I've known Myra since I was a little girl. She's told me so many fantastic stories. Still does when I have the time to go see her. I try to make sure I pop in at least once a week to check on her. Especially now that she's so old."

"That's nice of you." I took another sip. The warm bourbon splashed over my tongue and down my throat, tingling my senses with vanilla and caramel. "Good choice on the whiskey, by the way."

"Glad you like it." She looked toward the window for a second, as if contemplating something. "Myra doesn't just tell me stories. She gave me a whole collection of books on forgotten legends, mystical teachings, and ancient knowledge. I read some of them. They're interesting books. Some of the stuff seems pretty out there. I'd honestly never really considered any of it to be real. I thought they were all fairy tales, stories you tell kids to scare them in the night or to teach them a lesson. Then you walked into my cantina."

She turned back and faced me. "Would you like to see the books?"

My eyes widened with anticipation. "Absolutely."

"Follow me, then," she said, already moving toward the corridor behind me that branched off away from the main container.

"Okay," I mumbled, uncertain where this was heading.

I followed Vero up a flight of stairs to the second level. Bookshelves filled with tomes lined the wall at the end of the room to the left. Two more shelves mirrored each other on opposing walls. Between them, a small desk with a glass surface and metal legs stood in the center of the floor. To the right, a fireplace in the corner offered ambiance and warmth. A sliding door led out onto the balcony, where I imagined Vero sat many nights, looking up through the gap in the canopy at the moon and stars above.

"That's quite the collection," I said. I followed a subconscious call to have a closer look, and my feet obeyed, taking me over to the near corner, where I began looking over the book spines.

"She gave me most of them," Vero said. "Heaven knows where Myra gets them all."

"You have some stuff I've never even heard of." I shook my head in abject disbelief. One of the books was about the seven wonders of the ancient world. Another's topic was lost cities. There were books about treasures, monsters, mythologies, and legends that time had either left behind or forgotten.

"Did you say you've read all this?" I looked to Vero with the question.

"Most of them. But not all. I get sleepy when I read, so I don't get a ton of reading in each day, but I try."

I spied one book that seemed to call me. "Is it okay if I look through some of these?"

"Be my guest," she replied, raising the glass before taking another swig.

I pried one of the volumes from the shelf and pored over the cover. The faded hardcover told of its age. The embossed lettering on the front and on the spine had worn down, but the name of the book remained easily seen.

"*Forgotten Gods*," I said out loud, reading the title.

"Yeah, that's an interesting one. Talks about you in there, actually."

"What?" My head swiveled to face her. "Me?"

"Well, not Gideon Wolf. The chupacabra, though. He's in there. At least, I think it's in there. Seems like I saw the name. I haven't read that one through, though."

I flipped open the first page and felt a burst of energy course over me, as if I'd opened some book of spells and unleashed the magic's fury. Except this power felt good, and I welcomed it.

When I turned the page, I nearly dropped the book onto the floor. Fumbling it, I recovered just in time, and opened it back to the first page again.

"Uh-huh," she said.

I merely shook my head as I gazed at the image above the first chapter's title—"Medallions of Power."

I tore my eyes from the book, lifting my eyes to meet her knowing stare.

"Look at the next page," she suggested.

I wasn't sure I wanted to, but I had to know. I peeled back the next page and looked at the images drawn in old ink.

The first one was familiar. Too familiar. Goose bumps trickled across my skin. There, at the top of the page, was the same amulet I wore around my neck.

"Whoa."

25

"You knew," I said, holding her stare. "You recognized the medallion when you first saw me in your cantina."

"I did," she admitted. "At first, I wasn't sure about you. But when I saw that, my opinion quickly changed."

"And you knew about the story behind what happened to me?"

"No. Not all of it. Like I said, I haven't read all these." She waved a hand around to indicate the volumes surrounding us. "But I did see the pictures, and I recognized that amulet out of the seven on the page."

Seven. "That's right. The guide said there are seven heroes connected to ancient powers."

"Powers of forgotten gods," she said, motioning to the book. "That's what that one is all about. Xolotl is the ancient guardian connected to your family lineage. The Wolf family is one of the clans destined to protect humanity against the wicked, no matter its form."

"Form? What's that supposed to mean?"

"I don't know exactly. Maybe Myra can tell us more when we see her in the morning."

Suddenly, I found myself very much wanting to get to this Myra as soon as possible, and I didn't feel like waiting until tomorrow to do it.

I knew how ridiculous that was. Myra was asleep by now. And if not, she should have been. The hour drew long, and I noted the time on a clock behind the desk.

"Sorry," I offered. "It's getting late. But I have so many questions."

"I'm sorry I only have a few answers, Gideon. But yes, when I recognized the medallion on you, I knew there had to be something special about you."

"That's why you helped me." I spoke the realization with a slight hint of disappointment. To be honest, I didn't know where that sentiment came from. *Or did I?*

"It isn't the only reason," she countered. "I help people who need it. You needed it badly. But seeing the medallion helped me trust you. Trust isn't something that comes easily for me. Not anymore."

"I understand." My voice faded into the distance. "I understand all too well now."

Visions of the stupid pictures with Garcia and my wife resurfaced in my memory. I wished I could burn them away and never face them again, but they were there—probably for good. No sense in wasting energy on wishes.

"I know," Vero consoled. "I really do. And while I hate you had to go through that, something better is waiting for you. A greater purpose that will guide you to your destiny."

I huffed. "Destiny," I muttered. "I always blew that off, the notion that we had some kind of predetermined fate taunting us."

"Many of the ancient ways have been forgotten," Vero said. "We have only pieces of their teachings, beliefs, and knowledge."

"You're right about that," I agreed. "That's what I love about archaeology—the perpetual search for the truth, the reality about what happened so long ago. I believe we've been taught only fractions of actual history. I enjoy the search, and the discovery. There's nothing like finding an object that hasn't been seen in hundreds, sometimes thousands, of years. Being the first person to see something like that..." My voice faded off as I thought about some of the discoveries I'd made in my time.

The medallion pulsed against my skin, as if calling my attention. I looked down at the thing, pinching it with finger and thumb. The red eyes glowed, and I felt myself being pulled into them. They swirled like vortexes, drawing me down into some mystical abyss.

"And you were the first to see that in a very long time," Vero said.

"Yes," I nodded absently. "I suppose I was." I cast a sidelong glance at her. "And you knew way more than you let on, apparently."

"Yes, well, monsters and mythical heroes empowered by ancient spirits of the universe aren't really topics you bring up on a night out with the girls."

"I imagine not." I let the medallion fall and turned to study the emblems on the page. I recognized some of the creatures, ones that looked like animals I knew. The falcon was an easy one to identify. One was a strange beast. It had the face and head of an ape, but the eyes were so human.

"Forgotten gods, you say?"

"Yes. They were called gods back then, when people didn't know what else to call your kind. You weren't creator beings, like the Maker, but you were made by them, and given powers to fight the forces of evil."

"And now you definitely sound like you know way more than you let on before."

"I only know the legends, the ones Myra told me. And the tidbits I read from that book. In the early chapters, it makes reference to the time of creation, and the fall of mankind that happened after. Have you ever read Genesis 6 in the Bible?"

A cryptic smile creased my lips. "The one that talks about the Nephilim, the watchers?"

"Very good. Then you know how that book goes on to talk about the giants in the land that were there before and after."

"After meaning the Great Flood?"

Her shoulders inclined an inch them dropped. "Maybe. Maybe it was something else we haven't even heard of... or been told about. Either way, it also mentions men of might, men of renown."

She paused, letting me put the pieces together on my own.

"And you think that I'm one of those... men of renown?"

Vero lowered her head in a show of cynicism. "Don't get cocky. But yes, it would seem that the seven guardians sent to protect humanity were the same ones revered as gods, or demigods, by the ancient peoples. Or as the Hebrew text suggests, powerful people."

The mere thought that I could come from a lineage of ancient, superhuman warriors sent a tremor through my body.

"These guardians," I said. "What happened to all of them?"

She took a sip of bourbon before speaking up again. "They died, Gideon. Everyone dies. Just because you've inherited this power doesn't make you immortal. You will age. And you will die. Sooner or later."

"Yes, I get that." I pinched my lips together, focusing on what I wanted to say. "But the legends, they've been lost for so long. Reduced to fairy tales or ghost stories."

"That's how it works. Based on my loose understanding. The red saint shows up when he is needed. And when his work is done, he disappears once more."

She didn't bother trying to hide the correlation from me this time.

Part of me just wanted to kill Carrillo and be done with it. Maybe I would bring down his entire organization. That would appease the ancient... whatever was causing all this.

My mind raced with thoughts. I found myself wanting to pore over all the books in her library, but that would take weeks. Fortunately, I was a fast study and an even faster reader. Even so, I'd need time to learn everything, and I wasn't sure time was something I had much of.

A single idea kept ringing in my head until I couldn't ignore it any longer.

"You said Carrillo doesn't know about this place?" I asked, looking around.

"No. No one knows. I'm sure people see the trail, but there's an old gate that keeps out trespassers. And I have the security cameras on the house itself. If anyone comes here unannounced, I'll know it."

"Yeah, but how do you protect yourself out here?"

Her lips had flattened and taken on a nondescript, unemotional pall. They curled up again, though, and she walked over to the shelf near me. Standing inches away, I sucked in the smell of her hair and the light perfume she must have sprayed on her neck earlier in the morning. The scents still lingered on her like sweet nectar on a rose.

She pulled a particularly large book by the spine, and the bookshelf hissed, then began swinging out away from the wall.

I leaned my head over and looked behind the shelf to see an eight-foot-long gun rack built into the framework. Three AR platform rifles, two shotguns, and four pistols hung on a rack, along with several magazines stacked at the bottom in corresponding calibers. A hunting rifle hung at the end of the row with a scope attached.

"Wow," I said. "Impressive collection. You sure you're not an American?"

She laughed. "It took a bit of doing to get these. And you laugh, but an American friend was how I got these. He's based out of Portugal now, but he gets around. Whenever he had some extra inventory from his arms business, I would get a good deal."

"So, you're friends with arms dealers? That sounds safe."

She chuckled. "He's a good person. Doesn't sell to terrorists. Only sells to resistances, or groups trying to fight evil. Sound familiar?"

"The part about fighting evil?" I saw where she was going with that, and it started to feel more and more like this entire thing was set up. Not by her entirely, but the second she saw the medallion... I had to wonder if that set the gears in motion. Or if it was just a coincidence. Then again, her thoughts on those ran in my mind.

"You're still on the fence about all this, aren't you?" She asked the question point blank.

"Not as much as before. I don't know much about hunting down bad guys or fighting, but I do know how to do research."

My own gears were turning now, and there was no stopping them.

"Do you have anyone coming to stay here in the next few months?" I asked.

"No. I haven't had a visitor rent this place in six months. And that was only for a weekend. Nobody wants to come out here to the middle of nowhere. They want to see the historic places, like the pyramids or Tulum, or the mummies, or the big cities."

"Perfect. I'll rent it from you."

"I can't allow you to do that, Gideon," she said.

"Why not? I can pay you. Or is it too much of an intrusion on your personal space?"

She shook her head. "No, it's not that. I wouldn't feel right about taking money from you. If you stay here, and take on this mission, you won't be paid for it. Whatever money you make from your career will eventually disappear until you have nothing left."

Vero was right about that. I needed to make sure my income remained steady. Then again, another possibility bubbled to life. "Unless we use the cartel's money to fund the operation."

She considered it for a few seconds before nodding slowly. "They always have cash on hand. Lots of it. And it's usually untraceable, or at the very least difficult to track."

"Yes. Exactly. What if, as we take out the cartel, we use their own money to make this thing go?"

"Okay, I see what you're saying. But I don't understand what you're talking about using the money *for*."

At first, I was thinking of paying off my mortgage, my car, those kinds of things. But then I realized that those things were from my past life, the life that was no longer a part of who I was, or who I would become.

All those times growing up, people used to tell me that houses, cars, boats, motorcycles were simply material things—stuff that doesn't matter. Pile one more intangible item on top of all that. Career can become an obsession, too. I don't know if that was the cause for my marriage's failure, but—*Jeez, I'm getting introspective again.*

"Sorry," I offered, realizing I'd gone off in thought again. "You know about these medallions of power." I held up the book. "If you have this book, that must mean others do as well."

"Yes. That's true."

"Don't you see? The voice in the temple told me there were seven of these, from seven ancient clans. If Carrillo knows about these, then it's possible that elsewhere in the world someone is searching for one of the other amulets."

"Potentially, yes." Vero tried to stay with me. "What's your point, Gideon?"

I turned the book toward her, showing her the medallions again. "I think I just found my new purpose."

"And that is...?"

"I'm going to find the rest of these so they won't ever fall into the wrong hands."

26

Morning came too soon. Not that I could sleep much. My mind danced with the possibilities—tracking down six other ancient amulets of power.

The medallions could have been anywhere in the world, and while I would have stayed up all night reading through Vero's book, I could tell she needed to get some rest. I needed sleep, too, despite the adrenaline rocking through me.

Vero had a spare room at the other end of the second floor, complete with a queen-size bed and a collection of minimalist furniture—again from our favorite Swedish furniture company.

The fragments of sleep I achieved were strewn with strange dreams, nightmares of ancient battles, cities unlike anything I'd ever seen, and bizarre creatures from all realms of mythology.

A mishmash of cultures, religions, and people swirled through my view. During the last dream, I saw a churning darkness—a cloud blacker than anything I'd ever witnessed before. It rolled toward me as I stood on a plain. Within the charging darkness, flashes of purple light flickered and sparked, always consumed by the clouds folding in on themselves.

A powerful, hot wind blasted over me, and I felt myself change into the chupacabra, ready to fight the darkness.

Then I woke up.

I sat there in the bed with my head against the black headboard, staring out the window into the jungle.

It was disorienting waking up in this place—especially after the wild dreams and the reality that was easily as crazy.

I recalled the events of the previous night, the high-speed car chase, how I'd killed Carrillo's men. Everything was so surreal.

The smell of coffee filled the room, and I realized I'd been sitting there in the bed for too long. I climbed out and slipped into some pants, again remembering I definitely needed to get some new clothes.

I padded around the studio wall that separated the little bedroom from the rest of the second floor and then descended the stairs. The smell of coffee grew stronger with every step.

The sounds of dishes clattering echoed off the walls.

Vero set out two coffee mugs and a couple of plates, then tossed some eggs sizzling in a frying pan.

I walked slowly toward her, hoping I didn't frighten her.

She caught sight of me and smiled. "Good morning. Did you sleep well?"

I nodded. "Yeah. I think so. As well as could be expected."

She half frowned at the statement. "Bed not soft enough? Too soft? Too hot or cold in the room?"

"No. No, nothing like that," I said, waving a dismissive hand. "It's just, I have these weird dreams."

"Like nightmares?" she asked, tossing in a few beef sausages with the eggs.

"Sort of. The one I remember most is the last one I had before I woke up. I was standing on a plain."

"Like an airplane? Was it flying?"

I chuckled at the funny question. English could be a tease sometimes.

"No, sorry. I mean like flat land."

"Oh."

"Anyway," I continued, "there's this huge black cloud coming toward me. It's rumbling and churning and flashing purple lights inside it like lightning."

"That does sound like a nightmare. What happens?" She turned the eggs again. "Do you like your eggs medium? Or scrambled?"

"Either way," I answered. "And to the other question, I don't know what happens. I woke up before the cloud got to me. It was weird."

Vero shifted over to the coffee pot and filled the two white mugs. She took one by the handle and stepped over to me, handing it to me carefully.

"Thank you," I said, grateful to have my morning fuel.

I sat down at a little bistro table off to the side of the kitchen and looked out the giant window.

"This is such a nice spot," I observed. "So peaceful."

"You said that last night," she laughed. "If I didn't know better, I'd say you wanted to move in here."

I took a sip of the coffee. It was delicious. I raised the mug to her in thanks. "This is excellent."

"Thank you. I know the roaster in the village. He makes it special for me."

I nodded, pouting my lips to show I was impressed.

"Anyway. I meant what I said last night." I raised the mug to my lips and sipped again for dramatic pause. "I am going to find the other six medallions."

"Yes, I heard you. And I'm telling you, it's not that simple. Based on what you said about how you found that one, I'd say you got lucky." She crossed her arms with a look that a schoolmarm might give a pupil who misspelled *cat*.

I bobbed my head in agreement. "That's totally fair. And you're right. I did get lucky finding that temple. I happened to be in the right place at the right time."

"Yes. But it's more than luck."

Now I was confused. "What?"

"Sure, you may think you were lucky, but you need to let go of that."

"Yeah, but you just said—"

"I was messing with you, Gideon. Remember, no such thing as coincidences. You were meant to find that medallion. Is it possible you are supposed to find the others? Perhaps. I'm only saying don't expect it to be easy."

I huffed a laugh at the last part. "You know, you'd make a good archaeologist with that attitude. You're patient. That's something a lot of folks don't realize when they go into my line of work—that you have to be patient. We're dealing with slow processes, countless hours of research, and that's before we begin digging with spoons and toothbrushes."

She laughed—maybe politely—at the last part, but I felt like she got the joke.

"I will find the other medallions," I went on. "And if you could help me, I would appreciate it." I locked eyes with hers, letting her know I was absolutely serious.

"Yes," she said, her head nodding absently as she realized the gravity of my words. "I believe you will." She lifted her mug and took another sip. She set the cup down, turned the sausages, pulled the eggs from the frying pan, then placed them on two white plates.

A few minutes later, we sat down to eat the breakfast she'd prepared. The food, while simple, tasted better than anything I'd had in a while.

When we finished, I helped Vero with the dishes before we set out into the village. I wasn't sure about taking the SUV, but we didn't have another way to get there except walking, and that would have taken too long.

When we reached the outskirts of the little town, Vero parked the SUV behind one of the other businesses at the other end of the main street.

The flashy SUV would draw attention, and if Carrillo knew what his hit man had been driving, he'd recognize the vehicle the second he laid eyes on it.

I put the odds of that happening at 50/50.

After parking the car up the street, Vero and I walked around to the sidewalk and then crossed at the intersection. Then we skirted back around behind the row of buildings and continued toward the backside of the cantina.

Her car was still parked where she'd left it the day before. When we arrived at the back door, I looked around, scanning the area around us for an ambush.

She unlocked the door and started to open it, but I stopped her.

"Let me go first. Those bodies in there... I don't want you to see that."

"I'm going to have to if we're going to get them out of here. I know where the big trash bags are. I just hope no one see us hauling a couple of corpse-size plastic bags out through the back."

I laughed at the visual imagery. "Okay, but still. Let me go first."

"Fine," she conceded. "Be my guest."

"Thank you." I eased by her and pushed on the door. It didn't move.

"You have to turn the knob," she said, condescension dripping from every word.

"I deserved that," I admitted, blushing.

I turned the knob and pushed the door open.

At first, I didn't know what to expect. I wasn't accustomed to walking into places where dead bodies had been left overnight. Would there be a disgusting smell? Would it be so overpowering that I would throw up the second the odor hit my nostrils? What would the bodies look like? Would they be bloated? And if we moved them, would they—

I cut my thoughts off right there, immediately regretting volunteering to go first.

Slowing down to a tiptoe crawl, I maneuvered into the back hallway and waited, listening intently. A creak in the roof. A gurgle of a pipe. But no sign of trouble. If there'd been someone waiting there to catch us by surprise, I would have heard them breathing.

I continued moving through the hall until I arrived at the door to the kitchen. There I paused, waiting for a second. Stalling wouldn't change what I was about to find on the other side of that threshold.

I felt Vero come up behind me, stopping a few inches short.

I swallowed, wishing I'd let her go ahead of me. I went into archaeology, not biology. Medical stuff always bothered me, made me queasy. The dissection of animals in high school was something I would have rather skipped. Old bones were the only part of biology that interested me.

Out of time to stall further, I crept around the corner and poked my head into the opening. I expected to see two bulbous bodies surrounded by congealed blood, bloated to the point of making them unrecognizable.

The expression of concern on my face dissolved into one of total confusion. I shook my head, surveying the small kitchen from floor to ceiling and back again. "Stay here," I said, putting my hand up to keep Vero where she stood.

"What is it?" she asked.

I didn't answer immediately. Instead, I took one more step inside. I looked up on the shelves, and down under the stove, then shook my head in disbelief.

"Vero?" I said. "You might want to have a look at this."

She appeared in the doorway a second later. Her face mimicked my reaction exactly. Confusion colored her skin and filled her eyes. She turned her head back and forth, as if the answer to the bizarre quandary would appear somewhere else in the room.

"I don't understand. Where did they go?"

"I don't know," I confessed, poring over the kitchen with unbelieving eyes. The bodies, the blood, and any sign that the assassins had been there were gone. The kitchen looked as if it had just been cleaned.

"They couldn't have just disappeared," Vero babbled. "They had to go somewhere. Who got them? And why?"

All I could do was shake my head. "I have no idea. But maybe your friend Myra does."

27

We locked the cantina and walked around the back, again checking to see if any of Carrillo's men were lurking in the shadows. When we found no trouble waiting, we continued around the side of the building and then cut left across the intersection.

Every pair of eyeballs that noticed us felt like a threat, and it seemed as though everyone in the village was on Carrillo's payroll.

I knew that was absurd, but it didn't ease my worries as we found our way onto the next sidewalk and kept walking.

"Myra's place is just ahead," Vero told me.

I wondered how many places could be hers, since there were only a few shops and homes left on the neglected street.

Vero smiled at an old man sitting on a bench outside a hardware store. He wore a plaid farmer's shirt and an old straw hat. He offered a greeting to her, and she replied politely without stopping.

She kept going until we reached the end of the street, where the dusty road wound away from the buildings and disappeared into the jungle around the bend.

Vero halted outside an adobe house with wooden rods sticking out from just under the roof. The wooden door looked like it could be a few hundred years old, worn and smoothed by time and weather.

Vero reached out and put her hand on the door latch.

"Aren't you going to knock?" I asked.

Vero rounded on me and replied with her *aww, you're cute* grin. "She already knows we're here."

"What? But you didn't—"

Before I could finish, Vero opened the door and stepped in.

"Tell her we were coming," I said to end my thought.

"Hello, my dear," a creaky woman's voice said from inside. "Come in. Come in. You too, Gideon. Don't hover around the door like that. You never know what sort of people might come looking for you and that prize around your neck."

The medallion? How did she know? And how did she know my name? I haven't even seen this woman yet.

I had to know more.

I walked over the threshold and closed the door behind me.

The little hut was humble but cozy. A fire flickered in the hearth with a pot of something hanging over it that cast a savory, peppery smell into the air.

"Will you be staying for lunch?" Myra asked.

That's when I saw the woman. She was hunched over in a kitchen to the right, pressing tortillas out on a rolling table.

"I wish we could," Vero said. "But we're in trouble, and I don't want to bring any more problems to Santa Rojo."

Myra chuckled. Her long gray hair was arranged in braids that dangled past her shoulders. She wore simple garments—a green dress with a brown cotton belt that dangled around her hips. She was short and round, with a kind face that smiled from her eyes as much as it did her lips.

"Oh? Yes, I suppose you are in something of a hurry, my dear. What with that bad man looking for Gideon's medallion."

I stood there watching and listening with rapt fascination. Only when Myra spoke directly to me again did I realize I'd sort of faded off.

"It's okay, Gideon," Myra said.

"What is?" I asked.

"To ask questions. You don't have to just stand there in silent ignorance. You're a guardian. You want to know how I know your name and why I called it your medallion. You're probably also wondering how I knew you had that thing dangling around your neck."

"My first guess would be Vero here texted you," I indicated Vero with a finger.

Both women shook their heads.

"Right. Not much of a texter. So, yes. I'm wondering how you know my name and all the other stuff you mentioned."

Myra nodded. "And you saw the book I gave Vero?"

"Yes, ma'am. I saw it."

"And what did you think?"

I hadn't showed up here expecting to get a quiz. "Um, it's interesting. I'll say that."

The old woman laughed. Her wrinkled skin jiggled from her bones as she did. "Oh, it is definitely interesting, young guardian. You have no idea how far the rabbit hole goes, do you?"

"No," I confessed. "I don't know much about any of this."

"And yet you have decided you will do everything in your power to take on this mantle, to defeat the wicked and help the innocent."

"Yes, ma'am." I didn't sound sure. And I didn't feel it. "I mean, it doesn't seem like I had much of a choice."

"That's true," she said, holding up a bony finger. "You don't get to choose your destiny."

"Doesn't seem very fair."

"Ha! Life definitely isn't for most. Then again, that's why you and the other guardians exist, to balance the scales of this realm."

Realm? Did she say realm? That was a weird way of putting it.

"I'm going to find the other medallions," I said, uncertain where the words came from.

"Oh, is that so?"

She waddled over to the iron pot hanging over the fire. She stuck a wooden ladle into it and scooped out a reddish-brown liquid, then raised it to her lips and sipped the hot stew.

She nodded and placed the ladle back down on a wooden tray. "Needs more pepper. And more garlic." She picked up a wooden bowl from a stand next to the pot, sprinkled in a pinch of garlic powder, and then shook a pepper bottle over the pot a few times.

"Tell me, Gideon, what you're going to do with those other amulets when you find them? Do you believe they will give you the combined power of all the ancient guardians?"

The question caught me off guard even though I'd been considering what to do with them.

"No. Nothing like that. I don't want that kind of power."

"Are you certain?" She turned to me, and now the kind face that had been framed between her braids was gone—replaced by something dark and probing, almost otherworldly.

"Yes," I said, my voice trembling. "I don't have any desire for power, certainly not more than what this thing has given me." I held up the medallion.

Her face abruptly lightened. Only then did I realize that the corner around her, even the very fire, had dimmed slightly

"Good," Myra said. "Power is a dangerous thing. And it can corrupt even the most pious of souls."

She was right about that. I'd seen it in politicians back home, men and women who'd started on the ground floor with local school boards or city councils. As they climbed the political ladder, they forgot why they'd gotten into the game in the first place. Before they knew it, they sounded like all the others who'd come before them—the very people they'd once loathed for never having an original thought—only reciting spun speeches written for them by aides and consultants plagiarizing the same circular vocabulary.

This kind of power was even more dangerous.

With politicians, their strength was built on funding—financial gains on both a personal and business scale. Money was one thing. The power this medallion gave was something else.

I hated to imagine what could happen if any of these things fell into the wrong hands. World leaders, powerful businesspeople, gangs, cartels like Carrillo's, mobs, terrorists. The list went on, and the more I thought about it, the more certain I was.

"This artifact," I began, my fingers instinctively reaching for the amulet, "can't fall into the wrong hands."

"What makes you think it will?" Myra countered. "Those amulets have been hidden for thousands of years. Yours has only been gone a few hundred. Why do you think now, after all this time, the forces of evil will happen upon them?"

That was something I'd wondered, too. If the medallions were so difficult to find—and I'd found the first one in a few centuries, at least—then odds were no one would locate the other six. I could rest easy and not worry about some terrorist cell stumbling upon one.

"I know you're right," I said. "It was dumb luck that I found this one. I was running from Vicente Carrillo and his men. It was dark. I fell into a hole. When I looked around, I realized I was in an ancient temple."

"The temple of Xolotl," Myra added.

Vero had grown quiet in the kitchen, listening to the conversation with her arms crossed.

"Yes. But I didn't find it on my own. It's not like I'd been scouring over ancient maps and clues for years. I literally just fell into it."

She nodded, and I figured she probably already knew everything I was telling her. Maybe this was some kind of test.

"All the secrets of the medallions are in the book I gave Vero. If you are to seek their locations, everything you need is in that book." Her eyes filled with caution. "You must be careful, though. As you suggested, there are many who would seek those amulets for their own wicked gains. They must never fall into the wrong hands. Not even the ancient power that fills them can stop the one who carries it."

Two questions hung right in front of me, and I sensed my chance to ask. "Has that ever happened before? I mean, has one of the wicked ever gotten their hands on one of these?"

"No," she answered. "We were close, many eons ago. A man of

great evil—a king—tried to find the seven medallions of power. In the end, he never located a single one. The king spent a fortune in his conquest. Tens of thousands of soldiers were slaughtered, both on his side and on the sides of his enemies. In the end, his empire collapsed because of his obsession."

"And he never found a single one?"

"Fortunately. No. In the hands of such intemperate evil, the consequences would have been utterly devastating."

"Which guardian destroyed the evil king?" I asked.

She smiled humbly at me. "All of them. They united against him and the swarms of evil he'd summoned from the belly of the earth."

"Summoned?"

"You had a second question," she said, moving on from the one I'd just asked.

I guessed I better move on, too. "Two of Carrillo's men came to her cantina yesterday. We had to kill them."

Myra nodded. "Yes. A wise move."

"But we left the bodies there. When we went back just now, the two men were gone. And there wasn't a trace of blood or anything in there."

"They were consumed," Myra said plainly, as if that explained everything.

"I'm sorry? What?"

"They were consumed," she repeated. "The power that is contained in that medallion doesn't have to stay there. It can reach out and help you. Perhaps you've noticed the red mist that forms around the wicked."

I nodded. "Kind of hard to miss it."

"Red mist?" Vero asked.

"Yes," Myra answered, turning around to face the younger woman. "You probably haven't seen it. But when our friend here is near someone evil, the medallion senses that and wraps a scarlet fog around the threat. Keep in mind, that doesn't mean you need to go around killing everyone with a red aura around them. Try to keep it to self-defense most times."

That answered the question about the bodies. And about whether or not other people could see the mist.

"Do you see it?" Vero wondered, stealing my next question.

"I have seen it," Myra said. "It is like a ghost that comes to take the souls of the wicked off to the abyss where they will forever sleep."

"Forever sleep?" That sounded bad. Like, worse-than-hell bad.

"Yes. Some cultures believe in an afterlife, both good and bad. However, the teachings related to the medallions are different. When the wicked have been vanquished, they cease to exist and instead are relegated to eternal unconsciousness."

Nonexistence. That has to be a fate worse than death. At least in a hell, you were still around, even if you were in pain all the time. With existence came the chance to escape, to change things. Simply being gone eliminated all hope. And that was the starkest epiphany that I ever had.

"Myra," Vero said. "He will need something to wear that's more suitable to his... constant changes."

"She's right," I agreed. "Whenever I changed into the chupacabra, my clothes get ripped to shreds."

"Yes. I'm aware of that problem."

She turned and wandered through a narrow doorway into what I believed to be a bedroom. Two minutes later she reemerged holding a long gray robe.

"This is the garment of the Guardian of Xolotl," she said. "I've kept it hidden for many years. Now, it seems, is the time to take it out of storage."

"Wait a minute," Vero protested. "You've been keeping that thing here all this time, and you never thought to tell me?"

"It belongs to the guardian. Not to me, my dear." She disarmed Vero's complaints with a kind grin. "Besides, this is way too large for you, child."

Vero laughed at being called a child, and she relaxed. "Good point."

I accepted the heavy robe from Myra and inspected it closely. It had a hood that folded down over the back and a black belt around the waist.

"Try it on," Myra insisted.

I obeyed, taking off my rucksack and setting it on the floor before looping the hole in the top of the robe over my head.

The garment slipped down onto my shoulders. The bottom brushed against the tops of my feet. The fabric felt impossibly soft against my skin. Even wearing my ordinary clothes underneath, I felt remarkably comfortable.

"That is a special fabric," Myra explained. "It will grow with you as your body morphs during the change. And it will shrink back. The fabric is directly connected to the power in the medallion, so it will know."

"Smart fabric," I said. "What will they think of next?"

"Oh, this robe is at least six thousand years old, Gideon. It was worn by your ancestors. It's hardly new, as you suggest."

"Sorry. I was kidding. Just thought it was funny."

"Yes, well, you'll also find that the fabric is remarkably durable. It isn't bulletproof, but it will heal the same as you do. And no, before you ask, it isn't organic. It simply repairs itself."

I couldn't believe it. What was she telling me? That this cloak could fix itself? Then again, why was I questioning anything at this point? Every turn in my life had gone off the rails into some bizarre fantasy world where monsters are real and, apparently, I'm one of them.

"Thank you," I said, pushing aside all the other distracting thoughts. "I really appreciate it. And thank you for the information."

"Yes. And we appreciate you taking on such a difficult challenge on behalf of all those who cannot defend themselves."

I lowered my head and pulled the hood up so it hung low over my brow, hiding my eyes in shadow.

"Ridding this land of Vicente Carrillo is the first step," I said. "It's time for his reign of terror to come to an end."

Myra nodded. "And what will you do once your revenge is had? Will you feel complete? Will you finally feel a sense of closure? Or will you thirst for more?"

I had to think before I answered. This woman was a sort of oracle, at least that's what I surmised. She knew things and could tell if I was lying or being truthful.

"It isn't about revenge," I said. "Not anymore. Vicente is a wicked man. So are the people who work for him. The people need someone to stop him and others like him. They need to see that evil doesn't win. It has nothing to do with a quest for vengeance or to make me feel righteous. This is about protecting the people."

I felt an oddly familiar sensation radiating from the medallion, as if it fed my body with an ethereal energy from some other world.

"That is the right answer, Gideon," Myra said. She looked pleased. "May your work be blessed, and may you always be protected on your quest."

I felt the energy strengthen. I wondered if the blessing she gave carried actual power with it. Whatever she was doing or thinking, it had a very real effect on me.

The old woman closed her eyes for several seconds, and when she opened them, it appeared as though nothing happened.

She smiled at me and motioned to the kitchen. "Please, stay for lunch," she said. "You're going to need your strength for what's to come."

28

Vero and I walked out of the adobe home. When I turned to say goodbye to Myra, the door was already closed, and there was no sign of the woman anywhere.

"Where did she—"

"You'll get used to that," Vero said with a laugh. "She does that. The whole creepy door closing, her disappearing-behind-you thing."

"Oh." I stared at the door for another two seconds, then shifted my focus.

"If I'm going to find those other medallions, I'll need good internet. I have my computer."

"I have satellite internet at the container house," Vero said, stopping me in mid-sentence.

"You do?"

"Of course. I want to be out in nature, not totally off the grid. Besides, we're in Mexico. It's not like we have a bunch of spooks watching our phones like they do in the States."

She was making Mexico sound better every second.

"Great," I said. "Is it okay if I stay there for a while? At least until I get this thing sorted with Carrillo?"

"Yes. Of course. Stay as long as you want. And by the way, you mean we."

"We?"

"Yes. You said *if you're* going to find those other medallions. You meant we. As in you and me."

We walked toward the cantina and turned at the corner to cross the street and go in the back again.

"You have a business to run," I said when we reached the parking lot in the rear. "As much as I appreciate all your help, I can't ask you to give up what you're doing. And you've already done too much as it is."

"Yeah. Can't stay closed forever. People might get suspicious." She rolled her eyes. "This is Mexico, amigo. We take naps every day. If the cantina is closed every now and then, no one will think twice about it."

"You wouldn't say that if some of my drinking buddies were your customers," I joked.

"Your friends like to throw a few back, huh?"

"More than a few."

I followed her back into her bar and closed the door behind me.

"Lock that," she said.

I did, and then tailed her into the front, where the bar sat empty. Unoccupied tables and chairs were exactly where we'd left them.

She walked behind the counter and bent down. Vero flicked a hidden switch. A panel opened in the wall. Inside the secret door, a shelf contained four bottles. One of them was white and slender with a blue agave plant painted on the front.

She removed the white bottle from the hidden stash and set it on the counter.

"What's this?" I asked, admiring the bottle.

"My favorite tequila," she said. "Clase Azul."

"Out of all the super añejos and other stuff you guys have down here, this is the one, huh?"

"Yes," she said without a splinter of doubt.

Vero took two tumblers from underneath the counter and set

them on the bar, then popped the cork off the bottle and poured until the glasses were nearly half full.

"I guess it's tequila for brunch then," I said, slightly terrified of the heavy pour.

She leaned over the bar, letting her black tank top hang low. I averted my eyes, doing my best to be respectful.

Vero raised her glass to me. "To fighting evil," she said.

"Yes," I picked up my glass and clinked it against hers. "But I can't—"

"Drink," she ordered.

"Fine." I took a sip with her. But she kept going until the contents of the glass were gone.

"Okay," I said. "You all right?"

Vero nodded. "I'm good," she said, exhaling. "We need a plan to find Carrillo."

I looked at the glass, stunned at what was happening. "Is this how you start all your planning sessions?"

She smirked at the question. "All the best ideas come from a little inspiration, cowboy. My muse is in these bottles. Sometimes other places."

"Other places?"

"I don't think you're ready for that yet," she warned. "But maybe someday."

I had a feeling I didn't want to know what she was talking about. The cryptic way she brought it up only reinforced that sentiment.

I tossed back the warm liquid and let the spice crash over my taste buds before cascading down my throat.

The tequila was smoother than almost anything I'd ever had, short of some homemade stuff a friend brought home every year to the States. He ran a restaurant in my hometown and always brought tequila back from his village in Jalisco. And it was always in some random container. The last one I recalled was from a few months ago. He'd come out to where I sat in a booth—alone at lunch—and offered me a drink. When I said yes—since there was no other answer to that question—he disappeared into the back of the restaurant, only to reappear with a Hawaiian Punch jug filled with a clear golden liquid.

Vero's was superb, but my buddy's homemade tequila was still the best tequila I'd ever had. I didn't tell her that.

"So," I said, fighting the slight burn that still charred my throat, "do you have any idea how to find Carrillo? I heard about a boat and about some property."

"He owns many properties. And yes, his yacht out on the gulf is worth more than ten Santa Rojos. Maybe twenty."

"So, how do we get to that yacht? And how do we know he'll be on it?"

Vero popped open the bottle again and poured two more drinks. These were shorter than the first but still potent. Especially at this hour of the day.

"You don't know," she answered, raising her glass to me. "But you aren't going to have to find Vicente Carrillo."

"Oh?" I eyed the glass in front of me with both terror and curiosity. I didn't think I was ready for another shot yet. Normally, I would have been fine tossing a few back. But this girl was next level. "Why is that?"

She pounded the shot of tequila, jerking her head back in a flourish that would have made any bartender proud.

She slammed the glass down on the counter and exhaled. "Because, we won't have to find Carrillo. He will come to us."

"Wait. What?" I searched her eyes for further explanation. "Did you say he will come to us?"

"Of course he will," she reaffirmed. "He sent two of his assassins here. They haven't reported back in over a day. Honestly, I'm surprised he hasn't sent anyone here sooner."

"What?" Now I felt worried. I looked back over my shoulder, out the front window into the empty village street.

"I would say sometime today he will send more. If I had to guess, I'd say probably four this time. Could be more. But I doubt he'd send only two. Carrillo isn't the type to make the same mistake twice."

"How prudent," I said and lifted the glass to my lips. I suddenly felt the urge to drink a lot more.

I took half the tequila on the first go, and the rest on another tip. Setting the glass down on the counter, I studied her face as she thought.

"I hope you're coming up with a better plan than simply sitting here drinking all day. Because while I'm all for that, I don't think it will help us take down Carrillo. Quite the opposite, in fact."

"He won't come right now. Not in broad daylight." She stuffed the cork back into the bottle and then placed it back on her secret shelf. "He'll send his men closer to dusk."

"Why is that?" I asked, realizing I wanted more tequila as I spied the bottom of my empty glass. The last thing I needed was more booze.

"Because that's his style."

"But he sent those two in the middle of the day," I reminded.

"True. That was different, a house call. Or maybe it was just his men going rogue. Remember what they said? How they acted? I don't think Carrillo was one hundred percent behind their visit. They used finding you as an excuse to come here and pester me."

"Oh, I see." Her reasoning started to clear.

"Those two were the enforcers for Santa Rojo, and for other villages in this region. They'd come around every couple of weeks to make sure things stayed in line, and to make sure their boss got paid. They were early yesterday. But that doesn't mean Carrillo sent them. I think they were fishing. Now that they haven't reported in, though, the boss is going to want to know what happened. He'll track them to here. And if he has some kind of a tracking system on that second SUV we stole, he'll have two reasons to visit here."

"You probably should keep the tequila out," I mused. "Sounds like we're going to be in for a tough fight."

"Not from where I'm standing. I have the ace up my sleeve with you. After what I saw you do to their vehicles on the highway, I'm not worried about anything. You should be able to take all of them out.

The people of this town will be free again. And no one will have to worry anymore."

Her words carried a ton of pressure. Like a literal ton pulling down on my shoulders with the weight of hundreds of souls. Maybe more.

"Um, you're making some big assumptions there," I countered. "And you said they'd send four people. Now you're making it sound like Carrillo will send his entire army."

"He'll send four or so at first. Then again, he might send everyone. If he thinks that you're here, I wouldn't put it past him. It's well within the realm of possibility."

"I'm definitely going to need another drink now," I said, already feeling the effects of the first two. "You say you think they'll come around sunset?"

"That's how I would do it. Things will be slowing down here at the cantina at that time of day."

I made a show of looking around the room, searching for the mysterious customers I knew weren't there.

"Okay, you're funny. It actually does get busy in here during late afternoon. Some nights are busier than others. But this is a Monday. No one will be in here tonight, except a few of the old regulars."

"And Carrillo knows this?"

"He knows everything," she said, casting a *you know this* look at me.

Fair enough, I thought. I guess I should have assumed that.

The phone in my pocket started ringing. It wasn't my phone, though. It belonged to the assassin who followed me to my hotel room.

I took the device out and stared at the screen.

Vero looked at it, too, except her eyes filled with a fear that mine did not.

"Is that the hit man's phone?" she wondered.

"Yeah," I said with a nod.

"Why didn't you get rid of it?"

I shrugged. "Because..." I stopped myself, realizing I didn't have an answer that made any sense. "Actually, I don't know why I kept it. I just did."

Her eyes widened.

"Well," she put her hands on her hips. "You might as well answer it now, because he can track that phone's location."

Now my eyes grew wide. I hadn't even thought about that, triangulating the location of a cell phone through the towers or GPS or however it was done. I was just an archaeologist, not an IT guy.

"What should I do?"

"Doesn't matter now. If there was any doubt about Carrillo showing up here with his entire army, I'd say you've assured that now."

I felt immediate regret swelling in my chest.

"I'm sorry," I offered.

She shook her head. "Don't be." She thought for a second. "Answer him. Keep him on the line as long as you can. While you do that, I'm going to see if I can get everyone out of the village."

"Out of the village?" I asked, the phone still vibrating in my hand.

"Yes. We'll need to get them somewhere safe before Carrillo arrives."

I wanted to argue that there was no way we could be certain the cartel don would show up here, that we were just planning a worst-case scenario. But deep down, I felt a very real, tangible concern that she was right.

She nodded to me, pointing at the phone, and slipped out from behind the counter and down the corridor toward the back door.

I looked down at the device and then pressed the green button on the screen.

"Hello, Vicente," I said as coolly as I could. "I've been expecting you."

29

At first, I only heard a low growl come through the speaker. It was almost like a labored breath that might come from the maw of a dying animal.

"You've been expecting me?" Carrillo grumbled. "You? Have been expecting... me?"

"Should I not have been?" I deflected, falling back on my old wise-guy wit that seemed to get me in plenty of trouble during my years growing up in the education system. "Seems like a logical conclusion to reach, you know, since I killed one of your men and took his phone."

"You—"

"Actually," I cut him off, "I killed more than one of your men. Let's see. There were the ones in the forest. I forgot how many of them there were that morning. It was so dark out, and they died so fast, honestly it barely registers."

"I will—"

"And then there were the ones you sent here to Santa Rojo. I imagine you realize, by now, that those two are dead, too. Unless, of course, you didn't know they were coming here. Those two seemed to be on their own, a couple of loose cannons out to get something for themselves. If you know what I mean."

Only a breath came through the speaker.

"They're definitely dead, though, those two. Very dead. So dead, in fact, I'd say you'd do yourself a favor by not bothering to look for the bodies."

I waited to let my words stoke the fire. I had no idea where Vero was. Somewhere in the town, I assumed, but what was she doing? She'd mentioned getting the citizens to somewhere safe. But I had no idea where that could be. The church was my only guess, but I didn't know if cartels adhered to that whole no-bad-things-on-holy-ground concept or if that was just in the movies.

"All said," I continued, "you've probably lost, what? Ten guys? Seven? Honestly, I'm losing track of all your men I've killed, Vic. Can I call you Vic?"

"I know where you are, you fool." I could feel the steam sizzling off his fiery words. "I know you're in Santa Rojo. Right now, my men are heading to your location. If you are as foolish as you appear, you'll stay right where you are."

I laughed. "Seriously? You're sending more of your guys here? Did you just hear the words that came out of my mouth? I killed like, I don't know, a dozen of your guys. Including a couple of them that I'm sure were 'highly trained assets.'" I used air quotes on the last part even though I was the only person who could see them. "I mean, when are you going to learn, bro? Your guys, plus me, equals fewer guys for you. I'm just going to keep killing them." I paused for dramatic effect. "Until I get to you."

"You have something that belongs to me," Carrillo drawled, ignoring my subversive threat. "And I will not stop until I have it."

"Oh, the medallion?" I joked. "You think that belongs to you? See, here's the thing, Vic. It actually belongs to me. Yeah, turns out my family and this thing go way back. Like, thousands of years back. So, I'm going to keep it for now. Okay? Pumpkin?"

"You will die!" He shouted so loud through the speaker that it nearly burst my eardrum.

"Unlikely," I fired back. "You can send everything you got at me, Vic. Send all of them. Nothing will stop me from making you pay for what you did. What you've done to so many people."

Carrillo breathed through the phone in deep, percolating breaths. "You think there is a way out of this that doesn't involve your death? Do you truly believe that the medallion can save you from me? It cannot. You will die, and it will be mine. It is my destiny to possess it. It will be mine. Do you understand? Nothing can—"

"Sorry, I'm getting another call here from"—I picked a random name—"Encarnación. Is that a girl name or a boy name? Because I've seen it with both. And it's kind of a long name. Do they use like a shortened version of it, or is it just all those syllables every time you want to get that person's attention?"

"You will die today, Gideon Wolf. Mark my words."

"You know what? I'm so sorry, Vic. Seems like you're cutting out a bit here. Could you call me from a landline? It seems like your hit man's phone doesn't have good service out here in the sticks."

I stopped for a second. But quickly resumed. "Anyway, I hope to see you again soon, Vic. Be sure that you drop by. In case you missed it, I'm in Santa Rojo at the cantina. So, you know, if you want to send all your guys here with their guns and all, I'll be waiting for you."

"I know where you are," he stewed.

"Yes, and I know that you know." My joking voice cut out and turned deathly serious. "And yet I'm still here, Vic." I growled the last words. "I'm here, waiting for you and everything you can throw at me. But I'll tell you what I'm going to do for you. You want this medallion so bad. Come take it from me yourself."

The man laughed, mocking my offer. "I'm sure you would like that."

"Oh, I would, Vic. I really, really would."

"We both know that isn't going to happen, my young friend. Even though I'm sure you would love the chance."

"So, you have other people do your evil deeds for you, huh? Don't like to get your hands dirty, Vic? You didn't seem to have any problem getting a little blood on your hands when you told your goon to kill my wife."

"That is where you are wrong, Dr. Wolf. I don't mind getting my hands dirty at all. But I'm not going to face a monster. And that's what you are now, Gideon—a monster. Nothing more than a freak of nature who found something that doesn't belong to him. But I assure you, I will have that medallion. You can't stop it. You aren't immortal."

"Well, we both agree on that, Vic. You're right. I'm not immortal. I can die. I will someday. But I can tell you one thing right now. It won't be by your hand. Partly because I know you're too much of a sissy to do it yourself. Second, I don't think you've got the guts to show up in person."

"We will see, Gideon Wolf. Just stay right there. My men will be with you shortly."

"And then what?"

I decided to press the issue, and keep the pedal to the metal of the psychological warfare I was playing with him.

"Your men will kill me and take the amulet? Is that what you think is going to happen, that they'll rip it off my cold, dead corpse and bring it back to you like a bunch of Boy Scouts?" I shook my head. "You're talking about guys you pay to kill other people, who are on your payroll because you know they're a bunch of miscreants, killers, thieves, scumbags. Those are the ones you're putting your trust in to bring this medallion back to you safe and sound? One of us is definitely crazy, I'll tell you that."

"Yes. You make a—"

"Sorry, I gotta take this other call," I lied. "Tell you what, Vic. Why don't you have your boys meet me somewhere? I think there's a field not far from here; looks like nothing is growing there right now. Just a bunch of tilled dirt. Tell your men to meet me there this evening, and we can sort all this out."

"I don't think so."

The line went dead. I checked the screen to make sure he'd really ended it.

"What a jerk," I said to myself. Then I realized what I'd just done.

I picked a fight with one of the most dangerous men in the Western Hemisphere, who happened to run one of the most feared organized crime syndicates in Mexico.

The old me would have cowered in fear, or run away as far as I could go. Gideon from even a week ago would be banging down the gate of the US border, desperate to get back into the warm and safe security blanket I called home.

That home, that place on the golf course in Tennessee where I'd spent holidays, birthdays, anniversaries... all of it felt hollow now, fictional to the point of unbelievable. Nothing I'd built was true or real, except my career. That much was tangible, I supposed. My degrees weren't built on lies or mistrust.

I struggled with this new life that had been thrust upon me. Coming to grips with the shape-shifting piece seemed easy by comparison. And there was no telling how many times I was going to go through this sort of struggle in my head.

All of that could wait. I had the rest of my life to sort out those issues, and I felt sure there would be some kind of therapy in there somewhere.

I loathed the thought of sitting in a room with someone I didn't know, telling them about all my struggles, my failures, and my flawed marriage that ended with my wife's murder at the hands of a Mexican cartel.

"Ugh," I said, running my fingers through my hair.

I shook my shoulders to loosen the gray robe hanging from them. And then there was this new outfit. *What had I expected? Some kind of fabric that grows with me when I shift into the creature?*

I took another glance at the phone screen, just to make sure the call really was done, and then stuffed the device in my pocket. Through one of the front windows, I saw Vero pass with several people following her.

"She works fast," I muttered. "And the people trust her." It hit me that she trusted me, too, this complete stranger who took me, another complete stranger, into her bar, didn't kick me out, and actually offered me help.

I'd tried to convince Carrillo to send his men somewhere else to fight me, to take the battle away from Santa Rojo and the innocent people here. But he wasn't having it. And I got the impression that he wanted the showdown to happen here. Was it so everyone could see? Or was he staging the fight in this village so the citizens could learn a lesson—as in, never get out of line?

I walked over to the front wall and peered through the window at the people passing by. Vero led them down the street, beyond the last home—and the adobe dwelling where we met Myra. A humble church sat at the end of the street, between the edge of the jungle and the rest of town.

Perhaps it originally served as a spiritual barrier against evil spirits that might have entered the village. Now, its walls served as a very real barricade against the evil forces of Vicente Carrillo.

I just hoped they would be safe there. Because the devil was on his way. Or at least his demons were.

And I had to make sure hell was waiting for them.

30

The minutes ticked by like a blacksmith hammer on an anvil, clinking along at a snail's pace with every blow of the second hand.

Vero finished getting everyone to the church in quick order, leaving only a few stragglers who insisted on staying in their businesses or homes. Most of the people heeded her warning and followed her to the little church, where the priest was happy to take them in.

"That's everyone," Vero said when she returned to the cantina. "Everyone that wants to go, anyway."

I nodded. There would always be people who were stubborn against such warnings. Who could blame them? How many times had people been told to evacuate for a hurricane only to see a small thunderstorm make landfall?

"What about you?" I asked. "You going to stay at the church?"

Vero glanced at her watch and shook her head. "No, but we do need to go."

"What? Where?"

"We still have a few hours before Carrillo's men will show up."

"You don't know that," I argued. "They could be here any second. They might be here already."

She brushed off my warning with a faint smile. "They're not. And he won't come in broad daylight. He has before. But he won't this time."

"Carrillo is pretty bold. I wouldn't put it past him."

"You yourself said it earlier; he'll wait for nightfall."

I nodded. I knew what I said, and the reasons for it. That didn't change the fact that this guy could call an audible at the last second and decide to come in guns blazing before the sun dipped in the west.

"You not so sure anymore?" she pressed.

"I don't know. I don't know about any of this. I'm just an archaeologist." I looked down at the floor, dejected.

"That's the old you," she said. "The Gideon I know is confident. Right now, Carrillo is amassing his forces to come here, to Santa Rojo. We can either sit here in the cantina and debate whether or not it's going to happen, or we can do something about it. So, are you going to continue having this identity crisis, or are you going to help me stop him? I mean, it's your medallion he's after. I could just throw you to the wolves."

The comment caused my lips to crease upward. "But *I'm* the wolf," I said, thumping my chest with a thumb.

She smiled back at me. "That's what I hoped you'd say. Follow me. We have work to do and only a little while left to do it."

Vero set out a blank piece of paper. She drew a squiggly line across it from left to right. "This is the main street. Only two ways in and out of Santa Rojo. Carrillo's men will most likely be coming from the east."

"But what if they aren't?"

"Coming from the east?"

I nodded.

"They will be," she clarified.

"How do you know?" I pressed.

"Because Carrillo's property is to the east, and his yacht on the gulf is also east. You mind if I continue?"

"Nope," I said, pouting my lips as I shook my head. "Please. Continue."

She drew a circle next to the eastern end of the street. "The church is here. Hopefully, they won't go in there."

"You thinking we need to cut off Carrillo's men on the road before they get into town?"

"That would be best, yes."

"How do we do that?" I studied the rudimentary map, imaging the buildings along the street. "They'll be coming to the cantina, right?"

"Yes, and they will check my house as well. Not the one you went to."

"Unless they already visited your place and are on their way here right now," I countered.

"I'm pretty sure they haven't," she said, then went back to the topic of Carrillo's strategy. "I expect him to have an entourage. Could be a couple of cars, or it could be six or more. There's no way to know how he wants to play this."

And yet we have to try to figure out how he'll come at us.

"So, do you have another map?" I asked. "Like one that shows all the roads, everything around here?"

She nodded. "Yes. But it's at my house."

"And where is your house?"

"Upstairs," she said with a coy grin.

"Got it." I hadn't even considered that she might live upstairs. Then again, there wasn't an indoor staircase leading up to a second floor. A rickety metal set of stairs was fixed to the wall outside and led up to a small landing and a door. "That explains why you don't think they've already been to your place. So, can we get that map?"

"Yes. Follow me."

We went out the back and around to the side where the black metal staircase climbed up to the second floor. At the top, she unlocked the door and entered the little apartment. The home was clean and simple. Everything looked organized, and nothing littered the counters, the coffee table, or the furniture.

"You really love IKEA, don't you?" I asked as I stepped into the apartment.

"Other than having to build the stuff myself, yes."

I closed the door and stood there in the entryway. Vero walked to a hallway between the kitchen to the right and the living room on the left.

"It's back here. I'll get it."

She disappeared into the hall and left me standing there.

The room smelled of apples and cinnamon. I wondered about the source of the scents and found it in an open candle jar on the end of the counter. If it smelled that good while unlit, I wondered how much better it might be if the wick was burning.

Footsteps echoed from the hall, and a second later Vero appeared in the doorway holding a large map book.

"You brought the whole atlas," I said and moved toward the L-shaped counter where she laid out the map.

"Yes. Well, I always had dreams of traveling around the country, seeing all the historical places in Mexico. Haven't had the chance to do that yet."

I sensed the regret in her voice, a distant pain that beckoned to a nomadic spirit—the call of those who wander but are not lost.

Something about the way she said it—I sensed a longing in her, regret lacing her words. Half of my job was traveling to amazing locations for research or for public engagements—most often at a university that was willing to foot the bill for my travel and accommodations. With visiting so many other places all over the globe, I'd taken most of that experience for granted in recent years. Anything, I guessed, could become a job sooner or later.

Now, hearing the wishful sound in Vero's voice, the tone of disappointment, I realized how fortunate I'd been all these years. Vero hadn't even seen much of her own country. I wondered how many lived that life, wanting to do more, see more, but couldn't.

Vero flipped open the book and turned the pages until she came to the area where she recognized the names and the terrain. "Here we are," she said, pointing at Santa Rojo on the map. "Carrillo's men will approach from here." She indicated the road leading into town from the east.

"If you're wanting to cut them off," I said, "then I guess the place you'd want to attempt that would be right here." I stuck my finger on the map where it looked like the road twisted into the shape of a serpent, bending and winding. "They won't be able to drive as fast there due to the curves."

"Yes," Vero agreed. "And one side of the road drops off into a ravine. The other side is on the edge of the jungle. There will be nowhere for them to go."

"Sounds like you expect me to hem them in and take them out." I shifted my eyes to gauge her response.

"Don't worry," she said. "I'll have your back."

"Oh really?"

I faced her with a dramatic, questioning scowl on my face.

"I wouldn't send you out there on your own to take on Carrillo's men. I'm going with you."

"But—"

"And before you try the whole chivalry thing of trying to tell me it's too dangerous or I might get hurt, you need to know that this is happening. I'm going to take up a position at a distance and pick off Carrillo's men while you work them up close."

I suddenly didn't like the sound of this plan. "Okay, it sounds like *you'll* be safe. But what about *me*? How do I know I won't accidentally get shot?"

"You won't die, anyway. Bullets can't kill you. And besides," she said, taking her eyes away from the map to meet mine. She made no effort to look apologetic. "You probably wouldn't even know it if I was the one who hit you or one of them."

I raised both eyebrows and lowered my head, doing my best to look stern.

"Yeah, you know, I think I want to go with a plan that doesn't expose me to a hailstorm of bullets, if it's just the same to you."

"It'll be fine," she insisted. "You're in good hands. And I won't miss."

"Me or the bad guys?"

She laughed. "You, I'll miss. But if they send more than four or five guys, you're going to want me out there with you when the bullets start flying your direction."

I didn't feel good about the plan, but who was I to argue? I wasn't a military strategist. "Fine," I surrendered. "But if you shoot me—"

"I won't."

"It hurts, you know. Every single time. It's not like I don't feel it."

Her expression softened, and her eyes drifted down from mine to my chest. For a heartbeat, she seemed lost somewhere else. I wondered if she was thinking about the past gunshot wounds I'd absorbed. She'd seen two of them heal. As soon as the moment started, it ended, and she met my gaze once more.

"I know," she said. "And I don't want you to hurt."

"Thank you," I said. "I appreciate that."

I found myself closer to her than I had expected and abruptly pulled away. So, I kept talking to mitigate the awkward silence and to buy myself some time to figure out what was happening. "What do you think we should do to stop their convoy?"

"Good question." She tore herself from my gaze and reset to business mode. "I know the rancher who owns the farm right here," she said, pointing at a spot next to the road we'd discussed before. "The ravine is here, and it runs around behind the ranch to the southeast."

I wondered where she was going with all the talk about the ranch. *What did it matter if there was a farm there or a Piggly Wiggly?*

"The rancher has many cows," Vero added. "Hundreds of them. Every so often, they get out of the fence and wander across the road. It's a problem for people driving by car, but the road isn't very busy."

I started to see where she was taking the whole cattle ranch thing now. "Let me guess," I offered. "You're going to open the fence and let the cows out. The cows cross the road. They stop traffic—i.e., the cartel guys—and then we do our thing."

"Close. Except with one subtle twist."

I had no idea what she was going to say next.

"Have you ever been a real cowboy, cowboy?"

"Uh, no. I have not."

"Have you ever seen those dogs that run along by the herd and guide the cattle where they're supposed to go?"

"Yeah. Of course. Always thought that was cool, although I'm more of a cat person."

Her mouth froze for a second as she appreciated the moment. "The irony," she observed.

"No kidding."

"Anyway," Vero went on, "I'm wondering if the chupacabra might also be able to wrangle cattle in such a way."

Then it all clarified. She wanted me to be the cattle dog.

"So, you're telling me that your plan is I release the cows from their pen, and then I'm supposed to drive them out and into the road?"

"At the precise moment, yes."

I nodded, understanding the plan but also not sure I wanted to participate. "It's a little insulting, to be honest. I'm not a real dog."

"You're the next best thing. And if we're going to take out Carrillo's gang before they get to the town, then this is our best play. The cows will think you're supposed to be moving them somewhere."

"What difference does it make what the cows think?" I wondered.

"I don't know," she shrugged. "I guess if they didn't think you were their boss, they could charge."

"Wait. Is that a real thing? Do cows do that?"

She laughed. "Not that I've ever seen or heard of. You'll be fine. Just change into the... well, you know. And then corral them toward the road."

"And you'll be where again?" I crossed my arms emphatically.

"I'll be hiding in the shadows on the other side of the road. Once all the vehicles are stopped, you go around to the back and cut off their escape."

The plan made sense, as much as a plan involved me turning into a mythical dog-man could.

"Okay," I said. "So, I'm guessing we need to head back to the container house to get your guns."

"Correct," she said with a nod. "And then we get to work."

31

The day waned on for hours, and I wondered how everyone was doing locked inside the church. From what I could tell, there weren't that many people inside the little building, and overcrowding shouldn't have been an issue. Monks tended to the people, handing out pieces of bread and cheese, cups of water, and a pillow to one girl who slouched on a pew opposite of the doorway.

The room felt stifling and muggy .

We spent more than an hour at Vero's container home in the country. She collected her long-range rifle, a few dozen Creedmoor rounds, plus two pistols, two AR-platform rifles, and a utility belt to carry extra magazines.

She could have given me one of the rifles and a pistol, but we both knew my skills were going to be used in another way.

After a quick lunch, we loaded up her car and made our way back into town as the sun dropped lower in the west.

I hoped our assessment was right about Carrillo, that he would attack at night. If the man knew as much as he claimed about the medallion and its power, he'd know that coming to take his prize after dark was a big mistake. That told me Carrillo didn't know as much as he believed.

For now, I could use the ignorance to my advantage. I could only hope that edge never went away. I would be fine, but my concern was for Vero. And for the people of Santa Rojo.

I'd never want anything bad to happen to them and have that fall on me.

Vero drove us into the village and around to the back of her cantina. We noted the rear door remained closed as we'd left it before. Happy enough that the place was still secure, she continued out to the next side street, made a right, then a left, and kept going beyond Myra's humble home, the church, and the last of the shops along the main thoroughfare.

Beyond the village, farms rolled through the hills to the right, with the jungle ever encroaching on the left.

I spotted the warning signs on the side of the road cautioning drivers about the curves up ahead—along with a suggested speed for handling the terrain safely.

A weathered wooden fence lined the road to our right, stretching out acres in both directions.

"That's the ranch I was telling you about. We're getting close to the driveway. I recommend coming back once its dark, though."

I turned my head slowly to her, offering up the best *you don't say* look I could muster. "Thanks for the tip," I replied.

"You lean on sarcasm a lot," she observed. "Has that always been a thing?"

"Yes. Is that a problem?"

She smiled and shook her head. "Nope. I like it, actually. Makes me laugh. And it also shows me that you're covering up for some kind of insecurity, so in a way—it shows your vulnerable side."

That entire commentary caught me off guard like kibble in a Jell-O mold.

"I... guess I never really thought about it like that before."

"I'm going to take a position up here," she said, pointing to the left as we entered the first of what were apparently a series of curves. Vero slowed down to round the first bend, then accelerated to the next turn and repeated the process. When we reached the third curve, she slowed down more and pointed through the windshield. "Over there," she said.

A hollowed-out area of dark shade filled the seemingly endless sea of green tree leaves and shrubs.

"You sure you'll be safe there?" I asked. "Lot of animals out in the jungle at night. And not all of them are friendly."

It was her turn to offer me the *thanks, Captain Obvious* glare. "I've lived here my entire life. Pretty sure I know about the local wildlife."

I took my medicine like a man and only nodded.

"I'll be fine," she added. "Just make sure you get those cows through the opening before Carrillo's men arrive." She finished driving through the curves and then stopped when we were beyond them.

"Use this radio," she said, handing me an earpiece. The tech looked good, too good for a young woman who was only a bartender running a barely solvent cantina. "When I see them, I'll signal you."

"Okay," I agreed, but I still had reservations. I kept those doubts to myself, deciding I could deal with any additional worries if and when they arose.

She turned the car around and drove back down the winding road, passing the farm now on the left.

"There's the driveway," she said, pointing toward two gravel ruts that wandered away from the main road and over a hillside about a thousand feet away. "But you can cross the fence wherever you want. As long as you take it down in a place where we want the cows to get out." She searched the area ahead and then nodded once. "There," she said, pointing to a patch of bright green grass next to the fencing.

"So, disassemble the fence there, and then get the cattle to go through and spill onto the road." I repeated the plan out loud for her benefit. I knew I had it.

"That's the idea."

She drove us back into the village and stopped by the church. The old mission looked like it was a couple hundred years old, maybe more. Pieces of the twin bell towers had long ago crumbled, along with various portions of the walls. The heavy, wooden doors remained closed at the front entrance.

"What are we doing?" I asked as she shifted the car into park.

She killed the ignition. "Going to check on the people. They've been in there all day. I'm sure they're not going to be happy about it."

"So, maybe we shouldn't go in?"

"We need to put their minds at ease."

"How are we going to do that?"

"Come on," she ordered and stepped out.

I shook my head, confused, but also climbed out of the car and followed her to a door on the side of the building.

She rapped on the door four times in a unique rhythm, then stepped back and waited. A few seconds later, the sound of locks clicking inside escaped the barrier, and then the door creaked open.

An old man in a smock stood in the rood. He had a thick head of black hair and a pointy nose, and his dark brown eyes remained full of life even though his skin told the story of a person who'd been around for many decades.

"Hello, my child," the priest said, greeting Vero with a welcoming smile. "This must be the friend you told me about."

"Yes, Father. This is him. The man who will save our village."

She pointed at me with her palm up.

I didn't know how to respond to that, so I simply used the most cliché thing that came to mind. "Pleasure to meet you," I said, extending my hand to shake his as I would have a random person at a bar.

He looked down at my hand as if I'd offered him a spider, then took it after a moment of uncertainty. "A pleasure," he said in Spanish.

"How are the people, Father?" Vero asked.

His shoulders lifted slightly and then dropped.

"They are nervous, Vero. And they are frightened. How much longer will they need to stay in here? You know everyone is always welcome in the house of the Lord. I just worry about the children."

"I'll let you know when they can leave," Vero said.

I wished I shared her confidence. Truth was I didn't worry too much for myself. I had nothing to lose, and on top of that, was extremely hard to kill—unless someone got lucky and took my head off. Decapitation notwithstanding, my odds of coming out of this fiasco unscathed remained pretty good.

Vero, on the other hand, was a mere mortal. Bullets could take her out. She believed she'd be okay in her hiding place with her rifles, but if one of Carrillo's men sniffed her out, she could be in trouble.

"Thank you, my child. I understand this is a great risk for you to take."

At least the priest gets it.

"But the people trust you, and they listen to you. Even if nothing happens, they know you have the best intentions, and you would never mislead them."

"All true," she said.

Oh, maybe he doesn't get it, I thought.

"May we look in on them?" Vero asked.

"Certainly. Right this way." The priest stepped aside and let the two of us pass, looking out into the street before closing the door behind us.

Inside the church sanctuary, candles burned in all the alcoves. Light poured through a stained-glass window at the front behind the presbytery. The colorful panes displayed bright colors that danced on the floor near the pulpit. A wooden sculpture of Christ suffering on the cross occupied the center of the floor directly under the window and was surrounded by dozens of candles at the base of the vertical beam.

Families huddled in the pews. Mothers held small children. Grandmothers chipped in with that duty, too.

Some people were on their knees, praying for deliverance from the approaching scourge.

As I saw the fear in their eyes, and the desperation dragging their skin down, I realized quite clearly that I'd made the right decision—not only to go after Carrillo but to defend people like this wherever they might be.

Nothing had ever felt so clear in my mind as that did right then. Up until that moment, my life's purpose had been all about history and archaeology, uncovering the past to give the world a glimpse of how things used to be, how people used to live.

Now, my life's purpose had taken a massive detour. Instead of trying to show others the way people used to live, I was defending them so that they *could* live. So that they could write their own stories, leave behind their own legacies.

I wasn't sure them being here in this church was the safest place with the impending battle looming, but if I had anything to do with it, I'd make sure nothing happened to them.

I walked down an aisle, and a woman holding a little boy looked up at me and smiled, bowing her head in a sign of respect. The boy smiled, too, and reached his arms out as if to embrace me.

"Are you the Red Saint?" the child asked in Spanish.

Vero heard him from right in front of me and rounded to face the kid, then to me, I suspected, to see how I would handle the question.

I looked to her, then back to the boy, putting on the kindest, most confident face I could. "Do you believe I am?" I asked.

The boy bit his bottom lip, then nodded excitedly. "Yes. I believe you are him."

"Then who am I to argue with that?" I managed.

The kid continued to smile at me as I walked by to the other side of the church, meeting the eyes of more people than I ever intended. They all looked at me with this hopeful glaze in their eyes—a desperate yearning for the terror to end, to live a normal life. Whatever that was.

Living a normal life would never be on the table for me, not anymore. Not after I found the medallion.

I inhaled deeply and turned down the aisle against the far wall, walked around to the back, and then stopped. I looked toward the front of the sanctuary. Most of the people had stopped whatever they were doing and looked at me, as if expecting me to say something.

I wasn't much for speeches—even in my true element as an archaeologist.

"We're going to make sure you're safe," I said in Spanish, fumbling for the right words that would inspire a sense of safety in everyone there. "Just stay here, and everything will be okay."

I wasn't sure if anyone believed me. A few people nodded, and that was good enough, I supposed.

I turned without another word, figuring anything else would just be me trying too hard. I wasn't an inspirational or motivational speaker. I just told things how they were.

Vero followed me out the front doors and into a wide atrium. A black wrought iron candelabra hung from the arched ceiling above. Candles burned from its four tiers, and I wondered if the old priest had to light them every day. The doors closed behind us, and we made our way out the second set of doors leading outside.

"You see?" Vero said once we were back out in the quiet street. "They believe in you."

I glanced back at the door, unconvinced. "I don't know, Vero. Doesn't seem like they do. I mean, some maybe do."

"These people have been oppressed for so long, Gideon. They've forgotten what it feels like to hope. Our village is dying. It's been dying for a long time now. Some people have tried to move away, find work in the cities or on other farms. With every one that leaves, Santa Rojo dies a little more."

Maybe that was the answer. Why didn't everyone just leave, move somewhere safer? I wouldn't stay in a place where I was terrorized all the time, or bullied, or robbed by men claiming I was paying for protection.

I never understood that.

Then again, I didn't have deep roots to this place.

Being from Tennessee, I felt ties there, an attachment to who I was as a person. Tennesseans were a proud lot, glad to be from a free-dom-loving state. Beyond that, we loved the mountains and hills and our way of life. I know I felt a strong bond to the mountains, the culture, the music, the food, the people.

The light bulb blinked on in my head. These people obviously felt the same way about Santa Rojo that I felt about the Volunteer State.

"The people are connected to Santa Rojo, aren't they?"

Vero nodded. "There is something special here. It's a spiritual connection on some level."

I knew there was no arguing with that. I'd experienced something of a spiritual renaissance myself, or at the very least, a journey of self-discovery.

"Well, then. I guess we better protect them. And the best way to do that is to eliminate Carrillo's entire enterprise."

Vero's lips curled up on the right side. "Yes. This is the way it must be."

32

The sun slid slowly downward through the sky, making its way toward the horizon in the west.

I watched from my position on the edge of the cow pasture, waiting for the signal to spring the cattle. "You see anything yet?" I asked into the radio.

"Not since the last time you asked me three minutes ago, Gideon. And the two minutes before that. And the four minutes before that."

"Okay. Okay. I get it. I'll stop asking."

"You've said that three times."

I rolled my eyes. I guess I had said it three times. "Sorry," I apologized, probably for the third or fourth time. "I'm not used to doing this sort of thing."

"You'll be fine," she said. "Just stick to the plan. It's going to work."

I hoped she was right.

At the moment, and for the last hour since I'd been standing in the field next to the fence, I felt a tightness in my gut. I figured it was adrenaline, but it didn't make me feel good in any way. It was more like a fear-based thing that kept twisting and stabbing my abdomen.

I'd read and heard stories about soldiers who felt something they called battle energy. From the time of ancient Greek warriors to modern-day military personnel, battle energy was something I'd read about but never really experienced. Until now.

It was a sort of strange blend of the fight-or-flight response with a pinch of excited anticipation. I didn't like it. And the longer we waited for the convoy to appear, the worse it got.

Doubt started creeping into my mind. I wondered if we'd made a mistake. Would Carrillo come this way? What if Vero was wrong and he came from the west? Or would he come by land at all? What if Carrillo owned a helicopter and sent some of his men that way?

I considered voicing my concerns, but I'd already annoyed Vero enough throughout the late part of the afternoon.

I went back to my conversation with the cartel don, running over everything we said in my mind.

How did Carrillo even know I had the medallion? The last time the man saw me, I was running through the jungle trying to get away from his henchmen. Had I given it away?

And here's what really twisted my noodle—if Carrillo knew I had this thing, and he knew what it was capable of, he'd be a fool to send his men after me. Especially at sunset. Which is when it seemed like they would attack.

He'd made it clear that he had no intention of taking me on in person, so he knew the danger. Why waste his resources and considerable security forces if he didn't think he could win?

The conclusion was simple enough for me to reach. Either Carrillo was stupid or egotistical. I ruled out the stupid part. Maybe he did some dumb things, but no leader of a high-level operation—shady or otherwise—got there by being an idiot. The rise to power required deliberate calculation, planning, and foresight.

So, this was an ego play. *Right?*

Carrillo was a man accustomed to getting what he wanted. Like a spoiled child, he wouldn't accept no for an answer. And just like that child, he would throw a tantrum—or in this case, send all of his men after me to get the thing he so coveted.

I slowed my breathing using some techniques I'd picked up along the way to deal with anxiety. Usually, I didn't face a ton of stress or worry, except... with Amy. She had a way of making me feel anxious now and then. I never could put my finger on it, but now I wondered if it was because deep down, I always suspected something was going on with her.

Or that might have just been hindsight talking.

The breath exercises helped calm my nerves as I waited by the fence post.

Questions still lingered, dangling in front of my mind's eye like so many carrots in front of a mule.

Why would Carrillo send his men here at dark when he knows that's when I will be my strongest?

"Look alive," Vero said through the radio. "I hear something coming up the road."

"Visual contact?"

"Not yet, but soon. You in place?"

"Only for the last few hours!"

I couldn't believe how fast the time had passed. Standing around with the cattle, doing nothing but wait, should have made time crawl by.

"Cut the chatter."

"Yes. I'm ready," I said with a layer of irritation.

Everything about her plan required perfect timing. I could open the fence early, but then the cows could wander off into various parts of the surrounding area. I needed the bulk of them on the road.

"One vehicle confirmed," Vero said. "Eyes on target. We have a second. Third. Fourth."

I wondered how many more cars she was going to see.

"Eight. I count eight vehicles. They're coming your way, cowboy. Time to do your thing."

Yeah. It was time to do my thing. Except the sun hadn't set yet.

"Uh, so, problem. I can open the fence, but I can't shift into the... you know, until the sun goes down."

No response came for four seconds, and I wondered what she was doing.

"Stick to the plan," she ordered. "Take it down now. Do whatever you can to get those cows out onto the road."

I knew I didn't have much time. Even in the slow curves, the convoy would reach this point in the road in fewer than three minutes. With a quick look toward the horizon, I knew it would be close. The sun was more than halfway gone beyond the hills.

I pulled on one of the wooden pieces in the fence, dislodging it easily. I leveraged it up and dumped it to the side, then repeated the process with the second slat.

That was easy enough, I thought.

Now for the hard part.

I turned and ran around behind a group of forty cows. They all grazed lazily in the field, a few mooing occasionally. As I sprinted by the animals, they seemed to pay no attention to me—figuring I was no threat. Then again, when did a cow feel threatened? I realized I'd never thought about that before.

I shook off the random tangent as I reached the back of the herd and circled around behind them. The animals still paid no attention to me, as if I was a lunatic freshly escaped from the asylum.

I held out my hands and waved them forward underhanded, as if I could coax the cattle to move. They simply ignored me, except for one cow who stood relatively close by, chewing her grass methodically, a single eye focused on me with mistrust.

"Hey!" I shouted. "Get moving, you crazy animals! Yaw! Yaw now!"

I felt like an idiot shouting the words I thought I recalled hearing on cowboy shows and movies. It seemed even dumber when the cows didn't respond. So, I was nothing more than a crazy guy standing out in a field, yelling randomly at a bunch of grazing animals.

"This isn't working," I said into the radio. "I need more time."

"There isn't more time," Vero said, urgency trailing her words. "Get it done, Gideon. It's now or never."

"Fine."

I shouted louder, moving around in erratic, jerky movements to simulate a predator, anything I thought might frighten the animals enough to get them on the move.

They remained resolute.

I ran up to the one giving me the stank eye and leaned into the animal, pushing my shoulder against its side as hard as I could.

My shoes dug into the dirt, but the animal simply didn't move.

"They're halfway to you," Vero said. "Gotta get the cattle through the fence now. Are they almost there?"

"Yeah," I grunted. "Almost."

I inhaled a deep breath to give one final shove, and suddenly I felt a surge of power rush through me.

The cow bawled, then shifted, then lurched to the left, and I felt my balance nearly leave me. I recovered quickly, slipping a foot out in front of me before I fell as the animal lumbered away, mooing loudly.

A few of the others began making similar noises, and the cluster of cattle stirred restlessly.

I glanced to the west and saw the last cap of the sun had disappeared. Darkness descended from the east, and I noted the beams of headlights winding through the road.

I sucked in a deep breath, and this time when I yelled, it wasn't the sound of a crazed man that escaped my lips. Instead, a harsh howl burst through my fangs and boomed across the field.

My body changed under the robes. I felt the fabric stretching, but it didn't tear.

The cattle charged away from me, but they were heading toward the corner of the fence where the ravine dropped off.

The wooden fence continued around the corner and along the drop-off, but I doubted it would be strong enough to stave off a full-speed charge from the herd.

I sprinted to my right, pumping my legs as fast as I could. Looking around, I couldn't believe how fast I was moving. I passed the herd in seconds and rushed down to the fence just ahead of the lead animals.

The earth rumbled under their hooves. I was nearly to the corner they looked so dead set on charging through and looked to the front of the pack.

The air filled with dust and the sounds of hooves on dirt, blending with the bawling of terrified animals. I pushed myself to the limit. Tall weeds slapped against my furry shins, but the stinging barely registered.

Mere seconds before the first cows hit the fence, I skidded to a stop in the corner and roared as loud as I could.

The animals freaked out, planting their hooves in the ground to shudder to a halt, only to turn and take off the other direction.

The herd curved its route, all following the lead animals as they thundered up the fence line along the road.

To my right, I saw the headlights of the convoy approaching. This was going to be cutting it real close.

I didn't have time to circle around the herd streaming down the hill and then bending up toward the road again.

For a split second, my doubts paralyzed me despite one solution screaming in my head. *You're going to have to jump.*

I shook my head. "This is a bad idea."

Then, I reared back, pushed off the fence, and took three steps toward the herd. I jumped off my left foot and felt the ground leave me easily. Too easily.

I soared over the stampede nearly thirty feet above ground. I wondered what happened to gravity for a second, but then when I felt myself descending through the air, I quickly adjusted my feet for what I thought would be a painful landing.

Instead, I hit the ground running and kept my feet moving to stay ahead of the herd. I arrived at the opening in the fence with only seconds to spare, and stood to the right of the fence with my hands out wide. Uncertain that would be enough, I quickly picked up one of the wooden slats I'd dropped from the fence, and waved it around in my right arm.

A few days before, there was no way I'd have been strong enough to do that. Now, though, the board might as well have been a toothpick.

I slapped it on the ground to my right, waving it up and down to frighten the animals through the fence.

It was that, or they'd turn around and run back into the field. Or worse, back toward the fence at the bottom of the property and through the fence at the ravine.

My worries proved unnecessary.

The animals cut to my left, slowing down slightly as they rumbled through the opening and out into the road.

The cattle continued to spill out of the field, some spreading out into the grass alongside the road, and others out into the middle of the asphalt. Still more crossed the road to the patch of grass separating the pavement from the jungle on the other side.

The herd slowed down once they were clear of the perceived danger, except now many of them loitered on the road as the convoy approached.

I ducked down behind the tall grass lining the fence and stayed out of sight as the vehicles slowed down and came to a halt.

The driver in the lead SUV climbed out of the vehicle and threw his hands up in the air out of frustration. No way he and the boss could have expected a cattle crossing to slow them down.

And things were only about to get worse for them. I skirted the fence, keeping low as I moved.

My animal senses raged at full throttle. Downwind, I could smell the overused cologne the driver wore, and I heard the jangle of the gold chain around his neck.

I watched as the driver walked toward the cows and started yelling, waving his hands around in the same fashion I'd tried. And with the same result.

The animals didn't move.

One of the other men got out of the front vehicle and walked up to the herd standing around on the road.

He joined the driver, trying to shoo the cattle away but to no avail.

I waited, alternating my focus between the seven SUVs behind the first and the two men doing their pitiful best to try to move the animals.

The passenger reached into his jeans and drew a pistol. I noted the length of the barrel and immediately knew the guy had bought way too much hand cannon for anything practical. And I wasn't even a gun expert.

He aimed the pistol at one of the cows, as if to execute the animal.

The driver reached out and stopped him, lifting his arm by the wrist before he could fire.

"No," the man said in Spanish. "Are you stupid? If you kill the cow, then we won't be able to get by. Who would move the thing?"

The gunman nodded and then lifted the gun a little higher. I watched as his finger tensed on the trigger. He appeared unaffected by anything, only wearing an emotionless, bland scowl on his face.

He was about to fire the weapon in an attempt to frighten the animals when suddenly his chest burst open just below his neck. He fell forward without fanfare, landing prostrate on the asphalt.

The driver looked down at the entry wound in the wounded man's back, then drew his weapon and started aiming at random spots in the jungle.

Within two seconds of his reaction, a bullet zipped through the air, smashing into his chest and burrowing out through his back just below the right shoulder blade.

He spun around and fell onto his side, writhing on the pavement as he died.

The men in the SUVs reacted instantly, albeit chaotically.

They spilled out of the doors, each grasping for their weapons. Some carried pistols. Others shouldered submachine guns.

All told, there were thirty-two men—counting the two dead ones on the ground.

I hadn't expected Vero to take out the first two guys in the front of the line. Seemed like she said something about eliminating the ones in the back to keep the ones in the front hemmed in.

Screams at the back signaled the answer to my question.

I stood up and looked down the road, watching as two more men were cut down by Vero's deadly rifle.

Where did she learn to shoot like that?

I would have to ask her at some point, and I wasn't sure I wanted to know the answer. The woman was a dead eye, having already taken down four of the cartel's men within the first ten seconds of firing her initial volley.

One of the gunmen yelled, and the rest responded by opening fire. The cacophony of firearms going off filled the air with rampant, erratic pops.

In the jungle across from them, bullets tore through leaves and branches, cutting limbs from trees and splintering trunks with hot metal.

I hoped Vero was okay. She said she would be.

Now that she had their attention, it was my turn to work.

I stood up, basking in the light of the rising moon, and climbed over the fence toward the first of Carrillo's gunmen.

33

The first victim never saw me. I sped across the grass and asphalt in a blur. Red mist nearly covered the road, wrapping around the shooters' legs, swirling and pulsating.

I opened my jaws and snapped my fangs down on the first man's neck, ripping into his flesh with a savage bite. He screamed, then gurgled. His right hand raised up in the air to fire two more vain shots into the night sky, then dropped to his knees and fell on his face.

The man next to him saw the attack out of his periphery and spun around in time to catch a sharp claw across the throat.

Four down from the first vehicle.

I jumped onto the hood and howled into the sky like some kind of deranged wolf/dog/man hybrid.

The power from the fresh kills surged through me. And I felt my strength grow.

The howl was heard by the last men in the convoy, and every single one of them turned toward me to defend themselves, and to see what had made such a haunting sound.

Most of them took cover behind their SUVs, and their eyes blazed white in the moonlight as terror swept over and through them. The one nearest me trembled with fear, and stumbled backward into the man behind him. The two fell onto the ground, one on top of the other. A muzzle popped and sent a random round into the darkness.

To their credit, the other two men behind them—each taking a turn firing into the jungle from the corner—reacted somewhat better. The first took aim and fired, but he was too slow.

By the time the weapon discharged, I'd jumped down to the side of the SUV and darted over to the second in line.

The sounds of glass shattering and tires rupturing caught my ears from downwind, and I took a second to examine the vehicles at the end of the line.

Vero was disabling them with rounds from her rifle, while at the same time pinning the gunmen down.

The strategy was good. Really good. Part of me wondered if she had any military experience.

I let the thought go as I heard movement from the vehicle at my back. I turned, keeping the tire between me and anyone who might try to shoot at my feet or legs under the chassis. I squatted down and then leaped high over the truck.

The gunmen on the other side never saw me. All four of them were on the ground, peeking under the vehicle to see where I was.

I dropped out of the night with claws bared and landed on the first gunman with a sickening crunch. Most of my weight distributed through my paws into his skull, crushing it into the asphalt and killing him instantly.

The second in line twisted at the abrupt and sickening thud and crack from next to him. His face shook in terror. I could smell the reek as he wet himself.

Before he could muster a defense, I launched from all fours and pounced. I chomped down on his leg and jerked him toward me, then grabbed his head and stood up straight.

For a second, I held the man there, my massive arms extended out. I stared into his fear-stained eyes. He tried to raise his submachine gun, but he'd lost a lot of blood out of his right leg where one of my fangs had punctured an artery.

I twisted my hands abruptly and snapped the man's neck. His

body went limp, and as the third gunman from that vehicle took aim, I threw his comrade's body at him.

The dead man struck the last two guys and knocked them over.

Gunfire filled the evening air, and a thin, bitter haze hung in the air. The smell always reminded me of the Fourth of July when we would shoot off fireworks as kids.

Then a sting cut through my right arm. Then something hit my chest like a fist and I tumbled backward from the blow.

Men shouted, issuing orders amid the incessant popping. I rolled over behind one of the bodies and propped it up as a shield. The bullets couldn't kill me, but jeez they sure hurt.

I grimaced as I felt my body ejecting the round out of my chest. It was a strange thing to experience, like pinching folds of skin together, except my body was doing it on its own.

Bullets peppered the body and pinged off the asphalt around me.

I risked a look over the dead man's bloody shoulder and saw one of the other gunmen fall, taking one of Vero's rounds through the side of his neck as he focused his attention on me.

The remaining men retreated behind the SUVs for cover from her deadly aim. They ducked down, uncertain which enemy to focus on.

One of the men suddenly screamed in agony and grabbed at his knee. He fell over, flopping around in pain until he was silenced by a bullet through his mouth.

I furrowed my furry brow at the epiphany. *Vero just hit that guy's knee from a few hundred yards... between an SUV's frame and the ground... at night.*

"Who is this woman?" I muttered.

The gunmen, believing the monster dead, turned their attention back to Vero's position and resumed their attack.

That was a mistake.

I bounded from my kneeling position, flying toward the gunmen as they fired, took cover, and fired again.

The first man saw me out of the corner of his eye, but that was the last thing he saw.

I ripped the gun from him amid the swirling red mist, and turned it on him, planting the HK-5 muzzle under his chin.

I forced his finger to squeeze, turning my head slightly to avoid any splash that might occur.

He fell to the ground—his grip loosening on the submachine. I tightened mine, and then spun the weapon around, leveling it at the enemy.

The attackers turned and, again, looked aghast at the sight of me —me, this half dog, half monster standing before them in the moonlight. I'm sure they thought I was some kind of werewolf from their worst nightmares—holding a gun.

They opened fire, but only a second after I did.

I cut them down, holding my position even as hot rounds seared my skin and tore through tissue.

With the men from the third SUV dead, I stalked toward the fourth. They stopped and turned their full attention to me, pounding me with round after round. My gun clicked. Out of ammo. I dropped the weapon and ducked to one knee. The bullet storm rained on me, and I saw men from the fifth vehicle running to reinforce the ones from the fourth.

A bullet struck my cheek. The pain was worse than just about anything I'd ever felt. It burned and stung, and the shattered bone stabbed at the nerves.

I howled at the pain, but the enemy rounds still came.

I fell over next to one of the men I'd killed and lay on my back. Staring up at the stars, I felt a wave of emotions, thoughts, concerns —all smashing into me like the ocean onto a rocky shore.

The men barked out a slur of words, some giving orders, others swearing and shouting about how they got me.

More gunfire continued from farther down the road. I assumed— as I lay there looking up at the constellations, the moon, a cirrus cloud streaking through the night—the shooters were attacking Vero's position.

I breathed shallow, labored breaths. The pain subsided by the second, and I felt my body healing itself of all the wounds.

The robe Myra had given me was tattered and bullet riddled. I guessed clothing was going to be an issue for the rest of my life.

I caught more movement to my left, but I remained still. I'd healed from the assault on my body, and now I waited like a snake coiled in the leaves.

The first of Carrillo's goons ran up to me, a pistol in his hand—pointed at my face.

Two more joined him, then a third, a fourth, a fifth.

All of the men kept their weapons trained on me.

I held my breath, still waiting until I knew all of them were there that were coming. After the sixth showed up, no more did.

"What is that?" one of the men spat, disgust and fear written all over his face. He added a few expletives in there that all the others seemed to be using in spades.

"I don't know," another said.

"It's a monster," a third offered.

"No." This guy was the last one to arrive. His hair was done up in a mohawk, and he had diamond studs in each ear. He stared down at me in disbelief, his head turning from side to side. "It's the chupacabra," he said.

"What?" the second questioned, taking his eyes from me to look at his comrade.

"The chupacabra. It's him. I know it is."

"That's just an old story. Something they tell kids at night before they go to bed."

"And yet," I interrupted, blinking for the first time in a minute, "here I am."

"What the—" the first gunman started to say, but I rolled up onto one knee, sweeping the goon's feet with a powerful paw. I spun around amid the red mist, clipping every ankle until the men were all on the ground, trying to get back up.

Then I pounced.

I ripped through them with fang and claw, tearing limbs from bodies. The men screamed and fired their weapons helplessly, aimlessly, without a single round hitting me. I tore them apart amid the swirling, pulsing red mist until the last died with a snap of my jaws through his neck.

Then the mist sank into them, and I felt more power ripple through me.

I stood over the bodies and looked down the road at the remaining gunmen. They scrambled to escape, climbing in the remaining functional vehicles. The driver of one of them spun the wheel as one of the other guys was trying to climb in the back. He grabbed at the open door, hanging on to it while the driver pulled forward, then backed up.

Suddenly, the driver's head rocked back against the headrest, then slumped forward with the rest of his torso. A split second later, the familiar crack of Vero's rifle as the sound caught up with her super-sonic round.

The fifth SUV idled forward toward the ditch on the jungle side of the road. The first man trying to catch up to his ride shuddered, his shoulders twitching left to right. Then he fell onto his knees and into the grass next to the ditch—another victim of Vero's handiwork.

I darted after the SUV as it rolled into the ditch and stopped with a crunch.

The other vehicle was already turned around. Two men fired their weapons out of the driver's side window and into the jungle, hoping they were aiming in the sniper's direction.

I arrived at the wrecked vehicle in the ditch as the two remaining men inside tried to climb out and escape on foot. I caught the first one attempting to run down the escaping SUV, waving his hands in the air in desperation.

The men in that vehicle definitely didn't hear him over the sound of the roaring engine or the guns popping out the back window. Even if they had heard or seen him, there was no chance those men were turning back now.

They ran over bodies on the side of the road as they made their escape, with no attempt to slow down, instead winding their way back down the road and into the darkness.

I chased down the second man pursuing them and caught up to him near one of the disabled vehicles.

He skidded to a stop behind the SUV, hoping to take cover, but instead he found me, standing over him like a thunderstorm, dark and menacing. He looked up with fear in his eyes.

This guy was young, maybe no older than sixteen years of age. Just a kid, actually. He quivered under my gaze. His hands trembled, and I noticed he had no weapon in them. What puzzled me more than anything, however, was the absence of the red mist.

Where was it?

The living fog had surrounded all of Carrillo's men. Except this one. What was different about him? Why was he special?

I frowned, baring my teeth—ready to strike.

But I couldn't. An ancient voice spoke in my head—a reminder from something.

"Only the wicked," it said to me, as real as if it came from the young man cowering at my feet.

I breathed hard, trying to understand what was going on.

"But he works for Carrillo," I argued with the unseen voice.

The boy looked at me in confusion.

"Only the wicked," it echoed in my ears again.

I swore at the voice, but I let go of my aggression. Perhaps it was possible for someone innocent to be roped into working for someone evil.

I thought fast, noting the last man on foot had taken off in the direction of the town. I didn't know why Vero hadn't picked him off yet. It might have been she was focused on the escaping vehicle, but they were out of sight now, barely visible by the dimming glow of their taillights retreating amid the twists and turns of the hills.

Easing my breath, I calmed myself long enough to issue a warning to Carrillo's terrified little goon. "You," I snarled. "Stay right here. If you try to escape, I will kill you. Understand?"

He bobbed his head nervously.

I snapped my jaws at him in a half-full threat, and he retreated back against the car tire, squeezing his eyes closed.

When he opened them, I was already gone, running at full speed on all four paws. I saw the last gunman along the edge of the road, sprinting as fast as he could back toward the dim lights of the town just beyond the tree line.

The red fog chased him, wrapping around his ankles and feet. Even with my superhuman speed, the guy had a good head start, and catching him would require effort. I cleared my head of all other thoughts and focused on the mist around my quarry's feet.

My chest pounded. I felt a strange connection from heart to mind. It was real, tangible, like a cord strung from one end to the other, establishing a potent connection.

Abruptly, a surge of power flew out of me. I kept running after the man, the gap closing quickly. Then, as the energy connected to the fog around him, I felt it squeeze into a tight circle, enclosing around his ankles.

In shock, I watched the glowing mist trip the man and send him sprawling forward. The gun in his hand flew from his fingers and disappeared into the grass. Within seconds I was on him. The mist parted like an invitation to ravage my prey.

I towered over him, the mist still churning around us. This man wasn't like the boy by the truck. He was as evil as the others.

My fangs gleamed in the moonlight. He knew, as he stared into my blazing red eyes, that his end was near and that there was nothing he could do to stop it.

He drew a knife from his side, rolled to his feet, and thrust the blade into my midsection. I grimaced at the sudden pain, but I didn't allow him to see much of the effect. Instead, I cocked my head to the side, shook it for a second as if disappointed, then I backhanded him so hard I felt his skull cave on the left side of his head.

The man flew twenty feet and then rolled on the road like a rag doll.

I watched the body tumble to a stop. The red mist dissipated, some of it flowing into his nostrils before it was gone.

I figured the body would be gone within an hour, although the time frame for that little miracle still eluded me.

Now my attention returned to the kid I left by the vehicle. Even from down the road, I could see he still sat there on the asphalt, leaning up against the car tire.

At least he could obey.

I trotted back over to him and found the kid still shaking.

I inclined my head, unwilling to let him feel safe yet, but I'd already decided I couldn't kill him. I'd been instructed not to take the life of an innocent, and if the red mist didn't surround him, I had to take that as a sign. Before, I'd considered myself judge, jury, and executioner. Now, I realized I was only the latter.

The fog was the judge and jury. And it told me who I could kill, and who to let live.

"I have questions for you, kid," I said in a deep growl.

The young man still shook violently, no longer in control of his nerves. Fortunately, he still held control of his bladder, though for how long I had no idea.

"Where is Carrillo?" I asked.

"What?" He looked up at me in confusion.

"Carrillo," I repeated, leaning forward with the most menacing face I could muster. I imagined it had to be terrifying for the kid to stare up at such a creature—a beast who'd just ravaged his entire hit squad. "Where is he?"

"He's on his boat. Out... out in the gulf."

"Good." I nodded in approval. "What does he want with the town of Santa Rojo?"

The kid breathed heavily. I could tell he wasn't sure if he should answer.

"I'm not going to hurt you," I swore. "But I need to know exactly how to find him."

"You won't have to find him," the kid said.

"What?"

"He said you had something he wants. So he was going to take something you want."

I frowned at the statement. "Something I want?" I didn't want anything, except maybe a time machine. Although, now I felt like if I was going to go back in time, it would be to the time before I met Amy. Maybe I would skip meeting her.

This kid wasn't talking about Amy or a time machine. He was talking about something real. And for nearly thirty seconds, I couldn't figure out what.

Then it hit me.

"Vero."

34

I left the kid where he sat and leaped over the hood of the SUV. A single thought pulsed through my brain.

"Vero?" I shouted. My unusually powerful voice carried deep into the jungle. "Vero!" I yelled again.

Terrible feelings filled my chest. Feelings of loss, despair, anger, fear, sadness, all pumped with every pounding heartbeat.

I had just met this woman. And she was easily ten years younger than me. Why did I feel this... attachment? Is that what it was? Or was it something else? A connection?

I honestly didn't know. In all my life, I'd never really felt like I connected with someone—not in the traditional, romanticized way I'd heard it described.

But there was something about Vero—a mesmerizing, enchanting energy between us that pulled me to her, even now as I charged across the road, jumped over the ditch, and plunged headfirst into the dark jungle.

I searched the immediate area, thinking this was where I left her, but it all looked the same in the dark. Even with my enhanced superior vision, I couldn't make out any sign of her.

I stopped moving and listened, but all I heard were the stirring sounds of animals in the forest or the occasional bird in the canopy overhead.

"Vero?" I yelled once more.

No answer.

I scoured the ground around me. If this was the spot, there would be spent shell casings all over the place.

But I found none.

I looked back toward the road and tried to gauge the position she'd taken before the convoy arrived.

"This isn't it," I said. "She was farther up the road."

I turned that direction and stalked along the jungle's edge, scaling the earth for any sign of her.

A sickening thought percolated. *What if she was dead?*

I sped up, fearing the worst. What if she was injured by one of the bullets? The thought of her lying there alone in the darkness on the edge of the jungle sent a tendril of fear through me, and I quickened my pace again.

"Vero!"

I stopped when I reached a patch in the forest where the earth had been disturbed. I realized almost instantly that this was where she'd been. A closer examination revealed the spent shell casings I'd figured would be here. I reached down and picked one up, then looked back toward the road. To pick off the men from here had been an incredible feat of marksmanship. I knew there was no chance I could have done that.

I crouched down onto my haunches and searched the ground. Two narrow trails scratched the earth going deeper into the jungle.

I followed the little paths for thirty feet, then they veered off away from the road. I stopped and looked back at the headlights on the road, the vehicles now mostly blocked by the thick stands of tree trunks.

Where was she?

Had an animal taken her?

I sniffed the air but didn't detect blood. That was another new, unsettling skill I'd picked up that came along with all the other new powers. My sense of smell could pick up the faintest trace of blood. And I didn't like it.

Now, however, I wasn't smelling any, and I found myself at least slightly relieved.

I heard something to my right and darted through the woods in that general direction.

After running a hundred feet, I stopped again, skidding in the leaves until my paws dug into the earth. I sniffed again. Still nothing. Then I heard a sound that sent a chill through my bones.

It was faint, barely noticeable through the sounds of the night-time jungle. But I knew exactly what it was.

A slight shriek. From a woman.

I remembered the radio in my ear and instantly wished I'd tried that instead of running around in the woods like an idiot. "Vero?" I said, touching the earpiece. "Can you hear me? Vero? Come in?"

No response.

I took off again, running harder than I ever had. Low-hanging limbs and giant leaves smacked me in the face, whipped my legs, and scratched my arms.

The wind blew through my fur—still weird to say or think—as I ran harder and harder, pumping all four of my legs, arms, whatever they were.

I paused again near two large trees and listened. The sound of a car engine groaning filled my ears. They were close. Very close.

I snapped my head around to the right, tracking the sound to that direction.

"Vero," I said, and took off again.

Panting for air, I ran through the darkness. A thicket of bushes covered in thorns appeared straight ahead of me, and I nearly ran headlong into them. At the last second, I pushed off with my hind feet and sprang over the shrubs, only grazing a toe on one of the branches as I sailed over it.

I hit the ground at a dead sprint.

My mouth felt dry, but I could hear the sound of the vehicle now.

I burst out of the jungle and into a clearing. The moonlight appeared once more, shining down on a meadow filled with tall golden grass.

I didn't have to look long to find the source of the noise.

A black SUV sped away from the meadow and turned onto the road leading away from the village.

"Vero!"

I took off again, despite my muscles feeling heavy and my breath coming in huge gulps. Superhuman? Yes. All powerful? Apparently not.

You are not a god, the voice in my head reminded me.

"I never said I was," I argued as I charged toward the fleeing vehicle.

I had to be running nearly forty miles per hour, maybe faster. The fastest land animal on earth could only do sixty.

Clenching my teeth, I ran harder, pumping my muscles to their limits. The wind whistled in my ears, and I knew I had reached my maximum velocity.

Still, the Range Rover gained distance. I felt myself slowing down, unable to match the pace of the vehicle. I stopped, seeing the swirling red mist surrounding the red taillights and tires.

I squinted and focused on squeezing the vehicle with the fog. But it felt so far away. I reached out my hand as if to use a force choke or something. This, unfortunately, wasn't a George Lucas story.

I clenched my jaw and tried to unleash the same energy from before, the foreign power that had commanded the fog to trip the man I pursued.

Nothing happened, and within seconds, the SUV disappeared around the bend, its lights muted by the forests and hills.

I stood there, unbelieving, gasping for air.

I panted like an animal. Which was weird, not as weird as actually being some kind of animal, but it didn't help me feel better.

"Vero," I muttered.

I don't know how long I stood there in the road, under the moon and stars, in the middle of nowhere Mexico.

Just a few days before, my wife had been murdered by Vicente

Carrillo. Then he abducted and drugged me, tried to force me to find this medallion for him. Now, the one person in this place that seemed to genuinely believe in me, who had helped me and taken me in as some derelict stranger off the street, was now in deep trouble. With the worst kind of person.

My mind raced with solutions, most of them not plausible in the slightest.

Then I remembered the kid I'd left back by the SUV and what he'd said.

I whirled around and took off again, this time running at a steady pace down the road. Within a few minutes, I arrived at the back of the vehicle that had taken up the rear of the convoy.

I slowed down and inspected the shattered windows, along with the two tires on the passenger side that Vero had shot out. She really was amazing with that rifle.

I found the first dead men, two on the passenger side, another at the rear of the vehicle where he'd tried to take cover before Vero picked him off. Then I found who I assumed to be the driver. A hole through his right eye told me how he'd met his end, and I had to turn away from the gruesome sight for a second.

Irony hit me a heartbeat later when I thought about how I'd bitten into human beings with my dog fangs.

"Ugh," I spat, still more disgusted at the mangled, seeping ocular cavity than my new penchant for tasting blood.

I continued to the next vehicle, examining the bodies and moving forward until I reached the kid I'd left by the tire.

He still sat there, too afraid to move. I supposed he figured if he left the site, I would chase him down like I had his buddy.

But this one, he was different. The red mist still didn't appear around him.

He looked up at me, started at my monster-like appearance, and then swallowed hard. "Did you find them?" he asked.

"Find who?"

"The other truck." The kid looked confused.

"I did, but I couldn't catch up. They took my friend. That was a mistake on their part." I found it odd I wasn't fumbling for the words in Spanish.

The boy couldn't rip his eyes away from me. "I can't believe the stories are real."

"Hey," I snapped, startling him again. The sudden word pulled him out of whatever shock he swam in. "Where are they taking her?"

"I don't know. I only heard some of the guys talking about it in passing, about how they were going to kill you and take her alive."

I sighed, pondering everything he'd said. Carrillo knew he wasn't able to kill me, and if he knew anything about the medallion, he'd know that was doubly true at night. Unless, of course, he didn't know that little fact. Either way, I knew that Carrillo was aware that defeating me would be next to impossible.

He was going to use Vero as leverage.

The answer couldn't have been clearer. Anger rose inside me, and I felt my blood heat up. Whatever those feelings manifested on the outside must have frightened the kid because he shrank back at the sight of me.

"What?" I asked.

"Your eyes," he said. "They look like the eyes of the devil."

"Ah." I nodded. "I am not the devil. Except to men like Carrillo. What is your name?"

The kid licked his lips and swallowed back his fear like a shot of 120-proof bourbon. "Jesús."

"Well, I guess if anyone knows the devil," I joked.

The blank stare on his face told me he didn't get the joke.

"Never mind."

I felt something buzzing in my robe and remembered I'd stuffed the assassin's phone in a pocket inside the fabric. I couldn't believe the lone button on the pouch had kept the device from flying out, and in hindsight, maybe keeping it or anything else in there wasn't a great idea.

I reached into the folds of cloth, unfastened the button, and retrieved the phone. It had to be the weirdest sight the kid had ever seen—a dog-man creature holding a cell phone to his ear.

"Hello, Vicente," I snarled.

"Ah, so glad you answered, Dr. Wolf. I worried perhaps you lost my assassin's phone in the fighting."

"Nope."

"Good. I'm so glad. Because now you can bring me what's mine."

"Couldn't help but notice you weren't here for the battle," I jeered. "Too busy ruining lives, murdering innocent people, shipping dangerous narcotics across the border?"

"I'm sure you would have loved to see me there, Gideon. But I know what you've done. I know what you've become. The amulet is mine. And you will bring it to me if you want to see your precious Vero again."

"Put her on the phone."

A disturbing laugh came through the speaker. "Oh, Gideon. You are funny. I'll give you that. Vero isn't here yet, but she will be within the hour."

"If you hurt her—"

"You'll not be able to stop me. But you can keep her safe by bringing me what belongs to me."

"This medallion is my family's," I countered. "It belongs to the House of Claw and Fang."

"I'm well aware of the histories, boy." The last word scratched me the wrong way.

"Boy?"

"You have no idea what you're dealing with."

"And I suppose you do?"

"Yes." Carrillo demurred.

"Oh? And why is that?" I asked.

"Because I, too, can trace my lineage to the House of Claw and Fang."

35

"What?"

I couldn't wrap my head around it.

"Yes," Carrillo drawled. "You and I are distant relatives, Gideon. And the medallion is rightfully mine."

"You're not a Wolf."

"That's where you're wrong, Gideon. But we're getting off subject. You will meet me at my mansion on the coast of Tampico."

"Oh yeah?"

"Yes, if you want to see Vero alive again, you will come. I do hope you show up. It would be shame to see her pretty fingers, toes, arms, legs, all removed. I'm sure I don't have to remind you of my methods. Or perhaps word of my work hasn't reached the States."

I trembled with fury. "If you lay one finger on her—"

"I won't have to if you bring me the medallion. I swear, you will be free to go. Along with your friend."

An oath from a liar was no oath at all, and I didn't think for a second that this murderer was going to let us go. The best I could hope for was getting Vero out of there alive. But if I had to turn over the amulet, I couldn't guarantee it.

I looked down at the necklace touching my chest. It was as if the metal piece told me I couldn't give it to Carrillo, that men like him should never have access to this kind of power.

"Okay," I surrendered. "I'll bring it to you, Vic. Just give me your address. I'll have to find a ride—"

"No excuses," he said. He gave me the address for his beachfront home. "Be there by dawn, or Vero starts losing things. Things she needs."

The call ended, and for a second, I hoped he hadn't cut me off. The second thing I hoped was that I committed the address to memory. I spoke it out loud several times, and Jesús stared up at me like I was headed for the loony bin.

"What did he say?" Jesús asked.

After I repeated the address two more times, I had it. Then I looked to the boy. "He said I have to bring the medallion to him. To his place on the gulf. He's not on his boat, apparently."

Fear slithered through the kid's eyes. "I'm sorry, Chupacabra. I didn't know. Last I heard, that's where he was."

"Relax, kid," I soothed, holding out a paw. *No chance he was going to relax for the rest of his life.* "I'm not going to hurt you. I can't."

Jesús' confusion deepened. "What? I saw what you did to the others, how you killed them? Your powers are—"

"Superhuman?" I finished his sentence when it seemed like he couldn't find the words.

He nodded.

"Yeah, well, without the amulet I'm not. I'm just a guy. And Carrillo wants me to bring it to him at sunrise, which means this entire attack was a ruse."

"A ruse?"

"Yes. It wasn't real. If one of you could have managed to take me down and recover the medallion, then he wins. Great. No big deal. But I don't think he believed that was going to happen. Carrillo's plan all along was to get to Vero."

"The girl?"

I nodded.

"What are you going to do?"

"The only thing I can. I'm going to kill Carrillo and get her out of there."

"But if he makes you give him the medallion, how will you be able to defeat him?" Jesús looked at me with sincere worry in his mind.

I wondered how badly he'd been treated, the horrors he'd seen and been forced to commit. I'd heard about how young cartel recruits got "jumped in," a common term for initiation. Sometimes they were ordered to fight someone. Other times—in the more tragic cases—their acceptance into the gang was based on killing a member of another gang, or occasionally—a random, innocent person.

"You're right about that, kid. Without the amulet, I'll probably be killed the second it leaves my fingers."

He searched me for a solution, but I didn't have one. Not at first. Then, as I looked down at the bullet-riddled cloak draped over me, I had an idea.

"I'm going to take you to the village," I said. "You'll be safe there. I'm sure your parents are worried about you."

He lowered his head. "I don't have any parents. They died a few years ago. My sister and I... we've been..." His voice drifted away.

"Surviving," I said, ending his thought.

The kid nodded.

"Where is she?" I asked.

"Tampico."

Same place as Carrillo.

"Okay, new plan. I'm taking you with me to Tampico. When we arrive there, you get your sister and bring her back here to Santa Rojo. Understood?"

His eyes confessed that he didn't, but he nodded anyway. "Yes. I understand."

I loathed to think what his sister had been through and banished the thought to the remotest corners of my mind.

"Okay. Get up. Let's go," I said. I reached out my right arm, and my hand morphed back into human shape.

Jesús watched the transformation, and in fewer than ten seconds I was back to my normal self.

"Come on," I encouraged. "We don't have much time."

"When did he want you to be there?" Jesús asked, grasping my hand and hauling himself up. He looked down at his palm and fingers when he let go, as if he might catch whatever disease or mutation caused me to become a shifter. "Wow. You really are just a man."

"I know. Carrillo wants me there by dawn."

"Oh." Jesús sounded almost glad. "Then you will have plenty of time. It's still early, and the coast isn't more than a few hours from here."

"Yeah." I already knew that. "But we have to make a stop first."

"A stop?" He puzzled over my statement.

"Yes," I said with a foreboding look in my eye, nodding slowly like Jack Nicholson in *The Departed*. "A stop. And I don't know how long it will take."

We walked down the road, passing the wreckage strewn on the blacktop and on the sides of the road.

As we passed by, some of the bodies disintegrated into red mist that trailed up into the darkness, evaporating into nothing.

"What's happening to them?" Jesús asked, aghast at the sight of dead bodies vanishing into the ether.

"I don't know, kid. Whenever I kill one, a little while later their bodies just disappear. No clue where they go. Or why. I only realized that happens earlier today."

"Oh." He seemed to accept the explanation, and we kept walking.

After another minute or two, he spoke up again. "You said earlier that you couldn't kill me? Why? I would have been easier to kill than the others."

"Perhaps," I allowed. "Let me ask you something. Did you see anything unusual earlier when you and the others started your attack?"

Jesús cocked his head to the side in a show of thought. "Unusual like how?"

I decided to explain.

"What you just saw there, with the bodies of the dead. Did you notice the red mist?"

The kid nodded. "Yeah. What was that?"

"I don't know that answer. But I know that the same mist surrounds the wicked. It's how I know who is good and who is evil."

It took a minute for him to process. "So, there's a mist like that around people you're supposed to kill?"

"I don't know if I'm supposed to kill them. I doubt that would be something that went unnoticed if I went around offing people left and right. But it tells me who is a threat and if there is no mist, then there is no threat. You, it seems, are not an evil young man."

Jesús smirked uncomfortably. "I've done bad things. I'm not proud of them."

I saw that he truly felt remorse for the life he'd been plunged into living, and I sympathized.

"All of us have done bad things, Jesús." I thought about the irony of me telling a kid named Jesús that, and it made me chuckle. He didn't seem to notice so I continued. "Everyone does bad things. But bad actions don't make bad people. Sometimes good people do bad. And sometimes bad people do good. In the end, we're judged by our hearts' desires, and whether or not we do our best to help, not hurt others. I've hurt people."

My voice died off as I remembered a litany of things from the past —from childhood, teenage years, all the way through the present. There'd been too many moments of bad decisions, of actions I'd taken that hurt someone else. Still, I didn't consider myself to be a horrible person.

As I considered these things, I came to a crossroads in my heart. There, Amy stood in the shadows, watching with a face that begged to be forgiven. She looked at me, longing to touch me, wishing she could hold my hand or brush my face with her fingers. I sensed these things from the apparition in my mind and choked on the feelings.

"I forgive you," I whispered.

"What?" Jesús asked, looking over at me.

I realized I'd said the words out loud and cleared my throat. "Nothing. Just talking to myself. The point is what you've done doesn't make you who you are. Always remember that. Okay?"

The kid nodded.

We reached Vero's car, and I realized that the keys were with her. I swore under my breath and then put my hands on my hips.

"I just remembered she has the keys," I told Jesús. "You wouldn't happen to be able to hot-wire a car? Would you?"

A smile crept across his face as he assessed the vehicle. "Yeah. I can do this one."

Wow. This kid is full of surprises.

Another voice in my head said something else. "I told you not to kill him."

I snorted at the words, shaking my head. "Okay, kid. Let's see what you can do. And then we'll go see Myra."

"Myra?"

I nodded. "Yeah. I think she may be able to help with my situation."

36

Not killing Jesús proved to be a wise move.

The kid hot-wired the car within a minute of pulling the panel out from under the dashboard. He tapped the ignition wires together a few times, sparks flew, and the engine kicked to life like an old mule being yoked.

I drove us back into the village and stopped outside the church, pausing only for a second to consider what I was going to tell the priest and the other people inside.

With my short speech prepared, I stepped out of the car, telling Jesús to stay there.

When I reached the door, I knocked three times and took a step back to wait. In fifteen seconds, the priest opened the door and poked his head out, either feigning fatigue or genuinely exhausted. Either way, the guy looked like the proverbial hell he was trying to avoid.

"Gideon?"

"Hello, Father." I figured it was better to tell him and he could let everyone else inside know that it was safe to come out. Part of me was glad I'd been wrong about an attack from the west.

I could have returned to the village and found it in flames with towers of black smoke piling into the air. One particularly disturbing vision was one where the cartel had set fire to the church and killed everyone inside.

"Is everything okay? I heard some... sounds in the distance when I stepped out earlier."

I knew what he was talking about. He'd heard the gunfire, which from a distance probably sounded like nothing more than a bunch of kids shooting off fireworks—something that happened with uncommon regularity in Mexico, especially in traditional towns where so many celebrations of the old ways took place.

"The cartel is gone," I said. "And I don't think they'll be back to bother you or anyone else anytime soon. Vero told me what a scourge they've been, how they ruined businesses here, hurt people, and worse—I'm sure."

"Yes," the priest hung his head. "It has been very trying." He looked around and noticed I was alone. "Speaking of Vero. Where is she?"

"I'm going to get her now," I said, feeling like the old man didn't need more information. I wasn't lying to him. But I wasn't exactly telling the entire truth, either. If I told him Vero had been abducted by Carrillo, the man might have keeled over right there on the church steps. "Tell your people that it's okay to return to their homes, businesses, whatever. Carrillo isn't your concern anymore. Okay?"

The priest nodded.

I felt a twinge of guilt, but I pushed it deep down. I wasn't Catholic anyway, so what did it matter if I lied to a priest? He was just a man to me.

"Thank you," the old man said with a grateful bow. "If there is anything we can do, please don't hesitate to ask."

"I appreciate that, Father. You and everyone else get some rest. You look tried."

"Oh yes. Well, I suppose I am. I'll be sure to tell them. Thank you again, Gideon."

I nodded a goodbye at him and returned to the running car.

"What was that about?" Jesús asked, looking at me with a confused, curious gleam in his eye.

I shifted the car into reverse and guided it out onto the street, turning around the back of Myra's house to keep the vehicle hidden. She had plenty of gas in it, so we wouldn't have to stop before Tampico. And that was a good thing. I couldn't abide delays.

"The villagers all hid in the church. We were worried Carrillo would send some of you into the town and attack the people even though they had nothing to do with our issue."

"Oh," Jesús got real quiet. Too quiet.

"So, he *was* going to do that," I stated.

"Our orders were to get the necklace and then kill anyone who got in our way or tried to stop us."

I knew what that meant. Even if not a single citizen raised up arms to help me, they would have been killed anyway. Carrillo would have done it to set an example, to make sure no one else in his territory disobeyed.

I pulled the car into a parking spot behind Myra's humble home and shifted it into park.

"What is this place?" Jesús asked.

I struggled to explain, so I decided on the truth. "She's the local crazy lady who believes in magic, or something like it."

That's not true, the voice in my head argued.

After seeing the kid's response, I added, "She's a friend. And she's going to help. I hope."

I'd already noted Myra's absence at the church when I went in earlier, so I figured she had to be at home, though she could have easily left town or gone to visit a relative somewhere far away.

The more I thought about it, the more concerned I grew. I settled my nerves by telling myself that no matter the case, I would find a way to take out Carrillo.

I rapped on the back door and waited, hoping the woman was still awake. She may well have already been in bed even though it was still a few hours before midnight.

To my surprise, the lock clicked within a few seconds. The door creaked open, and I saw the same wrinkled, humble face from before.

"Well, hello again, Gideon. What brings you by at this hour?"

"I need your help."

"You mean we?"

I frowned at the question, then looked over my shoulder at Jesús. "Yes. We. Sorry. This is Jesús."

"Are you rescuing strays now, Gideon? Quite an odd hobby for a guardian."

I pinched my lips together, fully aware that her calling me that just opened up a can of questions I would have to answer on the way to Tampico.

"The mist didn't surround him," I said. "He was one of Carrillo's men. Not anymore."

"Is that right?" she asked, sounding happy about the kid's new state of allegiance.

"Yes," he said. "I didn't want to work for him. But I was forced into it."

"Then our friend here did the right thing," she said. "You look hungry, young one. Have you had any dinner yet?"

Dinner? It's late. And we need to get going. And why in the world would she have dinner on at this hour?

I wasn't sure if it was a regional cultural thing or just this woman's craving for a fourth meal, but as she opened the door wider I smelled something delicious inside. The scent of fresh baked bread and cooked meat wafted out and hit me right in the nostrils.

"I see your robes held up well enough," Myra noticed, looking me up and down. She poked a finger through one of the bullet holes. "I thought this might happen, which is why I made you a new outfit."

My furrowed brow wrinkled further. "You did?"

She nodded. "Yes, of course. Please, come inside. You'll need to try it on. And he needs something to eat. You look famished."

Myra stepped aside to let us pass. She patted Jesús on the shoulder as he entered; his head hung low as if in shame.

"Welcome to my home," she said. "Of course, Gideon has already been here."

"Thank you," the kid said.

"Well, I'm glad you're here, Jesús." She made her way over to the stove, where a frying pan sizzled strips of beef, onion, and bell peppers. Fresh tortillas were stacked on a platter to the right next to a bowl of lettuce, tomatoes, and avocado slices.

He stared hungrily at the food as she scooped the beef onto a plate and set it on the little counter by the rest of the offerings.

"There are plates right there," she said, motioning to the end of the counter. "Please, help yourself."

"You don't mind?"

"Of course not," Myra said, winking at me.

The kid shuffled over to the counter and took a dish, then set some tortillas on it, shoveled the beef into them, and then topped the street tacos with lettuce and avocado, finishing by sprinkling a little queso fresca on top, then a few diced tomatoes for color.

"You hungry?" she raised an eyebrow at me with the question.

"No, thank you, Myra. I'm okay. I'm curious why you're cooking so late."

"Oh, well, you know, sometimes you get hungry late at night. And I had all that meat sitting in the refrigerator, so I decided to make myself some tacos."

"Mm-hmm," I hummed. "You sure you didn't know we were coming?"

She blushed a little, her eyes squinting with her smile. "Maybe," she said with a shrug. "Come, try this on."

Walking to the corner of the room, she stopped at a dark wooden shelf. A silver pyramid with intricate designs on it, including—Scandinavian Runes? A light blue glow emanated from within the odd container. I figured it was some kind of unique lamp she'd picked up in travels as a young woman. Or maybe a tourist had given it to her.

She reached up to a sconce on the wall that held a dim light bulb —one of those vintage things that had regained popularity in recent years. Except I wasn't sure it was a replica. Based on the age of every-thing else in this little home, it well might have been an original bulb.

I shook off the notion. That bulb would have to be a hundred years old for that to be the case.

She pulled on the sconce, and suddenly, the wall next to me opened up, revealing a secret door I'd somehow missed.

"That's cool," I commented, looking into a hidden, unlit room. I didn't understand how the space was there. Based on the exterior of the house—what little of it I'd seen or considered—it didn't seem like there was enough square footage for the room.

"Yet here it is," she said, motioning with her hand into the closet.

"What?"

"I said here it is," she repeated.

But it sounded different than the first time.

"You said *yet*," I corrected, puzzled. Had she been reading my thoughts. Because that was starting to get a little weird, both with her and the voice in my head. And there were definitely places in my mind where I preferred to keep things private.

"Did I?" She giggled. "Sometimes I say things I don't mean to say. I guess it's old age."

She blew it off, but I wasn't buying it. Not entirely. Still, I let it go and peered into the dark room.

"Come," she said, motioning with a hand over her shoulder. She entered the closet and flipped a light switch. A dim bulb flickered to life on the far wall. I squinted, trying to discern if it was a light bulb or an actual candle. Because it looked like a real candle.

I hesitantly followed her into the tiny room. She stopped at a shelf fixed to the far wall under the candle and picked up an object.

I couldn't see what it was at first. Then, when she turned around, I saw what she cradled in her hands.

It was probably the most underwhelming thing I'd ever seen—as far as build up and expectations were concerned, although I wasn't sure exactly what I was expecting.

"Take this," she said, extending her hands toward me.

In her palms, a small piece of gray fabric that looked like it couldn't cover a doll rested on her wrinkled skin. The cloth looked like a sample swatch from a sewing store.

"I'm sorry? What is that?" I peered at the square with utter confusion.

"Oh yes. I apologize, Gideon. To you, this probably just looks like a piece of cloth."

I nodded. "Yes." Then I paused. "Wait. Isn't it?"

"Things aren't always what they seem, Guardian." Her eyes danced with mischief, but her face darkened, morphing into something serious, impending.

"I don't understand. Why are you giving me that little piece of fabric?"

Her lips parted in a thin smile. "This is no ordinary cloth, Gideon. This is a guardian cloak."

My eyebrows dove toward my eyes, the confusion only increasing. "What?" Now I really did think it was for a doll, like maybe a guardian action figure or something. Even then, it didn't look like any kind of clothing. Just a plain, gray cotton square.

"Come," she said, taking a step closer to me.

She pulled the neck of my robe down until the medallion was exposed. Then she lifted it toward her.

An instinct told me to stop her, to grab her hand and allow her to proceed no further. But I didn't. I trusted Myra. I didn't know why. The old woman was a kook, way more than just a little out there, but there was also something else about her—a knowledge, a wisdom, a kindness, a belief that begged me to trust everything was going to be okay and that she was on my side.

I wanted to ask what she was doing when she held the cloth in her right hand and pressed it against the back of the medallion with the other. But I kept it to myself and simply watched.

Out of nowhere, warmth radiated through me.

I didn't pull back, though I felt the instinct to. Instead, I stood there and watched, looking down past my chin as the cloth began to melt into the amulet, as if turning liquid before my eyes.

When the two were melded as one, Myra let go of the medallion. The metal fell against my skin underneath the folds of the robe.

Suddenly, I felt something slithering over my skin. It didn't hurt and I felt no threat, but the sensation was strange, almost like a faint tickle but without the need to shake it off.

"You can remove the robe now, Gideon," Myra said, a satisfied look in her eyes.

That look threw me off as much as the request.

"Um, what?" My right eyebrow climbed up my forehead. "I don't think that's a good idea. My pants are pretty shredded under this."

She sighed a laugh, her smile spreading wider. "I'm far too old for that sort of thing, Gideon. Trust me. Take off your robe."

I hoped Jesús didn't hear this conversation from the other room. I suddenly became very aware that the young gang member was still in the house, and I questioned whether or not he could be trusted. It only distracted me for a second before I returned to the issue at hand.

"Okay," I surrendered and pulled up on the bottom folds of the robe.

Just treat this like you're getting a physical at the doctor's office, I thought. *A very old, very female, very odd doctor.*

As the clothing went over my head and the light from the candle struck me, I realized I wasn't naked underneath but instead covered in a shirt and trousers that felt like lightweight long underwear.

"What is this?" I asked. "And how in the world did—"

"It is what guardians wear under everything else. It will expand with you when you grow into the chupacabra. And it will shrink back when you return to your human self.

"How?"

Her smile remained. "I do not know the science of it, if that's what you mean. I only know that it works. Also, bullet holes will no longer be a problem."

"It's bulletproof?" I held out my arms, examining the fabric. It was loose and airy, like Dry Fit on steroids.

"It's not Kevlar, Gideon," she said.

I wondered how she knew about Kevlar.

"It is woven from an ancient fabric, supposedly stitched with the vibrations of songs from the angels themselves."

"Angels?"

Her eyes narrowed to slits. "That is another story for another day, young Wolf. For now, know that you will always have these garments to keep you decent, which is more of an issue when shifting back into human form."

"Yeah." I marveled at the stuff. "But you said I don't have to worry about bullets."

She snorted. "You don't have to worry about bullet holes. The fabric doesn't tear. Bullets will pass through. Arrows, blades, anything of that nature can penetrate it. But those things won't kill you."

"Easy for you to say. It hurts like Hades. You ever been shot?"

She looked at me like I was filling a bin at the Planters factory.

"No. I haven't. Not with bullets anyway." She left it at that, and I sensed that I wouldn't receive an answer to the question that popped up. "Now," she said, touching my shoulders to spin me around, "you and Jesús need to get to Tampico."

"Tampico?" Had I mentioned where we were going? I thought I'd said something about finding Carrillo. I was sure of that. But had I said the name of the city? There was more to Myra than met the eye, and it was both unsettling and fascinating at the same time.

"You're going to find Carrillo," she clarified. "He has a mansion in Tampico."

That explained it. She wasn't a mind reader. Just a local with some knowledge about the regional warlord.

"Yes. His mansion is on the beach near Tampico. He—"

"Wants the medallion. Yes. I know."

And now I was back to believing she was a mind reader again. Or something else altogether.

"He is also of the House of Claw and Fang, Gideon. In every family, there are sides of light and sides that turn to darkness. Vicente's ancestors turned away from the light and found themselves constantly searching for the power of the guardians to use in their own selfish, heartless endeavors."

That was new information, as was most of everything that happened in the last few days.

"So, he really is a Wolf," I realized.

"Yes, in lineage. But the name remains only with those who stay with the light. Even Wolf women who married in times of antiquity kept their name because that is what is required of a guardian house."

Myra's head bobbed slowly up and down. "Carrillo will demand the amulet from you. It is of the utmost importance that you do not surrender it to him. No matter what."

She peered into my soul, prying truths from it I preferred to keep in the shadows.

"Even if he threatens to kill Vero," she added, her voice distant and sad.

A knife dug into my chest at the sound of the words. The tip twisted and carved through tissue and muscle, and it didn't seem like it would ever go away.

"But I—"

"Have to save her. I know, Gideon. I understand why you think that. But you don't. This is bigger than any one person."

"Even you?"

She scrunched her face at me like what I asked was silly. "Of course."

"Even me?" I asked, leveling my eyes to hers.

"Yes. Even you, the great guardian of the House of Claw and Fang. I know. Hard to believe, isn't it?"

"What do I do when he threatens to kill her if I don't hand it over?"

The mischief returned to her eyes. They gleamed in the light of her humble home, radiating through the doorway. "I think I have an idea."

37

I dropped off Jesús in the middle of town. The area seemed quiet and mostly residential with a few businesses and restaurants along the sidewalks. He said his sister was meeting him there in a half hour.

I worried about her, especially since she was about his age. Walking through the city at that hour of the morning would not have been a safe move in nearly any city. While I didn't know about the crime rate in Tampico, I knew no city was perfect.

The sky to the east foretold of sunrise with a dim hue of light barely touching the dark night.

The address I'd been given for Carrillo's mansion was another twenty minutes from where I dropped off Jesús. By the time I got there, the sun would nearly be over the horizon in the east.

I would have preferred to wait for night to fall again, or to get over to Carrillo's home before the sun came up. I'd have my power that way, and so far I hadn't seen any sign that Carrillo or his goons had any idea how to kill me.

Then again, I could have been making a deadly assumption.

I resisted the urge to go early, or to wait.

The latter was an easy decision. If I wasn't there at sunrise,

Carrillo would start torturing Vero. The thought of her in anguish stuck the tip of that knife into my heart, the same one I'd felt at Myra's place a few hours ago.

I'd stayed longer than I wanted at Myra's. She ended up forcing me to eat something, and after I'd done so, I felt incredibly tired—almost to a drugged level.

By the time I finished my third taco, Jesús was asleep on the leather sofa, and I was feeling groggy.

I woke up a few hours later and shot up, my eyes searching the room for threats. Instead, I found Myra standing in her kitchen over a boiling pot of something. It smelled good, like cinnamon rolls. Except why would something simmering in a pot smell like cinnamon rolls?

I rubbed my eyes and looked into the kitchen again, but this time it was empty.

"Myra?" I said in a groggy voice. But there'd been no sign of her. The apparition vanished into the ether, leaving me sitting there on a lounge chair, still blinking away the blurriness in my vision.

That couple of hours of rest cost me time but had been well worth it.

I felt invigorated again, ready to take on Carrillo and his entire army.

The rest of the drive went by fast. Too fast. And I found myself parked outside the front gates to the most opulent mansion I'd ever seen. The home was also egregiously ostentatious.

I got out of the car as the sun peeked over the gulf to the east. I felt my heart sink a little at the sight of it. The rising sun signaled that I wouldn't be able to call on my furry friend—the one who made me invincible.

I'd spent most of my life feeling vulnerable. I'd never felt great at anything until I found archaeology. Even then I spent most of my days feeling inadequate, never as good as others in my field, like Kara Cooney—world renowned archaeologist—or some of the teams of historians that I'd seen on television.

I should have been accustomed to feeling vulnerable, feeling like

I was exposed or weak. But after a taste of power, it felt like ash in my mouth—chalky and flavorless and impossible to stomach.

I took a deep breath as I approached the opening gate on foot, choosing to leave Vero's car out on the curb.

At least there, I figured, it would be safer than on Carrillo's property. I don't know why that even mattered. Neither one of us was getting out of here alive.

But I had to try.

Two guards stepped out from behind the white pillars of the gatehouse and grabbed me by the arms.

"Come with us," one said on my right.

They both wore sunglasses and black suit jackets. I figured they must have been sweating their shaved skulls off considering how hot it was outside. *Screw 'em. Let 'em suffer.*

The guards ushered me down the long brick-paved driveway toward the sprawling white-walled mansion. The main section in the middle was three stories tall, with two-story wings extending out on either side. Terracotta tiles on the roof contrasted oddly with the white exterior. It was like a mix between *Zorba the Greek* and *Scarface*.

"Couldn't make a decision, huh?" I said to the guard on my left, a man who was slightly shorter than the other and a good three inches shorter than me. I joked with him but found myself feeling the irrepressible need to rip his head off—which I could not do in this form.

The guard didn't say anything back.

"Because it looks like he was going for maybe coastal traditional plantation, but also wanted a splash of Italian Med in there. Of course, the white is pure Santorini. Just not sure why he—"

The guard on my right jammed his elbow into my middle back. My kidneys seized for a second. I grimaced, but the pain only lasted a few seconds.

I wondered about the garments I'd been given. The gray tunic had a hood that hung down my upper back. The black pants felt cool even as the first rays of light warmed them.

"Not much for HGTV, are you?" I spat, hoping blood didn't come out with the words.

Fortunately, none did, but I was left wondering if there would be blood in my urine later. Vegas would have laid odds on yes.

The two men led me between rows of ornately trimmed bushes—some in the shapes of exotic animals, others designed to look like cultural figures from ancient Mexican history.

Two huge walnut-colored doors flung open in the front of the house, and Carrillo stared down at me with a satisfied, smug grin on his face.

"What a piece of crap," I muttered in English.

The guards—apparently—didn't understand but still shoved me forward as punishment for what they deemed an offense.

Two more guards stood with Carrillo, one on either side—each carrying a submachine gun slung over his shoulder.

"What do you bet he says something stupid like, 'Well, well, well, there he is'?" I asked the guard to my right, but he shoved me forward.

I stumbled to a stop at the base of the steps and looked down at first, unwilling to make eye contact again for a minute. Maybe two. I didn't want to give him the pleasure.

"Well, well, well," Carrillo said. "There he is."

I looked back over my shoulder at the guard and laughed. "Called it."

The man didn't seem to think it was funny, but if he did, he didn't show it.

"I don't blame you for not laughing," I jeered. "But we both know it's funny."

Somehow I didn't see the guard on my left approach and kick me in the back of the knee.

The joint gave way, and I dropped to the ground. I winced for a second at the blow, but it didn't hurt much. I'd seen way worse injuries watching football and soccer. Nothing was torn. Not that it mattered. I chuckled at the thought.

"Is something funny, Gideon Wolf?" Carrillo asked.

I shook my head. "No. Nothing other than your weird taste in exterior design. I shudder to think of what it looks like on the inside. Probably like Graceland without the sense of modesty."

For a second, the man didn't seem to get the joke. I wasn't about to explain it to him. I thought I heard one of the guards chuckle, but it turned out to be a cough.

"I hope you brought my medallion, Professor," Carrillo drawled. "I would hate to have to hurt your pretty friend."

"Where is she, Vicente?" I punched back.

"Oh, she's right here."

"Hundred pesos he snaps his finger," I hissed at the guard to my right.

Within two seconds, Carrillo raised his right hand and snapped his fingers.

I shook my head. "Told you," I chuckled.

Two more guards appeared in the doorway. They wrestled Vero into view, and I started to leap forward. Two beefy hands clamping on each shoulder kept that from happening. Still, something felt stronger than before. *Is it possible that my human strength is much greater even though not quite to the level of the chupacabra?*

I didn't know, but I had a feeling I would find out soon. The red mist wasn't here, but I didn't really need it now. I was in the devil's den.

Vero struggled against the guards' grip, but she didn't cry. In fact, she looked plain pissed, like a snake with its tail caught under a rock.

"Let her go, Vicente," I said. "If you do, maybe I let you live."

That brought laughs from him first, then they cascaded throughout the ranks of his men.

I decided to join them and began laughing like a deranged hyena. The guards kept laughing for another ten seconds before they realized I was, too. Then Carrillo barked at them to shut up.

"Sorry," I apologized as a weird silence dropped onto the property. "I know. That's funny." I kept snickering, as if about to reveal a hilarious secret, like Carrillo's fly was open. "I'm really sorry. I know that was funny. But seriously, there's not a chance in hell I'll let you live."

My laughter died instantly, and I met him with my subzero stare.

Carrillo, to his credit, didn't flinch. A couple of the guards did, though, probably because they knew a little English, and that what I said didn't go over well with the boss.

"That's an interesting outfit," Carrillo mused with a cackle.

"I could say the same about yours. Maybe you didn't get the memo about white after Labor Day?"

His head bobbed like an apple on a toothpick. It went well with the look on his face that said he'd just gotten roasted. Then he stiffened. "Take the medallion from him," he snapped in Spanish.

The guards forced me over. The one on the left grabbed the top of my tunic and tugged the fabric down while the other one gripped me by the shoulder and back of the neck.

The guy searching me didn't have to look long. The silver necklace dangled between my shirt and my skin. The amulet glinted in the early morning light.

Without a word, the guard snatched the medallion and looped it up over my head. The other guy moved his hand out of the way and then clapped it back onto my skin.

My cheek twitched at the sting, but I didn't give him the joy of letting him see it hurt. Compared to the bullets, it barely registered.

The guard carried the medallion up the stairs to Carrillo, who waited, watching like a bird of prey high above the ground. His head tilted then straightened as the guard approached, the chain dangling from his fingers.

I wondered if the goon would do something stupid, like try to take the amulet and run. But he didn't.

He stopped one step below Carrillo and held the medallion out in his palm. Carrillo plucked it from his man's hand and held it aloft, inspecting it as he twisted it around and back again. He leaned his right eye in, examining every detail of the piece.

I sighed. Dejected, lost, and desperate for a miracle, I stared down at the ground, unwilling to take another breath.

When I finally brought my eyes from the earth, I saw Carrillo smile. A dragon's grin would have been friendlier.

"You have what you want, Vicente. Let her go. You can do whatever you want with me."

Carrillo nodded, the devilish smile still wrapped from cheek to cheek. He slipped the necklace over his head, and it fell to his chest. He closed his eyes, inhaling deeply, head tilted up to the sky as if about to receive Pentecost.

I snorted first, then chuckled loud enough and deliberately enough that he wouldn't be able to not notice.

A pained look washed over his face, and he whipped his head down to meet my eyes.

"It doesn't work like that, idiot," I derided. One of the guards shoved my head down farther. "You don't get to turn into the creature until the sun goes down. Until then, you won't feel a thing."

There were a couple of reasons I told him that. The first was that maybe, just maybe, he might wait until nightfall to kill me. Hopefully, on the very slimmest of chances, he'd let Vero go then, too. But by making the comment about nighttime, I hoped I was buying time. I figured we had ten hours until the sun set. Give or take. Probably take.

Carrillo shook his head. "You know, Dr. Wolf, I didn't realize what a wise guy you were. I don't like wise guys." His face turned sour, like he'd eaten a fly and couldn't get it out of his teeth. "Kill him."

I frowned, seeing the wishful future in my mind melt like ice cream in the desert sun. The guard to my left drew his pistol while the other guy held me tighter around the neck, and harder still on my shoulder.

I struggled, wriggling and trying to get free.

Vero screamed in protest, but her sounds died the second one of the guards smacked her on the face with the back of his hand then shoved his wrist against her mouth.

As the guard aimed his pistol, fury rumbled through me.

A hair of a second before the executioner fired, I let my weight pull me down. The guard behind me lost his balance and fell forward just as his partner's trigger finger twitched.

The suppressor muzzle puffed, spitting a round down through the falling guard's ear and out the other side.

I hit the ground first and rolled toward the gunman, who now felt a split second of shock at having accidentally killed one of his own.

I kicked my right foot up, smashing the butt of the gun with my toe. The gun flew into the air in what seemed like slow motion. It rolled end over end in a dramatic arc. My reflexes were faster than his, and I sprang from the ground, extending my left foot up as I twisted my body. The heel of my shoe drove into his jaw, knocking his head back to the left a few inches.

He staggered a step to the side.

I stuck my hand out and snatched the pistol before it hit the ground, and I turned and fired a shot through the back of his skull.

I didn't bother to watch him hit the ground. Instead, I whirled around and charged toward Carrillo, pistol extended at him as I took off.

Except I wasn't pointing the gun at him.

In the seconds it took me to kill two of his guards, Carrillo had grabbed Vero, who now stood between me and my revenge... my justice... the justice of everyone this piece of trash had hurt.

I only made it four steps before I froze five yards from the bottom of the staircase.

"So predictable," Carrillo chided. "Although, I have to say, I didn't realize you were an expert in hand-to-hand combat. A man of many talents, I suppose. It's a shame you turned me down, Doctor. It really is. I wonder what things we could have discovered all over the world. Oh well. I suppose I'll have to be satisfied with this." He held up the medallion.

I sensed another guard approaching from the right.

"Let her go, Carrillo. You have what you wanted. Kill me if that makes you feel better. But don't hurt her. That was the deal."

"I know the deal. Unfortunately, for our friend here, your definitions were somewhat vague and left up to interpretation."

My eyes widened in horror. "No. We had a—"

A pistol coughed a few feet to the right of my head.

38

The pain, for a half second, was the most excruciating I'd ever felt in my life. And that was including the dozens of bullets they'd previously blasted through my body.

Then, as quickly as my nerves howled, they suddenly silenced.

I hit the ground with a thud. The gunman hovered over me and fired two more shots through my skull.

Blood soaked the ground under my head. My eyes locked on a gargantuan fountain in the middle of a circular part of the driveway, and they didn't move even as the guard and another one of the reinforcements grabbed me by the ankles and dragged me away from the front of the mansion.

My bloody, mangled head bobbed on the pavers until they reached the grass then continued along a path that extended into a rose garden.

The two continued tugging me through the maze of flowers until they stopped at a hole that roughly matched my length and width. Without fanfare, they tossed me in.

Then the two took a minute to catch their breath before they picked up nearby shovels and began dumping dirt onto me.

The dirt must have been brought in from somewhere else because most of the soil this close to the beach should have been sand. Either way, when I hit the bottom of the hole, I made sure to roll onto my side with my head down, neck arched awkwardly.

When the guards were done covering me with dirt, I guess they went back in the mansion to stare at themselves in the mirror or do a few lines of blow. Either way, I was glad I'd altered my body position when I landed in the cavity. It allowed me to have a small pocket of air, as well as a little wiggle room.

Being buried dead is one thing. Being buried presumed dead is something else entirely.

If that had been one of the ways I could be killed, I'd have been terrified. The thought of being suffocated or starved or dehydrated to death in utter darkness that is literally pressing down on you every second wasn't something to fall asleep to.

I shivered my body for a minute. Took a break. Then repeated the process. I needed to loosen the dirt around me before I could dig my way out.

I felt the wounds in and around my skull healing as I worked. I didn't want to think about what that must have looked like. While it didn't bother the hardened cartel thugs, I imagined retching at the sight.

Then again, I'd been tearing into human beings with my mouth. As the chupacabra, but still.

The thought didn't sit well with me, but it also didn't nauseate me as it probably should have.

After about thirty minutes of intense labor, I shimmied into a position where my back felt like it was flat to the ground. The lazy way the two guards buried me made it easy to shake the soil, and it began to settle around my sides.

I jerked my hand back and forth until I could push it upward. Clawing my way through the soil, I dug upward, and did the same with my left hand. While digging, I continued to shimmy my body left and right while engaging my core to raise my torso higher.

This process went on for probably another ten minutes until I started to see cracks of light piercing the darkness.

I paused for a second, unable to catch my breath yet. Four more minutes of work, though, and my head emerged from the grave like a modern-day *Thriller*. Minus the zombie makeup.

I sucked in big gulps of air, suddenly realizing how much my lungs hurt from the lack. I stared across the patch of grass into the hedges and rows of flowers. The two guards were gone. I didn't know if Carrillo's security team did patrols. Or if they did, was this part of the garden on their scheduled route?

I had no intention of sticking around to find out.

I'd noticed cameras along the wall of the north wing, but out here in the rose garden, I doubted they'd have any such security measures.

After I rolled out of the dirt and brushed myself off, I was surprised to see how clean the fabric was—like it hadn't touched a grain of soil. My hair, on the other hand, didn't come out so lucky. It was still caked in dried blood from the head shots.

Crouching beneath the tops of the hedges, I made my way farther away from the house toward the northern perimeter. I wound through the maze of flowers and shrubs until I finally reached the other side, where a grove of palm trees and ornamental grasses filled a three-acre patch of land. I noticed tire tracks, maybe three feet wide.

"Four-wheelers," I muttered. The only question was, were the ATVs for patrols or for pleasure?

I squatted low behind the last of the bushes and peered out across the rolling terrain. About fifty yards away, I spotted a huge rock positioned between two bending palm trees. I was about to take off and run to the stone when out of the blue, a guard patrolling the edge of the garden strolled into view.

I retreated back behind the hedges and waited, holding my breath.

The man looked like so many of the other goons Carrillo employed—tattoos, the shaved head—although it appeared that wearing a uniform wasn't a requirement. Most of the men were haphazardly dressed, except for a few who wore suit jackets and button-up shirts like professional security teams.

This guy had on a gaudy Affliction T-shirt and matching jeans. Hardly subtle, his jeans featured sparkling silver patterns on the pockets that I assumed wrapped around to his rear, but I wasn't about to check. The shirt's pattern displayed skulls and swirling barbed wire all over it.

In addition to the clothes, he wore a perpetually pissed-off look on his face—lips set in stone in a downturn.

As he proceeded along the row, I continued creeping backward until I reached a corner and then ducked to my left behind another row in the maze. I couldn't know if he was going to enter the garden or continue around the outside of it, but I wasn't about to get thrown back into that dirt hole again. It hadn't killed me, but it felt enough like dying that I wasn't about to do it a second time.

I peeked around the corner. He turned his head my direction, and I retreated a few inches back.

I had no idea if he'd seen me or not, so I waited, unwilling to go farther back toward the mansion.

He lingered there, unmoving. I tried to see what he was doing through the foliage, but I could only make out bits and pieces of his clothes.

The anticipation killed me. I felt my heart pounding in my chest. My breathing came in quick, short bursts and I felt like the guard could hear every single one despite me doing everything I could to stay silent.

He turned as if to enter the maze, took one step toward it, and paused.

I was ready to go farther back down the line if needed, even though that would put me closer to the greater danger near the house.

Then, after what seemed like five minutes, the guard turned away from the mansion and walked back out into the open along the perimeter.

I waited until he'd exited the maze before poking my head around the hedge again to watch him leave. I had to make absolutely sure he was gone because the gag I'd pulled on Carrillo and his forces would only work once.

The guard meandered along the outside of the hedges, making his way toward the road.

I bear-crawled from my hiding place, back to the opening in the maze, and stuck my head out to watch the guard stop at the corner and look both to the north and south. Then the gunman reached into his pocket and pulled out a phone.

"What is this guy doing? Checking his Instagram account?" I breathed the words to myself.

The guard scrolled through something on the screen with his thumb. From my vantage point, I couldn't tell what it was, but he was fixated on it for at least a minute. I wondered what Carrillo would do to him if the boss realized one of his guards was screwing around on social media while he was supposed to be patrolling the perimeter.

With his addiction fed, the guard slipped the phone back into his pocket and continued to the left, heading south along the front edge of the garden facing the road.

I waited until he was twenty feet down the line before I took off, running as fast as I could while keeping my head down.

If anyone saw me, the alarm would have been raised. But no Klaxons sounded, and no angry shouts in Spanish followed me across the lawn.

I slid behind the big rock and pressed my back against it while I caught my breath, waiting. Then I peeked over the top of the stone and stared back across the yard toward the maze.

The patrol guard was still walking back toward the driveway, and thankfully, no others followed him.

I sat back against the rock and waited, looking up at the sun as it climbed into the sky.

This was going to be a long day. That much I knew. And I had no way to know if Carrillo's men ever came out this far on their patrols, but from what I'd seen, they kept to the edges of the garden.

I'd have to wait the entire day before making my move. I only hoped that Vero was okay. I could have gone in after her right then and there, but without the chupacabra, I would just end up right back in that hole again, probably next to Vero this time.

And if that happened, Carrillo would take the real medallion that still dangled around my neck, hidden under my clothes.

39

I'd been incorrect in surmising that the day would be a long one. It was exponentially worse than long.

The minutes and seconds crawled by at a turtle's pace. And I had no form of entertainment other than watching bugs skittering around on the ground or checking over the rock for the millionth time to make sure no one was coming my way.

Throughout the day, the same patrol guard paced the path encircling the garden, but no one came out to check any farther.

Finally, mercifully, after what literally felt like half of forever, the sun began ambling toward the horizon in the west.

My throat was parched, and more than once it felt like I'd swallowed dirt, which only made the thirst that much worse.

There was no way I could have prepared for something like this. It's not like I could carry a water bottle with me up to the front of Carrillo's mansion and then somehow manage to hold on to it when he killed me —or thought he had—and then dumped my body into an open grave.

With every inch the sun fell through the sky, the now-familiar feeling of battle energy continued to rise inside me, and it only increased by the second.

I shuddered to think of what Vero might be going through. My brain feared the worst, as it often did. Those thoughts distracted me from what I needed to do, so I choked them down like a bad whiskey and focused on staying out of sight just a little longer.

After what seemed like fifty hours, I looked to the west and saw the sun touch the horizon. A smile crept across my face. Power trickled through me at first, and I knew soon I could make the transformation.

I'd waited long enough.

I looked over the boulder and spotted the same guard from before. Now, a red mist swirled around his feet as he walked down the line of hedges and roses toward the road. I grinned, anticipating the first kill.

The sun was halfway below the horizon now.

I stood from my hiding place and stalked toward the guard, who had his back to me now as he approached the front north corner of the garden.

I scanned the rest of the property, spotting two more guards at the entrance to the mansion and the others out by the guard shack. I knew there would be more inside. How many? That didn't matter. They would all be dead soon.

I made no attempt to conceal myself now as I followed the patrol guard to the corner. With every step, the sun slipped lower and lower beyond the horizon to the west.

The guard stopped at the corner and proceeded to do the same thing I'd noticed him doing every time he reached that point. He stuck his hand in his pocket and retrieved his phone.

I guess he felt like he was far enough from the house to get away with checking social media without being noticed by his boss. Or anyone else.

Thirty feet from the man, the sun's last cap shimmered on the horizon. In the waning light, his cell phone glowed as he scrolled with his thumb, his eyes locked on the device—unaware that death was so near.

Twenty feet away, I picked up the pace, walking faster, pounding the ground with every step.

The ancient power pulsed through my veins now, and the red mist swirled brightly around my prey.

"Be sure to like and follow," I said when I was close enough to smell the overused cologne on the guard's skin.

His head whipped around. The device fell from his hands onto the grass. He spun and raised his weapon, firing four shots into my chest and gut.

As the bullets stung my flesh, I felt the change happening.

My face and head stretched. My fingers and hands morphed.

I imagined that to the guard it must have been the most frightening thing he'd ever witnessed.

It was also the last.

He continued firing the weapon. To my surprise, the fabric of my clothes did exactly what Myra said. The cloth expanded with my body, stretching over the fur as it grew from my skin.

Horror filled the gunman's eyes as he squeezed off the last round in his magazine. The weapon clicked three times. Then he dropped the gun, pressed on his ear to call for help, and stumbled backward toward the road.

"Help!" he shouted into the radio. "Chupa—"

I grabbed his neck with a meaty paw and cut off the rest of the word. The mist continued to churn around him, climbing up his legs toward his torso. I squeezed hard until I could feel his spine. His eyes bulged as he suffocated.

I held him a foot off the ground with a single paw. His feet jiggled and kicked as if that could somehow save him. He grabbed at my forearm, but it was too late. His fate was sealed.

The body went limp. The legs and feet stopped kicking. And I held on for another few seconds just to make sure.

Then I dropped him to the ground to let the mist consume him and jumped into the maze.

The other guards heard the gunshots—of that there was no

doubt. They also heard him cry for help through the radio. So I knew they would be coming.

I crouched below the top of the hedges, listening to the shouts of the reinforcements as they rallied to help.

I heard their footsteps as they ran, their feet beating the ground in a non-rhythmic staccato.

Looking up over the hedges again, I saw two men enter the maze, while two more ran around the outer edge toward the corner where they would find the one who'd called for help.

The two entering the maze split up, each going in a different direction.

Oh, this will be fun.

I crept away from my hiding spot, walking on all fours like the dog part of me. The hunt felt invigorating, exciting in a sick sort of way. *Am I actually enjoying this?*

I shook off the thought and stopped on the eastern side of the garden next to a shrub that had been shaped to look like a dolphin standing on its tail. I heard the guard coming from twenty feet away, despite the fact he was trying to stay quiet.

Stealth, it seems, didn't work on my new super hearing.

I lay low in the grass, nearly putting my belly on the ground. I saw the residual red light of the fog beating in and out of rhythm, flashing into the air around my next victim.

It was another handy trait I'd picked up, and a useful signal in the dark when enemies weren't in sight.

The footsteps drew closer, as did the glowing light, until the man's left leg came into view.

He looked to his left and saw me crouching in the darkness—a hideous and terrifying sight.

He shouted, turned his gun, and died as I surged upward, slashing his throat with a sharp claw. The guard fought death, wriggling and kicking, but I gave it to him with a quick snap of my fangs through his neck.

"Over there!" one of the other men shouted in Spanish.

With the kill, more energy coursed through me.

I heard the men coming, converging on my position, so I moved, slipping around the next corner and around behind them.

The second guy who'd entered the maze was the one I found next. He was making his way to where he'd heard the scream, moving slowly with his pistol raised high, eyes darting left and right to find the threat.

I circled around behind him, creeping after him for several steps. I felt power surge in me with the promise of another kill and snatched the man by his ankles as the red fog swirled around them.

I jerked him back, causing him to fall onto his face with a yelp. Then I dragged him to me. He tried to roll over and aim his weapon, but I leaped into the air. Putting both my front paws together, I dove into his chest, burrowing the sharp talons through him, crushing and cutting on the way to the ground below him.

The body shook violently as it protested imminent death.

The other two barked orders as they entered the maze. One of them called for help on the radio.

It would not save them.

Any of them.

One of the guards looped around to flank me. I smelled him, heard him, sensed him as he approached my position. I retreated toward the mansion, allowing him to work his way into the center where his partner also headed.

I smiled, watching from the shadows as the men swept their submachine guns left and right in hopes of finding the interloper.

I waited until they met in the middle before I circled around behind them, stalking on my haunches like a predator in the jungle.

The two came together at the fountain in the middle of the garden.

"Have you seen anything?" one of them hissed in Spanish.

"No, not yet."

"I have," I offered.

The two spun around and fired their weapons, but it was too late.

I stabbed my claws into their necks and twisted. The two men fell to their knees, the guns in their hands peppering the ground with bullets.

The dirt exploded around me as every round burrowed through the soil. Then silence descended on the garden with only the steady beat of the waves on the beach to interrupt it.

I stood tall and looked toward the mansion entrance.

"Your turn, Vicente."

40

For their part, Carrillo's men did all they could to keep from dying, and to protect their ungrateful and uncaring boss.

As I climbed the front steps, men poured out the front door, every one of them full of bravado and every one willing to die for a man who didn't care about them.

I slashed through them, moving at superhuman speed between each one. I cut them down with my claws, ripped limbs with my fangs, and even threw one of them against a marble column with such force the pillar shook on impact as the man's neck broke when his head struck it.

When I entered the mansion, I nearly laughed at my previous assertion about it being like Graceland.

Carrillo's taste—or lack thereof—oozed from the tacky zebra print wallpaper and the erratic and nonsensical displays of art that adorned the walls and floors.

Gunfire echoed through the halls as I continued forward.

Men took cover in alcoves or side halls, popping out sporadically to take aim. Not that it mattered.

Whether they missed or hit the mark, the end would be the same. And it was.

They all died, some more gratuitously than others.

I reached the end of the first corridor and caught one guard waiting behind the corner of an archway.

He fired a round into my forehead, and I staggered back, momentarily stunned by the bullet in my brain.

The haze quickly cleared, and I widened my eyes, beckoning the mist to take him.

The red fog obeyed, swirling around his legs and torso until it reached his neck. I stuck out my hand and squeezed, then raised it and watched as the guard lifted off the ground.

I stepped close, peering into his eyes with mine, noticing the two red glows reflecting in his.

Fear gripped him as tightly as the mist, squeezing him to the point that his face changed color.

"Where is he?" I asked.

The man swallowed, shaking his head and squirming to free himself.

I repeated the question. "Where is he?" This time, my voice deepened. "Where is Carrillo?"

"I don't know," he managed.

"Then I have no use for you."

I tightened the mist's grip.

"Your boss doesn't care if you die. Nor do I. This is your chance at redemption. You can tell me where I can find him, and perhaps save what part of a soul you have left. Or you can not, and I will get to him anyway. The choice is yours."

The man contemplated my offer.

Finally, he saw no other way. The fog constricted his chest like a python, unyielding to the air that he so desperately needed in his lungs.

"Upstairs," he coughed. "Third floor. Last room on the left."

"Good detail," I commented.

I lowered the guard down to his feet, loosening the fog's grip on him enough that he could free his arms.

His chance at salvation was lost when he raised his weapon at me again. I snatched the barrel and turned it up at his face. He shook his head vigorously, now realizing the mistake he'd made.

"No. Please."

"Your chance to beg for mercy has passed. Squeeze it." I said. "Squeeze the trigger."

"No. No!"

I pushed the finger, forcing it to twitch. The muzzle erupted, and the back of his skull ended up on the wall behind where he fell.

I turned to the staircase back in the front of the mansion. When I reached it, I looked up, anticipating more guards, but none came.

Bounding up the stairs two at a time, I flew to the second floor, paused to check the landing and the two halls that split out in either direction, and waited. No sign of anyone.

I wondered how that could be, but only for a second as I recalled how many men Vero and I had taken out on the road.

I rounded the curve in the staircase, running my paw along the golden rail that rested atop black iron bars.

Looking up to the next landing, again I saw no guards.

Either I'd wasted all of Carrillo's men, or he was keeping a few in reserve for me. My imagination saw him standing in his study with a gun in his hand, using ten men as human shields against the onslaught of violent death.

Not that it would help him. His fate was sealed.

I climbed the stairs and stopped at the landing. Looking down both corridors, still finding no guards, I turned down the hall the last guard had mentioned and hurried toward the end.

I didn't stop—passing several rooms, grotesque paintings, and opulent vases on plinths—until I reached a closed door on the left.

Only pausing for a second, I listened through the door for any sign of activity. I heard nothing. No voices. No movement. Not even breathing, which I felt confident I could detect under the right circumstances.

I took a step back, then rushed forward, barging into the door. The barrier exploded on impact, ripping from the hinges and shattering into splintered wooden chunks on the floor in the next room.

As I looked around amid the debris, all I found was an empty study. The long, ornately decorated room gave me no clue as to where Carrillo might have fled.

Except for one.

Two massive French doors hung open leading out onto the balcony. A rack of high-powered rifles, shotguns, and pistols hung from the wall near the doors. But the guns didn't draw my attention.

I heard something outside, amid the sound of the ocean waves crashing onto the sand. At first, I didn't know what it was until I drew closer to the doors. Then, in the breeze, I overheard a muted groaning.

Fear gripped me, and tightened when I saw the cord tied carelessly to the balcony railing. The taut rope dropped out of sight beneath the balcony, and before I looked over the edge, I knew what waited below.

I hurried to the edge and looked over, hoping I wouldn't find what I'd suddenly expected.

Relief curled around me.

Vero hung from the cord, dangling about five feet below the balcony. The rope wrapped around her ankles.

She wiggled, and the rope twisted. That's when I noticed the frayed piece just below the edge. Thread by thread, the cord was about to snap, threatening to drop Vero to a concrete pool deck below. The fall—feet first—would be extremely dangerous. But headfirst would be a death sentence. At best, she'd have serious brain and neck damage.

It was too late to pull her up.

As the rope frayed, I vaulted over the railing and dropped down to the ground, sailing past her just as the cord snapped.

Then Vero was falling, too, a split second behind me.

I hit the ground first, landing on my paw-like feet. In a flash, I spun around and stuck out my arms, just as Vero fell from above.

I sidestepped and caught her, bending my knees to cushion her fall.

It was hard to believe how light she felt, but my new strength was to thank for that.

She looked up at me as I held her. I peeled away the duct tape on her face, knowing it must have hurt for me to do so, but also relieved that she could finally speak and breathe normally again.

"Are you okay?" I asked.

It had to be weird for her to stare back at a monster with glowing red eyes.

She nodded. "I am now." Her breathing quickened as the weight of her near-death took over her body. For a second, she shook in my arms.

"Where is Carrillo?" I asked.

Her head twisted toward the beach. "He ran when he found out you were here." She looked down at my chest, spotting the medallion. "I thought you gave that to him."

I shook my head. "That was a fake. A little replica from our friend Myra."

Her eyes widened. "Clever."

"Yeah," I said. But my focus was still on finding Carrillo. "Where did he go?"

"Heading to his yacht."

For a second, I imagined jumping into the gulf and swimming like crazy through the waves until I reached the boat, but even with my new powers, I knew that would be a fruitless endeavor. If he got away now, I'd never be able to catch him, and Carrillo could disappear.

Staring out to the sea, I shook my head. "I can't get to him."

She followed my gaze. "I can."

I turned to her, locking eyes with hers. "What?"

"Get me back up to the third floor."

I looked at her with the unspoken question in my eyes, then stared up at the balcony. "Okay," I said. I trusted her. She'd earned that. "But can't you walk?"

"There isn't time for the stairs. You're going to have to jump."

"Jump?" I'd been afraid that was what she wanted. I knew I could make the jump on my own. I'd leaped at least that high, and probably higher.

"Yes. You can do it."

"How do you—"

"There isn't time. He's going to get away."

I had no idea what she was planning, but heading up to the balcony didn't seem like the right direction.

"Trust me," she said.

Meeting her gaze, I realized right there that I did trust her. I had trusted her before, but it was deeper now. I'd never established a bond like that so quickly with another person. It had taken years for me to surrender fully to Amy. But now, at this moment, I felt more trust with this woman I'd only met a few days before than I had with nearly anyone.

"Okay," I said. "Hold on."

She wrapped her arm around my shoulder. I bent my knees, summoning every ounce of power I could, and jumped.

The second-floor balcony sailed by, but as I neared the top, I wasn't sure I had enough to clear the third-floor railing.

I approached it as my velocity began to wane. When my head reached the level of the floor, I'd lost nearly all momentum. "Here," I snapped and shoved her over the rail at the last second. She flew over and landed on the floor as I dropped back down to the ground below.

Vero was okay, even if the landing was hard, because she immediately bounced up and looked down over the railing at me as I fell.

Again, I landed on my feet, and with a second burst, I leaped into the air again.

This time was much easier without the additional weight, and I cleared the balcony with aplomb, sailing over it with several feet to spare.

The floor shook under my monstrous weight as I landed.

Vero looked over at me with a smile. "That was awesome."

"Gracias, Señorita."

Then she turned and hurried into the mansion. For a second, I didn't know what she was doing until she reappeared with one of the long rifles, a scope attached to the top.

"Wait," I protested. "Where did he go?"

That's when I heard the thumping of the chopper in the air, and the whine of the rotor's engine.

"He has a helicopter?" I asked.

"Yes. And he's going to try to make it to the yacht."

"How are you going to—"

My question got cut off as the pounding air drowned out my voice. A second later, the wind from the rotors blew down on us as the helicopter rose above the house and tilted toward the yacht bobbing in the gulf.

The chopper flew right over us, and I felt the urge to jump up and grab the skis, but I resisted, trusting Vero knew what she was doing.

She lined up the barrel and looked through the scope, closing one eye as she zeroed in on the pilot.

There wasn't more than a foot of window she could see through, and I didn't think she could hit the mark.

The helicopter continued out over the property, then over the beach.

"He's almost to the water," I said.

"I know," Vero said, cutting me off.

She watched, breathing slowly, her finger tensing on the trigger.

Then she released the bullet in the chamber with a gentle squeeze.

The round sailed through the night and punctured through the back left of the cockpit.

Suddenly, the aircraft tilted to the left, then right, then started spinning. The machine went haywire, spiraling out of control as it continued toward the yacht.

Even all this time later, I like to imagine the last thing Carrillo saw before he died was his multimillion-dollar super yacht through the windshield of his multimillion-dollar helicopter just before it crashed into the obscenely expensive boat.

There was a momentary pause, and then a violent explosion. The bright orange burst consumed the helicopter, along with Carrillo.

I could only stare for a few seconds, half in disbelief and half in utter gratitude that the man who'd killed my wife and ruined everything for me had just died in a fiery blaze. When that realization melted, I looked back to Vero, who stood there with the rifle still mounted on the railing, like a golfer holding her follow-through pose after a hole-in-one.

"That was a heck of a shot," I said.

She pulled her eye from the scope and looked up at me. "Told you I had it."

41

I stood in the cantina at the bar, sipping on a Clase Azul reposado—or as I would have called it in college, a shot of tequila. Except this wasn't like the shots we did back in those days.

It was barely afternoon—too early, in some quarters, for tequila. If they had just been through what we had, they'd probably change their clocks to catch up with us.

"So," Vero said, leaning over her bar's counter with a similar glass in her hand. "What are you going to do next?"

The answer didn't take long. "Like I said before, I'm going to hunt down the other six medallions. I'm an archaeologist. If anyone can find them, I can. I hope." I winked at her with the last part then took another sip.

Everything from wild adventures in other countries to boring digs in the middle of the desert ran through my mind. Visions of subterranean tunnels, ancient temples, and spectacular vistas popped in and out as well.

"Do you think you will stick around here for long?"

I heard the hopeful tone in her voice. She wanted me to stay.

I'd been unclear about that sentiment, but now I knew for certain. At least I thought I did. I had never really been good at picking up signals from women, but this one was coming through loud and clear. I could see it in her eyes, hear it in her voice. Her posture at the bar, casual yet teasing, also gave away her intentions.

But I'd just lost my wife. Was I attracted to Vero? Absolutely. I'd have been insane not to be. She was naturally beautiful, and I knew I could trust her. That was a trait I realized I had been undervaluing for way too long, something I took for granted. Not anymore.

Still, I wasn't ready for anything like that. I still needed to process everything that happened, not just with Amy but all of this. Since I'd found the medallion, everything was happening at breakneck speed.

"I need to go back to the States," I said finally. "I could hang around here, but there will be questions—as in from police, the feds. Who knows who else? Amy's family and friends will want to know what happened. It won't be easy. They'll blame me. They always blame me for everything that goes... went," I corrected, "wrong in her life.

"That doesn't sound fair."

"I know. It isn't. But I still have to do the right thing."

She smiled at me, and I knew what it meant. It was the same kind of admiring expression one would wear while staring at a rare piece of art, or an exotic animal.

I realized right then that I didn't want to go. Could I get away with that, simply not returning to the US? I wondered what that extradition would look like, but only for a second.

Then it hit me.

"Just because I'm leaving doesn't mean I won't come back," I said. I looked around the cantina. "I have to do right by Amy's family and make sure everything with the authorities is cleared up." I blew air through my lips, flapping them loudly. "I don't look forward to any of that. Not sure how much any of them will believe."

"No?"

"I have to tell them that my wife was killed by a cartel and that I was abducted, somehow escaped, and then made it home after disappearing for several days."

She offered a disarming smile. "I guess you're going to leave out the part about the magical ancient medallion that turns you into the chupacabra."

I nodded. "Probably best if I leave that out."

She laughed.

"Then there's the part where Carrillo dies. No way they don't make a connection to that. At least, I would if I was in their shoes."

"Maybe you'll get a medal."

I snorted then shook my head. "Unlikely." I let silence take over for a few seconds before I went on. "I will come back," I said. "There's something about this place. I like it here. It's quiet. The people are kind. The pace of life is slower, too, and that's a nice change, even from Tennessee. And we know a thing or two about living a slower pace of life."

"Perhaps you will show me Tennessee someday." There it was. She risked it all on that statement. Or maybe she didn't. Maybe it was just a feeler bet, a way of testing where I was with things, or at least where I could be in the future.

"Perhaps," I teased. "I love the mountains and hills there, and the farms that stretch between them. It's a beautiful place."

"What about the amulets?" she asked. "When will you begin working on that?"

I'd already flirted with the answer. "Soon. I just need to know where to begin."

"I can help with that," a new voice interrupted.

I turned and found Myra standing in the doorway. Apparently, Vero hadn't seen her either.

"What are you, a ninja?" I asked with a huff.

"Not quite," she denied.

Myra walked into the room holding a leather satchel. She stopped at the bar and set the bag down on the counter next to me.

"If you are to seek the other six medallions, you will need to know their history, where they came from, and where they might have gone." She opened the satchel's flap and pulled out leather journals that looked like they were hundreds of years old. Some of the pages were made from vellum. Then she took out a few scrolls that I knew were papyrus, and immediately I felt panic fill me.

Just to be clear, I asked, "Is that papyrus?"

"Yes," she said with a pleased smile. "But you needn't worry about it being damaged by exposure to the air. These documents have an ancient blessing on them. No harm from nature will come to them."

I breathed a sigh of relief.

Those scrolls and journals could have contained nothing more than invoices for construction or someone's diary from hundreds or thousands of years ago. But they were still a piece of history, and even the smallest bits of that were important because they could give us clues into the way ordinary people lived their lives so long ago.

"What is all this?" I asked.

"Clues," she said. "These are the breadcrumbs that will lead you down the path. It will not be easy. And you must be aware, Gideon: No one person may hold all the guardian medallions. The power is too much, and will corrupt even the noblest of souls."

I nodded. "Okay. So, what am I supposed to do if... I mean, when I find them?"

"The way will be revealed to you. You must find the other guardians and give them what is rightfully theirs."

"Other guardians? How will I know?"

She smiled as if I'd failed to remember how to tie my shoes. "As I said, it will be revealed to you. When the time comes, you will know."

She left it at that, and I knew there wasn't going to be deeper explanation.

"So, what?" I asked. "I roam the world looking for these things and find the people they belong to? What happens after that?"

"This is the end of an age, Gideon, the final curtain for a great cycle. The Mayans knew about this. As did many ancient cultures. When the age ends, a great evil will emerge. Then the people of Earth will be at a crossroads. The planet can either descend into chaos or rise to a greater existence than we've ever known. But for the latter to happen, the great evil must be vanquished."

"What is this great evil?" I asked. "Are we talking about demons or something?" I wasn't sure what to believe anymore. I'd heard stories of angels and demons interacting in people's lives, but I'd never seen it personally. No angel had ever come up to me and spoken to me, that I knew of. And I was relatively sure no demons had been meddling in my life.

"It is unclear, but when it happens, you will know it."

I didn't like how she refrained from outright denying the demon question, but I left it alone.

"There are others who will try to take the medallion from you. Dangerous people who would use it for their own devices. And unlike Carrillo, many of them are not of the House of Claw and Fang. That doesn't matter. Understand that anyone who holds the amulet will receive the power of Xolotl. Always protect it. And always be vigilant. Danger lurks in every shadow."

"Okay," was all I could manage. I looked over the documents on the counter, still unwilling to touch them. "So, you're giving these to me?"

"I'm loaning them to you. Don't lose them." She held up a bony finger and put on a warning expression. But it didn't carry much weight when it cracked into a smile. "I'm kidding. If you lose them, they will return to me."

I wanted to know how that worked, but I left it alone. "Thank you," I said. "For all your help." I faced Vero again, who'd been listening quietly from behind the bar. "And thank you, too. You risked everything to help me."

"You're worth the risk," she said, suddenly shy and hiding behind her nearly empty glass of tequila.

I felt myself blushing and shook my head. "A week ago, my life was so simple. So mundane. Now... it's complicated. But I don't hate it. I never felt like I had a sense of purpose. I knew what I did for a living was good, and maybe it made a difference in the world. But this. This is something I could have never imagined. It's a lot to take in."

Myra put her hand on my back. "You will do better than make a difference. You're a guardian now. You, along with the others, will save humanity."

A cartel enforcer sat in the interrogation room on a metal chair at a metal table. He struggled, albeit mildly, against the straitjacket wrapped around him. It was no use. The drugs they'd given him at the asylum sapped most of his strength. And worse, most of his will.

All he could do was stare at the table surface, but even that reminded him of the horrors he'd seen just two nights before.

Two men walked into the room through a gray metal door with one of those windows infused with steel wire. The men wore matching suits and ties. They looked like some kind of federal investigators, but for some reason not FBI.

"Tell us what you saw," the one on the right said. He was tall, with dark brown skin and black hair cropped close to his head.

His partner, a guy with a light tan and dusty brown hair, sat down at the table and crossed his arms, ready to listen with his phone on the table set to record.

José looked at both of them, then shook his head. "I'm not crazy," he said in a sluggish voice.

"We know you're not," the white guy said. "That's why we're here, José. We want to help you."

"You worked for Carrillo, yes?" The black man asked the question in a deep baritone. It was to the point, but not unfriendly.

José nodded. "Yes. Until... the attack."

It was strange to see a hardened criminal like José, all tattoos and tough-guy exterior, looking like a sheepish child awaiting punishment.

"And what happened?"

José's head and eyes snapped up to focus on the two interrogators. "The chupacabra," he said. "The chupacabra killed everyone." He shook his head, lowering his gaze to the table again. "The chupacabra. The chupacabra. The chupacabra."

He kept repeating the words. They felt haunting in the dim light of the single-bulb room, surrounded by dark walls full of shadows.

"The chupacabra?" the white guy asked.

The question brought José back again. "Who is he?"

The two suits nodded.

José fought for the answer. It was a battle against vivid, terrifying memories. "I was there." he began. "In the house when he came. I saw him die. I saw him killed. And then, later that night, the monster came." The nightmare played out in his eyes, and both investigators saw it. "I didn't know what to do. So I ran. I had to leave."

A red mist swirled around José. It pulsed brightly as it snaked around his legs and lower torso.

"And you escaped," the black man said. "You were the only one who managed to get out alive."

"Yes," José said with regret.

The fog continued to rise, wrapping around him like the strait-jacket clinging to his body.

He began to shake.

The two agents looked at each other, puzzled.

"Who was he?" the white guy asked. "Who was this man that turned into the chupacabra?"

"Chupacabra. Chupacabra. Chupacabra." José said the words again in a trance. His eyes glazed over.

The mist swirled faster now, climbing up to his neck.

He began to choke, and fought harder against his restraints.

"Who was it?" The interrogators demanded. "Tell us who this man is."

José's eyes bulged from the lack of air getting to his lungs. "He was... a gringo."

"Yes. But what is his name?" the black agent demanded. "Tell us his name."

"His name... his name was..." The fog engulfed José and muted the words. "Gide... Gideon Wolf."

He slumped forward, the manacles connecting his body to the chair holding him up in a sort of weird, forward-leaning death pose.

The two spooks looked at each other in utter confusion.

"José?" The white guy reached out and touched him. No response.

"He's dead?" the other man asked. "How?"

The other stood up and shook his head. "Drugs? I don't know. But we got what we needed. Let's get out of here." He hit the red button on the recording and slid the device into his pants pocket.

The men walked to the door, opened it, and left.

That's when I woke up. I blinked my eyes several times to clear the haze from them, and from my mind. I looked around the bedroom and recalled this was to be my last night in Mexico before I flew out of Guadalajara the next morning.

I checked the clock on the nightstand and noted it was only 3:45 in the morning. I needed to go back to sleep, but what had that dream meant? It felt so real. And the mist. The mist was there, killing that guy. But I didn't know who he was, other than he'd claimed to be one of Carrillo's goons.

And who were the two spooks? They didn't present any credentials, or even make mention of who they were with.

An idea bubbled into my mind. I'd read about remote viewing before, as well as the projects that went on with MK Ultra. Had that just happened to me while I was sleeping? Try as I might, I couldn't come up with another answer, as if that one was the right one and there were no other possibilities.

I inhaled deeply, held it, then exhaled.

If that was true, then those men were looking for me. Now they knew my name. And if they knew my name, they would be coming for me.

THANK YOU

I just wanted to say thank you for reading this story. You chose to spend your time and money on something I created, and that means more to me than you may know. But I appreciate it, and am truly honored.

Be sure to swing by ernestdempsey.net to grab free stories, and dive deeper into the universe I've created for you.

I hope you enjoyed the story, and will stick with this series as it continues through the years. Know that I'll be working hard to keep bringing you exciting new stories to help you escape from the real world.

Your friendly neighborhood author,

Ernest

OTHER BOOKS BY ERNEST DEMPSEY

Sean Wyatt Adventures:

The Secret of the Stones

The Cleric's Vault

The Last Chamber

The Grecian Manifesto

The Norse Directive

Game of Shadows

The Jerusalem Creed

The Samurai Cipher

The Cairo Vendetta

The Uluru Code

The Excalibur Key

The Denali Deception

The Sahara Legacy

The Fourth Prophecy

The Templar Curse

The Forbidden Temple

The Omega Project

The Napoleon Affair

The Second Sign

The Milestone Protocol

Where Horizons End

Adriana Villa Adventures:

War of Thieves Box Set

ACKNOWLEDGMENTS

As always, I would like to thank my terrific editors, Anne and Jason, for their hard work. What they do makes my stories so much better for readers all over the world. Anne Storer and Jason Whited are the best editorial team a writer could hope for and I appreciate everything they do.

I also want to thank Elena at Lı Graphics for her tremendous work on my book covers and for always overdelivering. Elena definitely rocks.

A big thank you has to go out to my friend James Slater for his proofing work. James has added another layer of quality control to these stories, and I can't thank him enough.

I also want to offer a special thanks to Allison Valentine for her generous efforts to help promote not only my work in the United Kingdom and Europe, but other independent authors as well.

Last but not least, I need to thank all my wonderful fans and especially the advance reader team. Their feedback and reviews are always so helpful and I can't say enough good things about all of them.

Made in the USA
Columbia, SC
07 April 2022

58640351R00186